Chocolate-Covered Baloney:

Confessions of April Grace

Other Confessions of April Grace:

In Front of God and Everybody

Cliques, Hicks, and Ugly Sticks

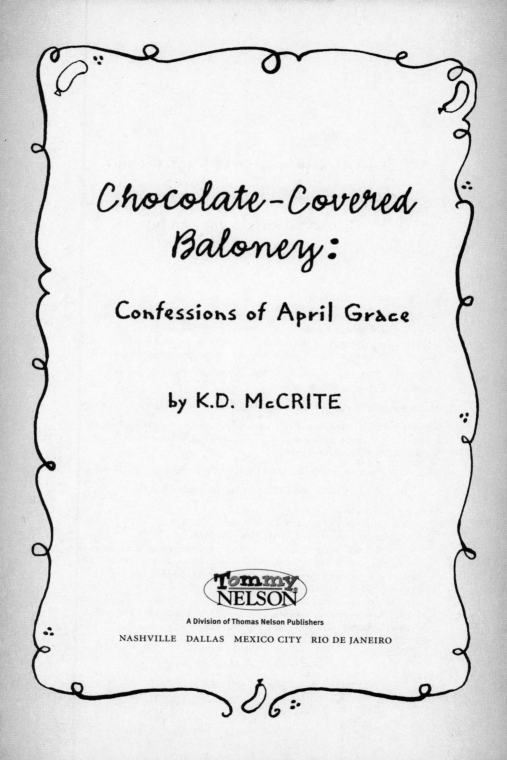

Chocolate-Covered Baloney:

Confessions of April Grace

by K.D. McCRITE

Tommy NELSON

A Division of Thomas Nelson Publishers

NASHVILLE   DALLAS   MEXICO CITY   RIO DE JANEIRO

Dedicated to my good friend and neighbor, Judy Lorenz, who goes the extra mile every day.

Published in Nashville, Tennessee, by Thomas Nelson. Thomas Nelson is a trademark of Thomas Nelson, Inc.

Author is represented by Jeanie Pantelakis of Sullivan Maxx Literary Agency.

Thomas Nelson, Inc., titles may be purchased in bulk for educational, business, fund-raising, or sales promotional use. For information, please e-mail SpecialMarkets@ThomasNelson.com.

All Scripture quotations are taken from the King James Version of the Bible.

Library of Congress Cataloging-in-Publication Data

McCrite, K. D. (Kathaleen Deiser)
    Chocolate-covered baloney / KD McCrite.
      p. cm.—(Confessions of April Grace ; bk. 3)
    Summary: 1987 brings more changes for April Grace when Myra Sue starts acting very sneaky, her new baby brother comes home, her neighbor Isabel becomes her gym teacher, and a long-lost relative suddenly appears.
    ISBN 978-1-4003-2068-4 (pbk.)
    [1. Family life—Arkansas—Fiction. 2. Farm life—Arkansas—Fiction. 3. Middle schools—Fiction. 4. Schools—Fiction. 5. Christian life—Fiction. 6. Arkansas—History—20th century—Fiction.] I. Title.
PZ7.M4784146Cho 2012
[Fic]—dc23   2012007531

Printed in the United States of America

12 13 14 15 16 QG 5 4 3 2 1

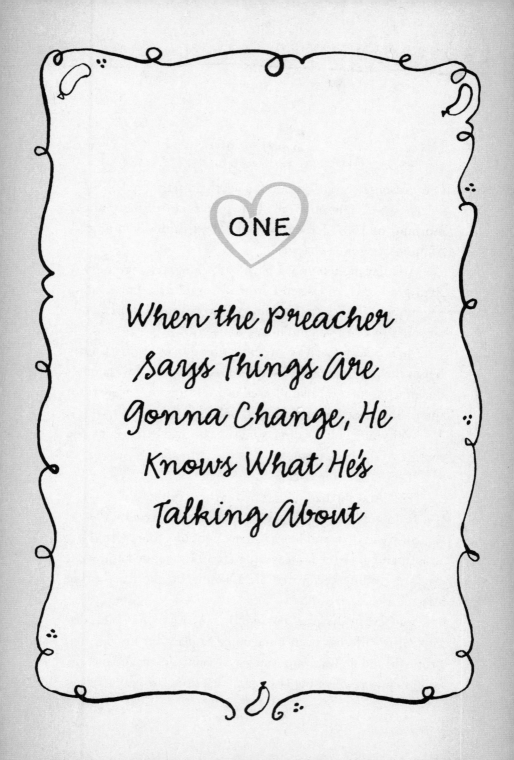

ONE

When the Preacher Says Things Are Gonna Change, He Knows What He's Talking About

♡

January 1987

Our preacher scared me out of a year's growth.

He stood right up there in the pulpit on that first Sunday morning of 1987, looked at us all, and calmly announced, "Things are gonna change."

Well, let me tell you, I have had enough change for any sixth-grade girl, and when Pastor Ross said that, I opened up a hymnbook and started reading the words to all those familiar songs just so I wouldn't have to listen.

Melissa Kay Carlyle, my best friend, was sitting on my left in the pew where we always sat. As long as we were quiet during church, our folks allowed us to sit together away from them. She passed me her church bulletin.

"Why are you reading songs?" she had written in the margin of the back page.

"B-cuz," I wrote back.

"???" And she had underlined it three times.

"I do not want to listen to the sermon," I wrote.

She read that, and her hazel eyes got big. She twisted her mouth and gave me a measuring stare. I shrugged and went back to reading the words of "Leaning on the Everlasting Arms."

You see, in the past few months, my home has been disrupted, my life has been interrupted, a place on my face has erupted, and I just want things to calm down and be the way they were this time last year. This time last year I was in elementary school, not junior high. My fourteen-year-old sister, Myra Sue, who is the biggest Blond-Haired, Blue-Eyed Drip you will ever meet, had not totally lost what tiny scrap of good sense she had. My grandma had still been a cookie-baking, old-fashioned lady with gray hair and ugly shoes who liked to sit in the rocking chair a lot, instead of getting her hair cut and dyed and going through a Total Makeover until she hardly looked like herself. Last winter at this time, we had never heard of the citified Ian and Isabel St. James, and there had only been two kids instead of three in our household.

Boy, oh boy, if there was gonna be more change in my life, I'd rather it were the kind I could spend on chocolate bars.

TWO

Myra Sue Reilly, the Sneak of Rough Creek Road

❀

That afternoon, after the family finished Sunday dinner, I washed the dishes and straightened the kitchen. This has become my Permanent Job, and let me tell you, it is *not* something I wish to make a career of.

When I finished rinsing out the sink, I looked out the kitchen window at Grandma's little red-roofed house across the hay field. Her white Corolla was *still* not there.

You want to know where she was? I'll tell you. She was at the Methodist church where she'd been invited by the minister, Reverend Trask Jordan, to come for the service and to stay for a New Year's potluck celebration afterward. We Reillys attend Cedar Ridge Community Church and have done so since time began.

Reverend Jordan likes my grandma. *Likes*, as in he'd *like* to be her boyfriend. He's been inviting her over and over again to visit his church. (Just *visit*, mind you. Not become a member or anything because he "doesn't want to take folks away from their own churches.") The other day, he drove his bright-red Mustang to her house while Daddy and I were there, and he invited her right in front of us.

Grandma's face got all red, and her mouth opened and shut a couple of times.

Daddy said, "I think you should go, Mom. You'll enjoy it."

She gave him a funny look and blurted out, "Yes, okay, thank you," like she was afraid she'd forget the words if she didn't say 'em loud and fast. Then Daddy laughed, and Reverend Jordan chuckled. I just sat there thinking about the whole thing.

I wish that preacher had invited me to go, too. If I'd gone to the Methodist church that day, I wouldn't have had to hear all that mess Pastor Ross said about changes. I like Pastor Ross, but I'll tell you something: he'd have done a lot better job if he'd just preached about the Sermon on the Mount or Jonah and the Big Fish.

Of course, if I'd gone with Grandma, I would've had to ride with her, and Grandma's driving is so scary it will make your toenails curl. Likely as not, she'd drive just as well if she sat upside down and drove with her feet.

I sighed, wiped my hands on a towel, and went into the living room. Mama was there, rocking my brand-new baby brother, Eli, and singing softly to him. Let me tell you something about that kid. He was born too early and had to stay in the hospital for a while. He's only been home with us a few days, but here's the thing: just because he's a newcomer doesn't mean he hasn't got things figured out around here. Every single time we sit down to eat, he starts crying to be fed at the same time, even when he was sound asleep two seconds earlier. I suppose he wants bacon and eggs or meat loaf or whatever we're having. Poor Mama hasn't had an entire hot meal with the family for a while.

Not that any of us are complaining. We're happy Eli is healthy and doing well. He's so cute and soft and sweet, it seems someone is smooching his little cheeks all the time. Poor kid. He'll probably grow up with permanent lip prints all over his face.

"I'm finished in the kitchen, Mama," I said softly, so as not to startle Eli, who was cuddled in her arms.

Mama looked up and smiled. Her red hair was all fluffy and soft around her face, and her green eyes shone bright and pretty. She has freckles on her face, and I reckon I inherited my freckles from her. For that matter, I got my red hair from her, too. I hope that when I'm a grown-up lady, I'm as pretty as my mom.

She'd been mighty sick for several months before Eli was born, and I was sure glad to see her feeling healthy again. And I admit I was kinda upset last year when I found out she was going to have a baby. It seemed like one more unnecessary event that turned our lives upside down. But once I got hold of Eli with his soft skin, tiny little hands, blue eyes, and bit of fuzzy red hair on his head, I knew I wouldn't exchange him, not for a million-gazillion dollars, so don't even offer.

"Thanks for cleaning up, honey," Mama said, holding the baby on her shoulder to burp him. "Did you remember to wipe off the stove and rinse out the sink?"

"Yes'm."

"Then you may go play or read or whatever you want to do," she said, getting up. She laid Eli down in his little white bassinet in the living room.

"Okay, Mama. Thank you."

❦

I went upstairs to read *Rebecca* by Daphne du Maurier. The school librarian—who looks and smells like a rotten lemon and does not like kids—said it would be over my head, but she does not know April Grace Reilly. I bet I have read more books than she has.

After I got to my room, I heard something out in the hallway and opened the door a crack to peer out. There stood ole Myra Sue. She was so close to my door that if I'd opened it all of a sudden, she'd have fallen inside like a big load of dirty laundry.

"What're you doing?" I asked, surprised as all get-out.

She glared at me. "Just mind your own business!" she snapped.

"Excuse me, but *you* were the one snooping around *my* door."

"Don't be dumb! I was just walking past."

"Yeah, I'm so sure! You were standing there, listening to see if I was doing anything."

"Leave me alone, you brat. I don't know why everyone in this family thinks they have to know all my private business when some things are nobody's business but mine!"

"Things like what?" I asked.

"None of your beeswax," she said. Then she gave me a little shove and closed my door, hard. By the time I opened it again, she was heading downstairs.

I stood there and thought about it for a minute. Why would that girl have any private business? She sure was acting funny, even for goofy Myra Sue. I wondered for a minute what could be up. Maybe she was thinking about dyeing her hair again, but the last time she did that, she got in Big Trouble. Did she start smoking? Some of her friends had been caught recently . . . Boy, oh boy. Not only would she barbeque her own personal lungs, but Mama and Daddy would hit the ceiling.

I walked over to the shelf by the window where I keep my library books, and what do you think I saw outside? I saw my sister sneaking down the driveway. When she got as far as the mailbox, she stopped and looked around like she was a bank robber casing the joint. I squinted so hard to see what she was doing that my eyelids hurt, and of course, my breath fogged up that cold glass at the very worst time. I cleared a circle with my sleeve just in time to see her pull something out of her coat pocket and shove whatever it was in the mailbox. Then she jumped away like the mailbox was gonna grab her or burst into flames.

"What's that girl up to? What'd she put in there, anyway?" I asked out loud. I leaned closer to the window and watched ole Myra come slinking back up the driveway. Then, just as if she'd felt my eyes on her, she looked up and saw me.

You shoulda seen her. She stopped hard, like she had run into a brick wall. She just stood there, staring at me. It was cold outside, but believe me, it wasn't cold enough to freeze her in place like that. That girl had to have been up to no good, otherwise she wouldn't be out there in that cold.

"What are you doing out there like a big dummy?" I hollered through the window glass at her.

All of a sudden, like my voice had spooked her—or maybe her brain had finally unfroze—she turned around and galloped back to the mailbox. She yanked out whatever she'd stuck in there and stuffed it into her coat pocket. She looked at me, then at the mailbox, then around the woods and up and down the road like the whole entire FBI was watching her, and then she tore off down Rough Creek Road like someone was chasing her. Myra Sue runs like a chicken chasing a June bug, her head leading the way and her arms out, bent in at the elbows like wings. I could see the world pretty good from my window upstairs, and I didn't see a blessed thing—not a grizzly bear or an ax murderer or even a three-legged wood rat on a crutch. What was that silly girl running from?

I watched her run off in the direction of Ian and Isabel St. James's house. My sister loves and adores Ian and Isabel, especially Isabel. That woman thinks my sister is a golden child, a pure angel, and a gift from heaven. Let me assure you, Myra Sue Reilly is no gift. In fact, she's more like the coal that Santa delivers to rotten kids at Christmas. I figured whatever secret that girl had been trying to hide was now gonna find its way into the hands of Isabel. In which case, the Big Secret she was hiding probably involved makeup or nail polish, and I didn't care *what* it was. But if you know me at all, you know my curiosity itches me worse than poison ivy and mosquito bites put together.

Now, here's the thing: it was cold outside. I mean, January in the Ozarks is not the balmy, sunny weather you might think. As Grandma would say, it was colder than a wedge outside. The sky hung above us like an ugly, gray curtain that needed to be washed, and the wind blew hard enough to force your teeth down your gullet.

What I *wanted* to do was stay in our nice, warm house, crawl up on my bed, wrap myself in the raggedy old blanket

I'd had since I was little, and read that book that was supposed to be over my head. That's what I *wanted* to do, but something inside me said, "April Grace Reilly, something is Going On, and you need to find out what."

THREE

The April Grace Detective Agency Is Now in Business

☺

I could've gone straight to my folks like a big, fat tattletale, but that's more Myra Sue's style than mine. I'd rather get the goods, sort out the facts, and then inform those who need to know—*if* there is anything they need to know. So instead of snuggling down and reading, I yanked on my heavy tan coat and thick, green-and-tan wool hat, ran downstairs, and called out to Mama as I headed to the front door, "I'm gonna go outside for a little while."

"Button up your coat," she said from the kitchen, "and come back in before you get too cold."

Boy, oh boy, some moms really do have eyes and ears in the backs of their heads. I buttoned my coat even though I hate being bundled up that way. It makes me feel like a burrito.

I would've taken along good ole Daisy, our huge, white Great Pyrenees dog, but she's old and the cold weather isn't good for her bones. She was sound asleep on her very own dog blanket on the service porch. Daisy likes to sleep back there near the little wall heater.

Outside, that cold wind sucked the breath right out of my mouth, and I wondered how in the world my wimpy big sister was able to buck up long enough to step off the porch, let alone walk to the mailbox and take off down Rough Creek Road.

I had almost reached the end of the driveway when Daddy pulled in, driving his nice, almost brand-new, bronze-colored pickup. He stopped next to me and rolled down his window. Mama says my daddy is the best-looking man in all of Arkansas, and I agree with her. He has dark hair and real blue eyes, and when he smiles, you feel warm and cozy right down to your very toes.

"What are you doing out here in this cold, little girl of mine?" he said. His breath came out in a mist.

"I'm getting some air," I said, making my own misty cloud.

He frowned a little.

"Mighty cold air, punkin'. Don't stay out too long. The temperature's dropping fast."

"Okay, Daddy. I'll go back in soon."

I watched him drive around to the back of the house. Then I nipped over to the mailbox and opened it. Of course there was not a single, solitary clue inside because that rotten Myra Sue had taken out her secret. I don't know why I even looked.

Arms akimbo, I stared at that dumb mailbox, wishing it could talk. Had Myra been writing love letters to Johnny Brittain, who lives up the road? Maybe she wrote a story and was sending it off to a magazine, but that idea was so all-fired crazy, I laughed right out loud and nearly froze my tongue.

Then I heard galloping footsteps pounding against the frozen brown dirt of our old road, and before I could say, "What's going on here?" I was yanked around hard.

Myra Sue stood there, panting like an army mule, glaring at me like she wanted to knock me upside my head. "What are you doing, you little brat?" she barked.

"I could ask you the same thing, Miss Smarty-Sneaky

Pants. First you skulk around my bedroom door, and then I see you hide something in the mailbox. What was it?" I peered down the road, looking for anything strange, but it looked like the same old dirt road to me.

"I didn't hide anything in the mailbox! And besides, it's none of your business!"

"Aha!" I hollered.

"Aha, what?"

"If you weren't hiding anything, then how could it be none of my business?"

I watched her try to figure out what I just said. Boy, watching that girl go through a thought process was like watching a snail run away with a turtle. I like to have grown a long, gray beard before she caught on.

"Oh!" she finally snarled, and she stomped her foot, which had to have hurt pretty good, seeing as how the ground was frozen hard as a rock. "I was not hiding anything. I was looking to see if we got any mail."

I crimped my mouth. "That's so dumb I shouldn't even reply, but I will: *The mail does not run on Sunday.*"

She blinked a few times, taking in this late-breaking news flash. Then she said, "So what?"

"Myra Sue Reilly, I saw you sneak something into that mailbox, and when you saw me see you, you went and got it out and took off with it. So it must be something sneaky and rotten that you don't want anyone to know about."

She waggled her mouth open and shut about 674 times and then said, with all the intelligence you can imagine, "Nuh-uh!"

"Nuh-uh, what?"

She stomped her foot again and grabbed my arm. She shook me hard and said, with her eyes all squinted, "You just keep your big, fat mouth shut and don't go blabbing to anyone, or I will tell about that box of chocolates you aren't supposed to have that you hid under your bed, and that math test you nearly failed right before the end of last semester, and how you tore your brand-new good church coat under the arm and stapled it back together so Mama wouldn't know."

"Ho-hum," I said, hoping to fool her into thinking I did not care if she told all my little secrets. But boy, oh boy. How'd she know about all that candy? I bought it with my very own allowance, even though I wasn't supposed to buy a whole entire big box of candy, especially as I'd already eaten all those Mint Dreams that Rob Estes gave me for Christmas. Rob Estes, by the way, is another one of my grandma's gentlemen friends, or at least he was. But I'm not sure if he is now or not because I think they had a little falling-out on account of Grandma having another boyfriend, Ernie Beason, who owns Ernie's Grocerteria. He liked Grandma first. And now there's Reverend Jordan to consider. But I'll tell you the honest truth: I don't want to think about that right now. I'm in the middle of telling you about Myra Sue and all the dumb things she was saying to me right then.

"I will tell Mama and Daddy," she said, all bossy and mean, "and you will be grounded *forever* just for not mentioning that math test, and you know it."

I did know it.

"All right, then," I said. "But you better tell me what all that sneaking was about."

"I was not sneaking," she said, looking all prissy. "Maybe I was ordering a present for Grandma's birthday, so you just better shut your trap, April Grace."

Well.

If she'd said right from the very first that she was ordering a present for Grandma, we wouldn't have had to go through all that mess. That girl is about as smart as a box of rocks.

"What did you order for her?" I asked.

"None of your business, that's what." And she flounced off, up the driveway and to the house.

I stood where I was a little longer, even though the wind was bitterly cold and little stinging bits of ice started to pelt my cheeks.

Myra Sue's explanation sounded reasonable enough, but something told me she was lying like a rug. Number one: She would never think to order a present when she could pester Mama to take her to Wal-Mart in Blue Reed. Number two: She spent every cent of her allowance on dumb stuff, like cheap lipstick and hair clips. Number three: She was acting far too sneaky to be ordering a present.

You better believe I was gonna keep my eyes and ears open.

FOUR

Grandma Comes Home in the Sleet and Lives to Tell About It, Thank the Good Lord

♫

The front door opened, and my mama stepped out onto the porch. She hunched up her shoulders and rubbed her arms against the cold.

"April Grace, honey, come inside. It's beginning to sleet."

"Yes'm," I hollered, and trotted the rest of the way to the house.

She held open the door for me.

"You and your sister! Why in the world did you want to go outside on such a cold, dreary day?"

I didn't know what to say, so it was a good thing she didn't wait for me to reply.

"Go hang up your coat, then get yourself some hot cocoa in the kitchen. And don't go outside again today, honey. The weather is turning really nasty. I hope Mama Grace gets home before the roads get slick."

I hoped my grandma got home soon, too. She was a scary enough driver in the middle of August on hot, dry roads, and here it was, January, with sleet coming down.

And I hoped that as soon as she got home safe and sound, we'd get a snowstorm so gigantic, school would be canceled until the Fourth of July. You see, I do not like junior high, not even a little bit, which is sad, because I do like learning things. But Cedar Ridge Junior High is about as awful a school experience as you'll ever hope not to have. It's smelly and noisy, and cold in the cold weather and hot in the hot weather, and the teachers all have an Attitude Problem. So you can see why I dreaded going back tomorrow for my first day back after Christmas break.

Upstairs, the door to Myra Sue's room was closed. Not that I cared. She could lock herself in there until she was a great-great-grandmother and I'd be perfectly happy, but a minute later she came out of her room and went into the bathroom. A second later I heard water running. I tell you, the way that girl takes two or three showers a day, you'd think she'd have washed herself down the drain by now.

As I hung up my coat, I thought of something. I figured maybe what Myra Sue had put in the mailbox and then taken out might still be in her coat pocket.

I listened at the bathroom door and heard her splashing around in the shower, so as quick as possible, I went into her room.

Boy, that girl lived in the biggest mess of a bedroom anyone ever lived in. I'm telling you, a person would need a gas mask, leather gloves, and a blowtorch to get around in that mess. How in the world my mama, who is the world's neatest housekeeper, allowed my dumb sister to have a room that disastrous is something I do not understand. One time I heard Mama tell Grandma that everyone should have some private space, and if Myra Sue chose never to clean up her space, she'd just have to live in it as it was.

Once I got past the idea of all that filth, I went in and opened her closet door, and there was her coat, on the floor instead of being hung up like it should've been. I picked it up and thrust my hands into the pockets.

I found a piece of gum, still in the wrapper and unchewed, thank goodness, two Kleenexes, a candy-bar wrapper, a broken pencil, the blue cap off a Bic pen, a safety pin, and a folded piece of paper. I left all that trash and junk in her pocket but unfolded the paper. When I read that list, I figured I had a clue—but a clue to what? I had no idea.

1. Midnight Cruise
2. Treehouse Rendezvous
3. Never on Sunday
4. Cream Cheese in Florida

I read that list at least twelve times and still did not know what it meant.

I heard the water in the shower turn off, so I stuffed that paper into my jeans pocket and got out of her room, but not before I threw her coat back on the closet floor. If I'd hung it up, she'd know I'd been in there.

Back in my own room, I left that paper with the weird list in my pocket, grabbed my book off the shelf, and headed back downstairs for some hot chocolate. Then I settled down to read in the living room, where Eli was sleeping peacefully.

The telephone rang, and Myra Sue, all wet and wrapped in her robe, came thundering down the stairs to answer it.

"Hello?" she said in a voice that did not sound like her. She always did that. A la-di-da voice that sounded like she was thirty years old and living in New York City. Then she said, "Hello? Hello?" Then, "Hello, hello, hello! *Helllllloooo!*" which did not sound mature, sophisticated, or ladylike *at all*. In fact, she was yelling like a dipstick. I jumped up and went into the hallway where the phone was to see why Myra Sue was yelling like that.

Daddy came right out of the bedroom. He had changed

into a pair of sweatpants and a T-shirt, and he had been lying down for his usual Sunday afternoon rest. He did not have a happy look on his face, I'm here to tell you. His blue eyes practically glowed.

"Myra Sue Reilly, what on earth are you yelling about?"

"Nobody answered when I picked up the phone," she told him.

"Shouting doesn't help, but it does wake up people in the house! You do that again, and you will be grounded from the phone for a week. Got it?"

She gave him a sullen glare. "Yes, sir."

In the living room, Eli set up to howling, and I went to get him.

Mama came into the living room. "Just when I thought I might take a little nap myself," she said with a tired smile. "You want me to take him, honey?"

"That's okay, Mama. Why don't you take a nap, and I'll watch Eli? I can rock him back to sleep."

She put one arm around my shoulder, and with her free hand, she tickled his cheek.

"Actually, April, I think he probably needs his diaper changed."

Oh.

She took him right out of my arms and carried him into the hallway where Myra Sue stood, looking like a reject from a Pepto-Bismol commercial. At least her face was that pink, and she was still giving our daddy a sour look.

Mama said, "You woke him, Myra Sue. You change his dirty diaper."

I like to have busted a gut laughing, especially as up to that point, ole Myra had avoided changing diapers of the poopy sort.

Daddy and I exchanged a look.

"You girls be quiet, you hear me? Your mama and I need a little rest."

As if I had been the one to galumph down the stairs to the telephone and stand there screaming at no one on the other end. But I said, "Yes, sir, Daddy. I'm sorry you got woken up."

Myra Sue went off to change Eli, but Daddy just stood there, eyeballing that telephone.

"Mike?" Mama said, a slight frown on her face. "Something wrong?"

He heaved out a big breath, frowning deeper than she did.

"I just don't like it when someone calls and hangs up. It's like they're calling to find out if someone's home . . ."

Mama was shooting looks at him, then at me, and back to him, and he broke off what he was saying.

"What d'you mean, Daddy, about someone calling to find out if we're home? If they do that, it's dumb to hang up when we answer. Why don't they just ask . . . ?" And then I understood. If some rotten ole person wanted to rob our house, they might call to see if we were gone. Well, that riled me good and proper, and I started to say so, but Daddy put his hand on my head.

"Don't worry about it, punkin. It was probably someone who just got a wrong number and was too rude to apologize."

I sure hoped it was a wrong number, 'cause I hated to think of sitting up all night, wide-awake, watching for rotten ole burglars.

♫

The weather did not look good outside. Sleet started pouring down, and I almost got a knot in my stomach worrying about my grandma. Thankfully, just a little while later, the front door opened and Grandma walked in, safe and sound, toting her three-tiered pie carrier. I was never so glad to see anyone in my life.

"Grandma!" I said as soft as I could, given my relief to see her. At least I didn't holler out like a wounded warthog.

"April Grace!" she said in the same awed tone of voice I had used.

"I'm glad you're home!" I said.

"Me, too. The roads are getting bad." She glanced around. "Everybody asleep?"

I nodded. "Except Myra. She's upstairs, probably sulking like an old possum."

"Mercy me," Grandma said, walking toward the kitchen, toting her pie carrier.

I trailed along behind her, hoping she had a piece or two left over from the three she'd made for that Methodist church potluck.

"What's that girl pouting about this time?" she asked, so I told her all about Myra screaming into the phone like a doofus.

"Goodness' sake," Grandma murmured, like she was about half-listening.

"What do you think about people who call and hang up?" I asked her.

"I reckon they got nothing to say."

"Do you think they might come to rob your house?"

She looked at me like I had just asked to have worms for tomorrow's breakfast.

"Where'd you come up with that wild notion?"

"Daddy said sometimes people do that."

She waved a hand like she was waving away a fly.

"Maybe it happens in the city, but you don't need to worry about things like that on Rough Creek Road. Put those thoughts out of your mind. I'm surprised your daddy said such a thing to you."

"He didn't. He said it to Mama."

"Don't give it another thought, April. And your daddy shouldn't worry about such piffle, either."

Suddenly, a thought occurred to me. "Are you gonna leave our church and start going to that one?"

She rested one hand on her hip and frowned at me. "What in the world makes you ask such a question?"

"Change!" I hollered, then clapped my hands over my big hollering mouth. "I mean, *change*!" I whispered between my fingers. "In his sermon this morning, Pastor said things were gonna *change*. Grandma! I don't want any more change."

"Well, I reckon you better just go move into a cave and stay there," she said unreasonably, "because life is nothin' but change."

FIVE

Telephone Etiquette 101

✻

Grandma sliced me a piece of pie, made some fresh coffee, then looked out at the weather.

"I should have had Trask—er, Reverend Jordan—drop me off at my house," she said. "Walking across the field in this stuff won't be fun."

"Grandma!" I said, scraping any speck of pie that might be left on my plate. My tongue ached to lick the last bit of taste, but I knew better than to even try such an uncouth trick. "You can't go outside in that cold and ice."

"Mebbe it'll stop soon."

Just then, Myra came dragging into the kitchen, looking like the bloom from a skunk weed. Grandma gave her a big smile.

"There's Myra-Susie-Q." She held out her free arm and hugged that sulky girl. Myra endured the hug like she was being tortured.

Daddy, Mama, and Eli weren't far behind her, having just woken up from their naps.

"Good afternoon, sleepyheads," Grandma said. "How about some fresh coffee?"

"That would be real nice, Mom," Daddy said.

"Thank you, Mama Grace," Mama said, nuzzling Eli's cheek. But it seemed like as soon as all the adults settled down with their fresh cups of coffee, someone knocked on our front door. Mama handed Eli to me and went to answer it. I wondered who in the world would come to visit on a day as raw and ugly as that one.

"Hello, Lily," Ian St. James said. Next to him stood his missus, Isabel. Behind the St. Jameses, grinning happily, were their next-door neighbors, Forest and Temple Freebird. The Freebirds are old hippies from up north but have lived here in Arkansas for a gazillion years, and the St. Jameses are transplanted Californians who moved here last summer.

"Well, hello, everyone," Mama said, bright and friendly, just like she expected a quartet of neighbors to show up on her doorstep during a winter storm while she was in her sweat suit and house slippers, her hair all mussed up from her nap. "Come in this house where it's warm!"

They trooped inside, bringing in cold air and plenty of sleet on their coats and heads. Mama shut the door and said, "Go on into the kitchen and get yourselves some hot coffee."

I trailed along behind everyone and entered the kitchen just as Ian was saying to Daddy, "So I'm here to help with the milking until Brett gets to feeling better."

Mr. Brett has been our hired man since before I can remember. Usually he was healthy as a horse, but that day he had the creeping crud and was sicker than a dog.

"I'll pitch in, too, Mike, and Temple is going to take Brett some of her tea," Forest said.

My sister stood on the far side of the room, arms folded, a pouty expression on her face. This was unusual only because Isabel was in the same room, and Myra Sue had *not* flown to her side like a starving homing pigeon. Looking at Isabel, I'm not sure she had yet noticed her darling's sourness.

She came over to where I sat holding Eli. She touched his

cheek with her fingertip, then held his tiny fist. She spread open his hands and looked at all his fingers.

Finally Isabel noticed Myra Sue. "What's wrong, darling?" she asked. "You aren't getting that awful flu that's going around, are you?"

Mama laid a hand on Myra Sue's forehead, then she shook her head and dropped her hand.

"No fever. I think Miss Myra is still just a little put-out because she had to spend most of the afternoon in her room."

Myra's mouth flew open and then clamped shut. Her face turned red, then she hollered, "Everyone in the entire world hates me, and no one would miss me if I just fell off the face of the earth and disappeared forever!" And off she stomped, out of the kitchen, thundering up the steps and into her bedroom again, where she slammed the door so loud the house vibrated.

No one said anything for a moment, but from the look on my parents' faces, I would not want to be Myra Sue Reilly after our guests went home. Well, to be perfectly honest, I wouldn't want to be Myra Sue Reilly *ever*.

"My mother would have swatted my bottom," Grandma declared. "She never put up with any sass or nonsense."

"Myra Sue needs a good tonic," Temple said. "I have just the thing back home, and I'll brew some up for her."

Isabel gave Temple the Big Eye—which are the big staring eyes that do not blink at all—but Mama just said, "Temple, you're always so thoughtful. Thank you for your concern."

Now, I knew good and well that Temple Freebird was gonna bring some awful-looking, gross-smelling, nasty-tasting stuff, and I'll tell you here and now, I wanted to be there when my sister had to drink it.

Eli stirred and squirmed again in my arms, but he didn't wake up. I gave him a soft kiss on his tiny forehead.

While I sat there cradling my baby brother, I got to thinking about that business with Myra's secret again—a secret so secret she'd run around in the icy cold to take care of it.

I wondered if Temple had a tonic that would cure *that*.

SIX

Howling Wind, Frozen Thunder: Are We Having Fun, or What?

*

The three men all trooped out of the house and into the cold, going to take care of the evening milking. Temple had brought some kind of tea for Mr. Brett's creeping crud and insisted on walking to his house, although Grandma, Mama, and finally Isabel offered to drive her there.

She waved them off, laughing.

"He just lives around the corner. A little bit of cold and ice won't hurt me, friends!" she declared. And off she went with her tea, cheerful and bright as a day in May. She did not smell like a day in May, though. That's because she and Forest apparently saw no reason to bathe more than once a month or thereabouts

Right as Temple headed out, Mama opened the kitchen window the teeniest little bit. The air was cold, cutting right into that warm kitchen, but it was fresh and clean, and we all took a deep breath. Not a single one of us said a cotton-pickin' word about why we were sucking in fresh air.

Eli sneezed.

"Scat!" said Grandma. She often says "Scat!" when someone sneezes. I reckon it's her version of "God bless you" or "Gesundheit." "Let me have that little bundle," she said. "I'll take him to the front room and out of the draft."

I handed him over, real careful, and after she nuzzled him a few times, Grandma went right out of the room with that baby.

"I'll be in there in a minute, Grace, as soon as I finish my coffee," Isabel called after her. "And you better relinquish that child to me when I do."

Grandma laughed.

"All right, if you insist. For a few minutes," she replied from the other room.

"And I better get her a fresh diaper and some baby wipes. I think she might need them," Mama said with a chuckle as she left.

Isabel and I were alone in the kitchen. The teapot started whistling, so I got up and turned down the flame so that steam didn't sound like Coach Frizzel's whistle when he gets mad at us during PE relay races.

And thinking of that, I asked, "You looking forward to your first day of teaching tomorrow? 'Cause I'll tell you the truth, I'm pretty much looking forward to not having ole Coach Frizzel as my gym teacher for a whole semester. He scares the daylights out of me, with his big, red face and the way he hollers and yells and blows that stupid whistle."

Isabel raised one eyebrow. Although she would be teaching drama at the high school two days a week, one day a week she would be teaching dance at the junior high, and they were calling it PE.

"You don't plan to yell and scream and blow whistles at us, do you, Isabel?" I added, sitting back down and leaning toward her earnestly.

"Of course not," she sniffed.

"Good. 'Cause you won't need to do that, I'm thinking. I remember you had a good, strong voice when you were directing our Christmas play last month. I think everyone will be able to hear you just fine."

"I'm sure they will." She blinked a bunch of times, then sipped her coffee. She seemed a little nervous all of a sudden.

"April Grace," she said, putting down her cup. "I've never been a teacher, and I've had very little experience with young people. Do you think . . . that is, will those children cooperate with me?"

She looked right into my eyes, just like I was a grown-up having a grown-up conversation with her.

"Isabel," I said with all the maturity I could muster, "knowing you, I don't think you will give them a choice."

I watched her think about that, then she seemed to shed that nervousness as she drew herself up all straight and prim.

"Thank you, my dear. I intend to be a teacher, not a doormat."

I doubted she'd ever been a doormat for anyone or anything.

"Good for you, Isabel, 'cause I gotta say, those kids in junior high are not the easiest kids you will ever meet in your life."

She blinked about twenty times.

"Oh?"

"No."

She twitched. "Well. We'll see about that."

I smiled inside myself, 'cause I knew Isabel was gonna clean those kids' clocks if they got out of line in her classes. She might put Coach Frizzel to shame. I was afraid of Coach, but I knew Isabel, and I understood her. When you understand someone, you have no reason to be afraid of them.

"Isabel?" I asked.

She was drinking her coffee, all proper and dainty, but when she heard the tone of my voice, she put down the cup and looked at me.

"Yes?"

"Isabel, did Myra Sue come to your house earlier today?"

She frowned. "No. What makes you ask that?"

Okay, so Myra had not gone running to the St. Jameses' after all. Since that was the case, then where had she gone? I sincerely doubted she went to the Freebirds', even if they didn't live much farther down Rough Creek Road than Ian and Isabel. And there was no one who lived between us and the St. Jameses.

Hmm.

"April Grace?" Isabel said, interrupting my ponderings.

"Yes'm?"

"Why did you think Myra Sue came to our house this afternoon?"

Oh boy. What was I supposed to say? I knew, sure as the world, if I told Isabel my sister was acting peculiar, she'd tell Mama and Grandma, and they'd tell Daddy, and Ian would overhear, and maybe the Freebirds, too, if they were anywhere near, and then there'd be a whole lot of drama and carrying-on over something that was probably nothing, and then Myra would be so ticked off at me she'd probably blab about my chocolates and my coat and that stupid, dumb math test, which I never should have told her about in the first place because she has a big mouth sometimes.

Maybe Myra was back to doing all that awful mess of exercises she did last summer. She'd ended up being sick because she'd starved herself and exercised herself until she was the size of a skeleton because Isabel and her own thinness had not had a positive influence. But if Myra was doing that and she'd told Isabel, I'm pretty sure Isabel would've told Mama and Daddy. She doesn't want Myra getting all sick again.

"She's been all mopey, and I thought she might've gone there to pour out her heart and cry on your shoulder 'cause you're her role model."

Isabel shook her head.

"Myra hasn't been coming around much lately, but it's completely understandable, what with darling little Eli here in the house." She drank the last of her coffee. "I miss her, of course, but if I were her, I certainly wouldn't be hanging around with old folks when I had a baby brother to play with. And speaking of that . . ." She stood up and smiled. "It's my turn with that sweet baby. Grace, prepare to relinquish your hold," she said as she walked out of the room.

So that was that. Until I had some kind of solid proof that my sister was being a sneak, I figured I'd just keep things to myself.

That evening, as soon as the men came back from the barn and Temple returned from Mr. Brett's, all us women had a hot supper on the table for everybody. We had hamburgers and fried potatoes and brown-bean and ham soup with corn bread, and for the sake of Forest and Temple and Isabel, who have peculiar eating habits, there were also baked sweet potatoes and plenty of garden vegetables that had been frozen or home-canned during the harvest season. Ian had learned to eat normal, like the rest of us.

Right smack-dab in the middle of that meal, the telephone rang, and Daddy got up to answer it.

"Stay there," he said to my sister.

Now, you would've thought Myra Sue would have leaped outta her chair like a toad on a hot stove. She twitched and moaned and had the most severely pained expression you can possibly imagine.

"It's probably Jennifer or Jessica wondering why I haven't called them *all day*!" she said, nearly wringing her hands.

"Then I'll tell them you'll talk to them at school," Daddy said as he walked out of the room.

Myra looked so mad, I thought her head was gonna explode right there at the supper table. But I reckon for once in her life she had enough sense not to do something dumb, like scream or kick something. That lower lip like to have sprained itself by sticking out so far.

Daddy came back to the table, shaking his head.

"No one there."

"They hung up?" Grandma asked.

"Guess so."

"I *told* you someone called and hung up," Myra Sue said, all snippy. "And I got punished for it!"

I guess her brief lapse into good sense was over.

"Myra Sue," Mama said, coming into the dining room after putting Eli into his bed, "we believed you when you said someone hung up. You're being punished for screaming at the telephone and for screaming at us."

"You getting prank calls?" Forest asked.

"Maybe you should call the sheriff, Mike," Ian urged.

"Well, we'll see how it goes," Daddy told him, casually. "Like I said, could be someone just called the wrong number or changed his mind."

"I have something that will ward off all negative energy," Temple said, bright and happy. "It works wonderfully well.

You just pour it around the house and over the threshold and across your driveway . . . I'll mix some up for you as soon as I get home."

If she brought us some of it and *if* Daddy or Mama let her pour it around, I sure hoped it didn't stink to high heaven, or look like something one of the cows might've regurgitated.

"That's kind of you, Temple," Daddy said, with a nice, friendly smile, "but that won't be necessary."

A silence fell over us just long enough to hear the wind howl like a wounded ghost.

"Mercy!" Grandma said, shivering. "Listen to that!"

She didn't have to tell us. We couldn't help it. And it was creepy, let me tell you.

Ian said, "I think we'd better get home before the weather gets worse."

Right then the biggest old thunder-boomer you ever heard shook the whole entire house. The telephone rang one short ring, and then every single light went out.

Just as suddenly as they went out, they came back on.

"Gracious!" Grandma said. "I hope we don't lose power completely."

The telephone rang again, and I thought ole Myra might come right out of her skin, but she didn't. I started to hop up and run for it, but Daddy said, "*I'll* get it."

Well, ever' last one of us sat still and listened when he picked up that phone out in the hallway.

"Hello?" He didn't say anything for a couple of seconds, then, "Hello? Is anyone there?"

A moment later, he came back into the dining room.

"I don't know," he said, shaking his head. "The storm might be causing problems with the phone line."

Thunder shook the house again, the phone pinged twice—*Ping! Ping!*—short and sharp just like that, and Daddy frowned. He went right back into the hallway. "Is anyone there?" he said into the phone.

"I think the storm has knocked out the telephone," he announced as he came back. "It's dead as a doornail."

"Oh noooo!" Myra Sue moaned like she'd just been informed soap operas had become illegal.

"Well, there you go, then," Forest said. "Ice building up on the lines most of the day most likely caused your phone problems, not some prankster."

Boy, oh boy, you can't believe how relieved I was that some robber probably wasn't planning to carry off our VCR and all my books and stuff.

"No phone at all?" Myra whined. "But if Jessica or Jenni—"

"Myra Sue Reilly," Mama said, "if I hear one more word about you and the telephone, you won't be using it for a month of Sundays. Do you understand?"

Boy, oh boy, Myra's eyes got bigger than two blue dinner plates. I reckon she figured out that she'd finally got on Mama's last nerve, 'cause she gulped and nodded and said, "Yes'm." She hushed, and I was exceedingly glad to hear nothing coming from her mouth.

One thing was for certain: with all that ice coming down outside, there'd be no school tomorrow. But sooner or later, Isabel's class would begin, and I was gonna be there when it happened.

SEVEN

Isabel's Class Gets off to a Rousing Start

After that ice from that awful ice storm melted, school started up again on Tuesday. On my way to Isabel's first class, I reminded myself over and over that at least Coach Frizell would not be there.

The entire sixth-grade class, all fifty-seven of us, filed into that old gym and settled onto the bleachers. We all sat like wriggling worms on fishhooks, waiting for Isabel to show up. Let me tell you, if everybody had not been chattering like a bunch of monkeys in the jungle, we'd probably have heard her before we saw her, because she came marching across the polished oak gym floor in those tall, skinny high heels.

"Why is she dressed like *that*?" Melissa said as we watched the woman approach.

"I dunno. She always dresses that way."

"April Grace, she looks *scary*."

Now, I will admit, Isabel is scary-looking, what with her slicked-back hair, long, thin nose, and bony body. But she is not actually a scary *person*.

"You were there while she directed the Christmas program," I said hurriedly, because by then Isabel was standing in front of the class. "She didn't bite then, and she doesn't bite now."

Isabel stood there, straight and narrow as a crowbar, her lips pulled in tightly, her eyes traveling over the entire group.

Now, my own personal self, I could see plain as day that she was nervous, but I don't think anyone else could tell. They did not know her like I did, and nerves on Isabel

St. James do not show up like they do on normal people. In fact, if goose bumps were people, they'd have Isabels on their skin when they got spooked.

Here's the thing: Isabel was gonna have to teach dancing to a bunch of rowdy kids who didn't know a dance step from a soccer kick. All this dance stuff was new to us.

"May I have your attention?" she said more politely than you might have expected. But she didn't say it real loud, and most of the kids just kept yakking.

I could see a coach's whistle in her hand and figured she'd blow it to kingdom come when she realized what a good attention-getter it was. I should've known better, 'cause I remembered how she took over directing our church play. Instead of tooting that whistle, she pulled herself even stiffer and taller.

"*People!*" she said, not so politely. Her voice seemed to come from all corners of that gym.

Wow! She sure knew her business about voice projection. All that yakety-yak dried up like a snow cone in the desert, and everyone gawked at her. In a second, some of the boys snickered, and she pinned her killer gaze right smack-dab on them.

They shut their traps.

"All right, people," she said, and she didn't even have to holler. "I have handouts." She pointed to two girls in the front row. "These young women will pass them out. You absolutely must put these handouts in a binder and must not *lose* them. There will be tests."

She stopped speaking and let this sink in. We'd never had tests in PE before. She continued with her lecture.

"We will be discussing dance history and theory *before* you learn any actual dance." She paused to rake that cold gaze over everyone again. "You will *not* be learning clodhopping, line dancing, break dancing, disco, the moonwalk, or any other so-called dance that is nothing more than the undignified gyrations of hicks and other lowlifes."

I squirmed, wanting to gallop down off the bleachers to the place where she stood and clamp my hand over her mouth. I could only pray she'd remember some of the talks we'd had about her saying things like this.

Mutterings ran through the class like hot wind. Some of the kids glared at me, just because they knew that I knew Isabel personally.

"Quiet!" Isabel said. "You will be learning the basics of ballet, ballroom, and some of the Latin steps. Just because we live in Arkansas, that's no reason you should wallow in ignorance and gracelessness."

"Oh, Isabel, stop talking!" I screamed in my head. She had just taken one huge, gigantic, enormous step backward.

One thing's for sure, I would never in a hundred million years tell any of my classmates that this whole situation of her being our teacher had been *my* suggestion last summer. Boy, oh boy, sometimes I just needed to keep my brilliant ideas to myself.

By the way, those handouts must've weighed three hundred pounds, and Isabel, as she launched into the very first section that morning, did not so much as *glance* at her notes. She knew her stuff, and from all appearances, she was gonna make sure *we* knew all of it before the end of the semester.

At least we weren't getting out there on the gym floor doing twirly toes and pirouettes in front of one another and looking like complete goofs. Yet.

⊚

When Myra Sue and I got off the bus that afternoon, I walked toward the mailbox to pull out the day's mail, but ole Myra nearly flattened me like she was a steamroller with arms and legs.

"Hey!" I yelled, getting up and brushing the dirt off my pants. I picked up my scattered books. "Are you crazy?"

She pulled every bit of mail out and flipped through it. Then she frowned real big and stomped off toward the house.

Boy, oh boy. "What were you lookin' for, Myra? A love letter?"

"Be quiet, April Grace!" she snarled, and just kept walking.

"Who'd be writing to *you*, anyway?" I hollered at her. "The president of the Drips of America Society, wanting you to join?"

She turned around and walked backward, glaring at me good and proper. It was then I noticed she was wearing so much makeup, it was a wonder her face didn't fall off. With bright-blue eye shadow, mascara so thick her lashes looked glued together, and bright-red blush with matching lipstick, that girl looked like some of those women on the soap operas.

"I am not expecting any letters from anybody, so just drop it, you brat."

"Then what's the big deal? You went skulking and sneaking out here Sunday—"

"I did not, and you better stop spying on me."

"Myra Sue Reilly, if you're doing something you hadn't ought to be doing, Mama and Daddy are gonna pitch a fit when they find out."

"They aren't gonna find out!"

"Wait till Mama gets a load of you and that makeup, Myra Sue. What were you doing, practicing to be on *Silver Linings*?"

"I want to be on *Days of Our Lives*, April Grace!" Then, as if my words soaked into her tiny brain, she stopped dead in her tracks and slapped one hand to her face. Then she screamed.

"I forgot to wash it off!" She gave me a wild-eyed look. "Don't tell Mama! I'm going down to the washroom in the barn to scrub it off, and if you tell, I will make you sorry."

"What do you do, Myra, put on five pounds of makeup when you get to school every day?"

"I have to look glamorous!" she squealed, then took off toward the barn. If Daddy happened to be in there and caught sight of that mess, she was gonna get it.

I stood right where I was for a good long minute. Everyone always told her how pretty she was, so it seemed to me she wouldn't want to go around looking like a reject from clown school with all that junk on her face. Maybe she thought wearing lots of makeup would make her glamorous and impress Johnny Brittain or somebody. I don't know what was going on with her, but I'm telling you, that girl was up to No Good.

EIGHT

Myra Sue's Room: The Pit of the World

That very same Tuesday night, Ian and Isabel had supper with us to celebrate Isabel's first day as a teacher. Mama was in the other room changing Eli's diaper, and Grandma had gone to the movies with Reverend Jordan. I hoped they didn't go see something all romantic because I really did not want to witness any kissy or moony-eyed business in this house when they came back. It is Totally Embarrassing.

"I have never had such a case of nerves!" Isabel declared. "The stage is not nearly so frightening as a class of sixth graders." She glanced at me. "What did you think, April Grace? Did you enjoy my class?"

Uh-oh.

I squirmed.

"Well, um, Isabel, you did fine," I said. "First days are always hard, and none of us are used to sitting still on the bleachers for PE. But you kept everyone nice and quiet while you talked."

She smiled. "Thank you, dear. Did my nerves show?"

"Nope! You looked very calm."

My little comment seemed to satisfy her.

Isabel tilted her head to one side and looked at my sister, who was poking her food with a fork. "Are you feeling all right, darling?" she asked.

Myra Sue glanced at her. "Yes'm, just fine, thank you."

Mama gave that girl a steady look, even reached over and laid her hand against Myra's forehead. "She's not warm," she said, dropping her hand.

"I feel fine, Mother," Myra Sue said.

Isabel and Mama exchanged glances.

"The high school drama classes begin tomorrow," Isabel reminded Myra. "I hope you're looking forward to it."

"How about that?" Daddy said with an encouraging grin. "You'll like that class!"

Would you believe my sister just shrugged, as if she did not live and breathe drama and all sorts of theatrical baloney? But you know what? At the Christmas play, she got even more nervous than I did and flubbed her small part pretty badly. She was so embarrassed that even I felt sorry for her. I wondered if that experience changed her mind about becoming a world-famous actress.

Isabel blinked twenty times or thereabouts, laid down her fork, and gazed at Myra Sue.

"Aren't you eager to start the class, Myra?" she asked.

Myra poked at her broccoli with the tip of her fork, then she sucked in a lungful of air and heaved it out.

"I might not take your class," she mumbled.

Well, this was news to every last one of us. Isabel sort of reared back in her chair.

"I beg your pardon?" she said.

Myra Sue finally lifted her head and met Isabel's eyes.

"I might not take your class."

"Why not?"

"Because . . . because . . . maybe I want to be a TV star instead."

"Oh brother!" I hollered. "TV stars are actors, Myra."

"Oh, darling," Isabel said, looking kinda snooty, "television performance is not on the same level as real acting. For that matter, neither is being in movies. Live theater is the only *real* acting."

That was news to me, 'cause I thought acting was acting, even if you're selling toilet paper on a commercial.

"Even *Days of Our Lives?*" Myra asked in a voice so quivery you'd swear she had a mouthful of Jell-O.

"Oh, darling, goodness yes. Soap operas are, well, low-class."

You shoulda seen my sister. Her lip pooched out, then she drew it back in. Then she blinked a hundred times because I think she was fixin' to cry but didn't want Isabel to see. With her back as straight as a board, she said, "Maybe I will be a brain surgeon or join the navy instead of being an actress."

"Are you kiddin'?" I hooted. "Number one, you would never make it in the navy because you puked up your socks that time you were in Mr. Brett's rowboat on Bryant Creek, and number two, to be a brain surgeon, you have to have a *brain.*"

"April Grace," Mama said. "No more talk like that or you'll be doing the supper dishes every night this week without any help from your sister."

I crimped my mouth. "Yes'm." I don't understand why I get scolded for telling the truth.

"But you're already enrolled in Drama I, aren't you?" Daddy asked my sister.

"Yes, but it isn't a required class, like history," she said, kinda snippy.

Then, so uppity it would make your toenails curl, she

said, "May I please be excused now? Mr. Harmony wants us to choose topics for our term paper by the end of the week, so I need to decide what I want to write about."

Mr. Harmony was the ninth-grade history teacher, and I had never heard Myra ask to be excused from the supper table to do homework. It sounded fishy to me, but Daddy nodded and Mama said, "Yes, you may go."

Myra said good night to everyone, just as polite as anything, then she walked out of the dining room so stiff you would've thought Mama starched her drawers the last time she did the wash. When Myra Sue leaves the room like that, you know she's in a Mood. But we were all used to Myra Sue and her moods, so it didn't mean a whole lot, although I noticed Isabel looked a little hurt and a lot confused. But her expression cleared when her glance fell on Eli, and she reached for him. Mama handed him right over with a big smile. That poor kid only sleeps in his bed when no one is awake to pass him around.

As soon as I finished my supper, I said, "Mama, I've got homework, too. May I be excused?"

"Yes. I'll wash the dishes tonight."

I told everyone good night and trotted off upstairs. I had good homework that night. Mrs. Scrivner had assigned us a story to read, and tomorrow she was going to give us a list of questions to answer in class. But, wouldn't you know, right in the middle of my reading, words and music hammered right through the wall that separated my room and Myra Sue's. I liked Huey Lewis and the News well enough, but not so loud, and not when I was trying to read. I got off my bed and went to Myra Sue's door. I knocked on it, but I reckon she didn't hear because she did not say a word.

I opened the door, and guess what? My sister was sitting on her bed, reading and writing. But she was not reading history or writing down topics for a term paper—unless all those dumb magazines with celebrities' pictures in them were what they were teaching in world history. Plus, she had a dreamy smile on her face, and I don't believe people have dreamy smiles while they are doing homework.

I also noticed a dress I'd never seen before lying across the foot of her bed. It was red and spangly and sparkly, and Mama would never in a million years let her wear something like that. Or the spiked high heels that were on the floor next to it. That awful outfit looked like something one of those girls on the soap operas might wear, but not girls who live on Rough Creek Road.

"Hey!" I said, above the sound of horns, drums, and singers hollering about how hip it was to be a square.

Myra looked like she'd been caught. She yelped and splayed herself across her notebook and all those magazines and that dress as if she thought I was going to swipe them. Yeah, like I care about who is doing what on *Another World* or *Growing Pains*.

"What are you doing, you brat?" she shrieked. "Can't you knock? *Get out of my room!*"

"I knocked, but you didn't hear me! Where'd you get that dumb dress? And why are acting like you're hiding money in your mattress?"

"You shut up about my dress, and you better stay away

from my mattress, April Grace Reilly!" She was grabbing up all that mess on her bed like a starving man grabbing every biscuit on the table.

I eyeballed her mattress. "Why? You hiding somethin' under it?"

"Quit spying on me! I'm not hiding anything. And stay out of my closet, too!"

I was nowhere near her closet, but since she warned me, I figured she had something hidden in there, and if you think I wasn't going to prowl around in it as soon as I got the chance, you need to think again.

Of course I couldn't do a bit of snooping with her in there, and I had homework to do, so I said, "Will you turn down your radio?"

"No!" By this time the papers were mostly under her blankets. "I'm listening to my music, so get out of here."

"But it's too loud, and I need to study."

"No!" she shouted, so I just went right over to that radio and turned it off. She launched herself off the bed at me, but I stepped back, and she ended up on the floor like a big goof.

"What's going on?" Daddy called, and we heard him coming up the stairs.

Myra scooped up the magazines on the floor and threw them under the bed so fast, my eyeballs whirled.

"Don't you say a word about my magazines," she hissed at me like a nasty, old snake.

Daddy came into the room and glared at us.

"What in the world is going on up here? It sounds like you're tearing down the house."

"No, sir, Daddy," I said, gulping, 'cause he looked pretty put-out.

"No, sir, Daddy," repeated Myra.

He narrowed his eyes. "Then what's going on? Why all the racket?"

"I have a story to read for my English class, so I just came in to ask Myra to turn down her radio." I pointed at the silent thing, wishing now ole Huey Lewis was belting out his squareness so my daddy could see how hard it would be to read with all that mess going on.

"I need the radio on so *I* can study, Daddy," Myra said, looking all big-eyed and innocent.

And that right there, my friends, is how Myra Sue Reilly gets away with so much. By looking pretty and innocent.

But Daddy didn't fall for it. He gave her a hard look, then he gave me one.

"Go to your room, April Grace. And Myra, keep your radio turned down to a reasonable volume. If you don't, I'll have to take it away from you."

Myra pouted, and I went to my room and didn't utter a sniveling word about that dress and those shoes, or her reading magazines instead of her history book or hiding things or anything. I kept quiet for three good reasons. Number one: Daddy looked irritated enough that I did not want to rile him. Number two: She'd tattle on me. Number three: Who cares if she does flunk history this semester? Maybe when she was twenty years old and still in the ninth grade, she'd study more.

The next day after school, the moment she got off the bus, ole Myra was airborne, heading toward the mailbox.

"Boy, oh boy. What is it with you and the mailbox?" I said as she pulled out the handful of mail that was in here. "Are you *in love* with it?"

"Don't be so dumb," she muttered, then looked up. "Just because I want to be a help around here, April Grace Reilly, is no reason for you to get snippy. I don't see *you* going out of your way to help anyone."

So now she was Miss Happy Joy Sunshine, full of good deeds.

"At least you aren't covered with clown makeup."

She snarled at me but kept rifling through the mail.

"All I want to know is why you're all of a sudden so interested in the mail. 'Cause to tell you the honest truth, I'm not so all-fired sure you ordered a present for Grandma. I think that is probably just a big fat lie."

Boy, she got mad. I'm not sure if she was mad at me, or the fact that she did not get a speck of mail for herself. That silly girl stomped over to me and thrust every bit of mail into my hands and yelled, "There! You may carry it, since you're so desperate to show your intelligence and good-deed doing!"

"Are you expecting a love letter?"

"I am saving all my love for Bo Brady," she sniffed.

"*Who?* Is he that new boy with those big blue glasses?"

"Bo Brady! On *Days*! Get real, April Grace. Why would I want a boy from this horrible neck of the woods when I can have a boyfriend from Salem?"

"Huh?"

"And I'm not expecting love letters, anyway, so turn blue."

Then with a royal sniff of disdain, she turned and marched to the house, leaving me to shake my head at the way her mind works.

As soon as we got in the house, we found a note from Mama stuck to the fridge. She said she had taken Eli for his checkup, but she'd be home soon, and we could have some of the banana pudding Grandma brought over.

I got us each a bowl and spoon from the cabinet as Myra Sue took the pudding out of the refrigerator. I shoved aside the books we'd plunked down on the table and noticed on the top of Myra's stack was one titled *Theater for the Young Mind*.

I reached over to pick it up, but Myra nearly dropped the pudding in her rush to slap her hand down on the book.

"Do not put your grabby little fingers on my books, April Grace Reilly!"

"I was just looking," I said. She knows how much I like to look at books. "I thought you weren't taking Isabel's class."

She gave me a look so snooty you can't possibly imagine it, then got a serving spoon from the drawer. She plopped it down right smack-dab in the middle of that banana pudding so that the handle was half-buried.

"I changed my mind," she said. Boy, if her voice got any more hoity-toity, her larynx would probably freeze that way.

"So you aren't mad at Isabel anymore?"

Myra Sue blinked twenty times and laid one hand against her chest. "*Moi?* Mad at Isabel?"

"Duh, Myra Sue. You used to follow her around like a homesick puppy, and now you practically ignore her."

"I do not. Don't be daft." She shook back her hair and stuck her nose in the air. I sincerely doubted she even knew what *daft* meant.

"You do so! And don't think she hasn't noticed it."

Her gaze flew to me, and for a moment she forgot to be a snotty snoot.

"Nuh-uh!"

"You either ignore her or you're cool to her, but you aren't all adoring like you used to be. It's plain as day you're hurting her feelings."

She got all teary-eyed and lower-lip-poochy.

"Well, that's just peachy!" she squealed. "First I flub up in that play and then Isabel says the kind of acting I want to do is *low class*. I don't want to take her class and embarrass her with my low-class presence, and now I hurt her feelings. Isabel must *hate* me!" She ran out of the kitchen and upstairs to her bedroom.

I stared down at the mess she made with the pudding. I could only see part of that spoon sticking up, but I didn't care if I got pudding on my hands to get it. There's not much you can do to ruin banana pudding for yours very truly.

NINE

The Romantic Appeal of Certain Reilly Women

☀

When we got home from school on Thursday, we had phone service again. And it rang right at suppertime. Myra nearly broke all her metatarsals and both femurs to get to it. You woulda thought she'd been dying of thirst in the desert and the phone was a jug of water.

She chattered into the mouthpiece, giggling and hollering, "No *way!*" and "Like, I'm *so sure!*" and "*What* did she *say?*" every three seconds.

You know what else happened that very night? I'll tell you. We got another one of those weird phone calls where the caller hangs up the minute someone answers. Daddy got upset, and he did something that surprised us all. He hung up the phone and came into the living room where Mama, Myra, and I were watching *The Cosby Show*. We are allowed to watch one hour of TV a day, and I have to tell you, I was surprised as anything that my sister sat right there on the floor next to me, giggling as Sondra and Elvin tried to convince the family how well they were getting along.

Daddy came back into the living room, walked right over to the TV, turned it off, and stood in front of it, glaring at Myra Sue.

I stared at him, and my eyes were probably as big as Myra's baby blues as she gawked up at him.

"Myra Sue, is there some boy calling you who thinks it's fine to hang up if I answer the phone?"

She gulped.

"No, sir, Daddy."

Daddy narrowed his eyes. "Are you sure?"

"Yes, sir, Daddy. I've only been talking to Jessica and Jennifer, and sometimes to Rachel and Fiona. And Tracy-Lynn. And Christy Sanchez. But that's all."

"No boys?"

"No."

"Yeah, Daddy," I put in, because I couldn't seem to help myself when there were things in this world that were so obvious. "What boy in his right mind would ever want to call Myra Sue?"

The girl gave me the dirtiest look you ever saw, and all I was trying to do was help her. Some people have no gratitude.

Daddy turned to me. "Would some of *your* friends think it was a funny prank to call folks and hang up on them?"

My friends? Melissa was my very best friend, and she'd never do such a thing.

"Daddy, the only people I know who'd do something that dumb are Micky and Ricky Tinker. They might prank-call some folks, but I don't think they'd do it to us."

Daddy raised his eyebrows and still managed to frown. I didn't know how he did that, but it was a good trick, and I was gonna learn it if I had to stand in front of a mirror for a thousand hours like Myra does.

"Oh? Why not us?" he asked.

"Because they know if they pulled that stunt on us Reillys, I'll clobber 'em good. I don't put up with any nonsense from those two boys, and they know it."

His face cleared. "I see."

He sighed and said nothing else while he stared at the

floor. Then he looked up at Myra, who was still gawking at him like a dumbstruck old hen in the chicken yard.

"Here's something you need to know, Myra," he said quietly, but in a voice like steel. "When boys do start calling here, or want to come by and see you, I want to know about it. You hear me?"

She gulped again. "Yes, sir, Daddy."

"You make sure they know you won't be dating until you're eighteen."

"*Eighteen?*" she hollered. "Daddy! Eighteen? Nobody waits until they're that old!"

"Mike," Mama said with a giggle, "eighteen is a little extreme. I think sixteen is a good age."

He looked at Mama, sitting in Grandma's soft, old rocking chair, Eli sleeping in her arms, and he smiled.

"We were sixteen, weren't we, honey?" he murmured. She gave him a flirty smile and nodded.

Oh brother. Were they gonna start getting mushy?

"Sixteen, then, Myra Sue," he said, turning back to my sister. "Two years from now."

She nodded.

"And both of you tell your friends if they call here, they better not hang up if I answer the phone. Got that?"

"Yes, sir, Daddy. Okay, Daddy," we said, sweet as baby lambs. What was the point in bringing up the fact that no boy would ever want to date a drip like my sister, and there was not a boy on the face of the planet that I would ever want to date? Especially if it was gonna involve mush and moony eyes.

✸

Grandma came in the back door Saturday morning, hollering, "Good gravy, it is some kind of cold out there!"

She was wearing full makeup, with her skin already bright from the cold. Her nose was red as a maraschino cherry. She held a small paper sack in one hand and unbuttoned her brown tweed coat with the other.

"You got a date, Grandma?" I asked, because I couldn't see any other reason for running around with her face like that and wearing her new blue, velvety slacks and sparkly, white sweater. Plus, she had on those shoes she wears only for dates. She doesn't even wear them for church!

"Trask is taking me to Blue Reed for lunch at the Mill House."

"Oh, I hear that's a nice place," Mama said, putting down a fresh cup of coffee for Grandma.

"Is he gonna drive that Mustang over there?" I asked.

"I don't know. Why?"

"'Cause if he does, may I ride along with y'all to Blue Reed?"

"No!" Mama said firmly before Grandma even had time to open her mouth. "April Grace, you are not going to intrude into your grandmother's . . . outing."

I guess Mama thought the word *date* was inappropriate.

When the phone rang, Myra Sue screamed, "I'll get it."

"Oh no," I said quietly, politely, not moving a muscle except my lip muscles, "allow me." I was just being facetious, but Mama and Grandma gave me the stink-eye, so I guessed they didn't think it was funny.

Myra came dragging into the kitchen about a minute later looking Utterly Dejected.

"It was one of those pranks."

"Again?" Mama said.

I looked outside, and it was not snowing or storming or anything to mess with the phone lines. I kinda shuddered, thinking about somebody calling us and hanging up like that.

"Lily," Grandma said, "mebbe you might oughta call the law about it."

"Think so?" she murmured. "I'm not sure anyone could do anything to stop prank calls. And really, it hasn't happened that often. And some of what we thought were hang-up calls the night of the storm were not calls at all, according to the phone company; they were caused by power surges coming through the phone lines."

"Well, I don't like hang-up calls," Grandma said stoutly. "It takes someone with crude manners or no upbringing to do that."

"Yeah, and another thing, we don't want robbers coming to our house!" I said.

"Why, honey," Mama said, "even if someone like that came to our house, they wouldn't come in. Someone is always home. And if they saw Daisy, why, she's so big, they'd be too afraid to come any closer."

I took all this in, trying real hard to believe it. And I did feel a little better.

From the other room, Eli made his presence known. For someone with such a tiny mouth and itty bitty lungs, that kid surely could raise an awful racket.

"You're right, Mama Grace," Mama said as she left the kitchen to get the baby, "but I really don't think there is a blessed thing anyone can do to stop prank calls."

Just about then someone knocked on the front door.

"That will be Trask," Grandma said.

"I wonder if he drove that Mustang," I hollered, forgetting myself for a minute.

"Hush that," Grandma scolded. "You want him to hear you saying nonsense like that?"

"I reckon not," I said, then went skittering into the living room to look out the front window. Boy, oh boy. There sat his Volvo, as boring as the tan crayon in the Crayola box. I turned away, just as Grandma invited him inside.

Mama came from the bedroom with Eli in her arms, and she smiled real warm and welcoming at that man.

Now, the Reverend Trask Jordan has been the minister of Cedar Ridge Methodist Church for as long as I can remember. He was all dapper and cute as a bug in his dark dress coat and shiny shoes. He wasn't much taller than Grandma, with curly gray hair and round glasses. His figure was what is described as "portly" in some of the British stories I've read. That is, he was kinda chubby but not fat.

"Good afternoon, folks," he said, all friendly and preacherly. Our own Pastor Ross at Cedar Ridge Community Church smiled the same way and said almost the same thing when he'd come to visit. I guess you learned to greet people just that way in preacher school.

"Won't you have a seat, Reverend Jordan?" Mama asked. "Would you like some coffee?"

He shook his head. "Thank you kindly, Lily, but no. Grace and I have a lunch reservation for one o'clock." His gaze went to Eli, and his smile got bigger as he approached. "May I?" he asked, holding out his arms.

"Surely." Mama handed the baby over, and Reverend Jordan acted like he'd been handling babies every day for the last fifty years.

"Now, this is a fine specimen of a young man! Look at that. I don't believe I've seen a better-looking boy than this one, Lily."

Mama smiled proudly, and I warmed right up to that fellow.

"He has red hair," I announced.

Reverend Jordan brushed his fingers across Eli's head.

"I noticed that," he said, then ran those same fingers across his own personal head. "I used to have rather red hair myself."

I could feel my eyes bug.

"You did?"

"Sure 'nough. Got teased about it all the time, too."

"*You did?*"

Boy, oh boy, did this feller go right to the top of the list, and he didn't even have to bring chocolate like Rob Estes, or flowers like Ernie Beason did a time or two.

"Freckles, too?" I asked.

"Some." He handed the baby back to Mama. "That is a fine

boy," he said again, "and I'd love to keep him with me all afternoon, but if Grace and I are going to get there by one o'clock, we better go."

I want you to know, the second those two senior citizens drove away, Mama put Eli in his bassinet in the living room and was dialing the telephone. She was grinning and her eyes sparkled.

"Isabel, it's Lily," she said. "She's gone. As soon as you can get over here, we'll get started on our plans."

Plans? What plans? I even said, "What plans?"

But Eli set up howling, and Mama took off to take care of him.

"What plans?" I hollered.

"Answer the door when Isabel arrives," Mama said, "and please don't yell like that in the house."

Well, good gravy, excuse me all over the place for having an inquiring mind.

One way or another, I was going to have to start solving some of these mysteries before I turned plumb goofy with curiousness.

TEN

Curiouser and Curiouser

I went to my sister's closed bedroom door and knocked so politely, you could have written to that etiquette expert lady, Emily Post, and sent her an illustration of it. When she did not respond, I knocked again, louder, but politer than all get-out. The sound of Hall and Oates came wafting out from under the door.

She opened the door a crack and blinked at me from one blue eyeball.

"What do you want?"

"What are the plans Mama and Isabel have?"

The blue eye blinked five or six times, then Myra Sue stepped back and opened the door.

"What are you talking about?"

I walked into her room, and let me tell you, I nearly got lost among the piles of dirty clothes and *Tiger Beat* magazines, *Soap Opera Digests*, *Current Soaps*, and other junk all over the floor. How could she even sleep in that mess without worrying that something would crawl out of it and chase her around the room?

She had a bunch of notebook paper with lots of writing on it scattered across the bed.

"You're actually writing a paper for history?" I asked, surprised. "What're you writing about?"

She followed my gaze, then flew to the bed and gathered up those pages.

"It's none of your business!"

That's when I knew she was writing something that had

nothing to do with George Washington or the Monroe Doctrine or World War I. And one thing about it: she wasn't gonna let me see what it was, even though I strained my eyes as hard as I could.

"Why are you here?" she said, stuffing all those pages in her backpack, then hanging on to it like it was full of gold, frankincense, and myrrh. Let me tell you something: that girl would never pass for a Wise Man, even if she grew a beard and rode a camel.

"Mama just now called Isabel, and she told her to come over here while Grandma is gone so they can make plans."

"I haven't heard anything about secret plans. What do you think they're planning?"

I shrugged. "I thought you might know."

We stood there and stared at each other.

"Maybe they're going to send us off to boarding school," Myra whispered.

"*Boarding school?*" I yelped.

"Shhh! Yes."

"Where'd you get a crazy idea like that?" I whisper-shouted.

She looked all uppity and put her hands on her hips. "Well, I don't know, April Grace. *You* tell *me*. You're the one with crazy ideas all the time. Where do *you* get them?"

"From my imagination! But Myra Sue, you have *no* imagination. So why would you even think something as silly as us being sent to a boarding school?"

She huffed. "Because it happened on *Silver Linings* two years ago. Colton and Amber were going to—"

"Myra Sue, why can't you understand those dumb soap operas Are Not Real? They are *stories*."

She bugged out her eyes at me. "You don't have to keep telling me that."

I had to force my teeth to unclench because that goofy girl had frustrated me so much that I like to have fused my jawbones together.

"You might as well believe that we're all moving to South America," I told her.

"Really? Why would we do that?" Her eyes got bigger and bigger. "Daddy would have to sell the farm. And where would Grandma live?"

Now, at this point, I nearly had to sit on my hands to keep from choking my own personal throat out of pure aggravation.

"Well, Myra Sue," I choked out, "maybe they're planning to send us to boarding school in South America."

Boy, oh boy, I thought her eyeballs would pop right out of her skull.

"No!" she said. "I won't go to South America. It's too far from—"

I perked up right quick, thinking she was about to spill the beans on some of her mysterious behavior. But I guess she heard her own dumb words because she broke off all of a sudden.

"Too far from what?" I asked.

Her brain must have steamed with all the thinking she seemed to be putting it through.

"Too far from here!" she finally sputtered.

Oh brother. She is always and forever whining about living on the farm, so I'd think South America would be just peachy to her.

"I refuse to move!" she hollered.

"Good grief, Myra, don't be so all-fired dumb. No one is moving to South America, and we are not going to boarding school. Number one: Only rich people send their kids to boarding school. Number two: Mama and Daddy wouldn't do that anyway. Number three: None of us can speak Spanish or Portuguese, which is what most people speak in South America."

Her bottom lip, which had been pooched out thirteen feet or thereabouts, shrunk back to normal, and the wildness drained from her eyes.

"Well then, what are Mama and Isabel planning that does not include us?" she asked. Then she got all pouty again. "This just proves Isabel doesn't like me anymore. If she did, she'd want me right there while they were doing that planning."

"Maybe they're planning to clean out the cellar, Myra Sue. You want to be included in that?"

That took the pouty expression right off her face and replaced it with a look of horror.

"Myra Sue, I can almost guarantee you that whatever they're planning has nothing to do with boarding school, South America, or cleaning the cellar. But it is curious that *you* don't know what Isabel is up to."

She sniffed.

"I told you before. I embarrassed her into utter humiliation at the Christmas program, and I refuse to do it to her again."

"But, Myra, you were the one who was humiliated, not Isabel."

Her expression said she did not believe me, not for a minute.

"Has Isabel ever once told you that she no longer dotes on you, or dislikes you, or anything that dumb?"

"No," she said in a small voice. "But she wouldn't. Isabel is the very soul of discretion and manners."

"Oh brother! Where have you been? I will admit that Isabel has made some progress in manners, but she still does not hold back from blasting off somebody's eyebrows if she decides to tell them off."

Just about then, someone knocked on the front door.

"There's Isabel," I said, "and Mama told me to let her in as soon as she got here."

I hurried downstairs, but Myra did not follow. I shot a look at her when I reached the door, but she continued to hang around at the head of the stairs like she was waiting to be invited. I raised my eyebrows, asking silently if she was coming down, but she just shrugged and stayed where she was.

"Hi, Isabel," I said as I let the woman inside. "Mama's taking care of Eli. I'll tell her you're here."

"I think I'll wait for her in the dining room. I brought my notebook." She waved it at me like it was some kind of trophy.

"What're y'all planning, anyway?" I asked, cutting a glance upstairs at Myra. She leaned forward on the banister, listening. As if she had any right to eavesdrop, that secret-keeping brat.

"Darling child, if you don't know already, then I daresay your mother has chosen not to tell you," Isabel said, as uppity as you can possibly imagine, as she went into the dining room.

I opened my mouth to take exception to that observation, but I ended up saying nothing 'cause Mama came into the dining room, toting the baby in one arm, a notebook and pen in her free hand. I narrowed my eyes. The last time those two women had notebooks and pens and sat at the dining room table, the result had been a Christmas program, and I had been roped into participating in it like nobody's business.

"You need something, honey?" Mama asked me.

"Just wondering what you're planning, is all."

She twisted her mouth, thinking. She and Isabel exchanged glances, then both of them looked me up and down like they'd never seen me before.

"What do you think, Isabel? Should we let her in on our secret?"

Isabel let out a breath. "Can she keep a secret for two weeks?" She looked past me. "What do you think, Myra darling? Are you curious, too?"

I glanced behind me. Ole Myra Sue had come downstairs, and I hadn't even heard her. Instead of rushing to Isabel or anything you might expect from her, she just shrugged.

"April Grace has a big mouth sometimes," she offered, which I did not appreciate even a little bit, especially as I had been trying to make her feel better. I crossed my eyes at her, then turned back to the two women.

"I can keep a secret as good as anyone," I declared. And I

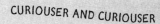

gave that sister of mine another dirty look because she knew I was keeping a secret about her and whatever sneaky thing she was up to. She just looked at me all big-eyed and innocent. D-R-I-P.

There was a short silence broken only by the grunts and other baby noises emitting from my little brother. Once again Mama and Isabel exchanged looks as if they were reading each other's minds. I just waited, acting like a good child who could keep secrets and make good grades and eat spinach without barfing.

"Well, I guess—" Mama said, and was interrupted by the ringing of that stupid telephone.

"I'll get it!" Myra Sue screeched like a barn owl being chased by a vampire. Eli jumped a little in Mama's arms, whimpering.

Mama sighed, then tried to hush him by patting his little bottom and rocking him gently in her arms.

"I declare, Isabel, the way that girl shrieks every time the phone rings, I am about ready to disconnect it permanently!"

The two of them laughed a little, although I didn't see anything funny about Myra hollering about that dumb phone. Besides that, I wanted to know the plans they were fixing to make.

"A-hem!" I said. "You two are making plans for . . . what? And why did you wait for Grandma to leave? Why don't you want her to know about these plans?"

"Will you promise to say nothing about any of this to your grandmother or around her?"

Grandma and I have always been close, almost best

friends, and keeping secrets from her did not sound like a good idea to me.

"I don't know about that, Mama. Why don't you want Grandma to know these secret plans?"

"I am not telling you anything without your promise to keep the secret."

"All right. I promise." I even crossed my heart.

The two women looked at each other again and grinned. Their eyes sparkled like they were getting ready to open presents on Christmas morning.

"We decided last night that we want to give Grandma a surprise party for her birthday," Mama said.

"Oh, wow!" I hollered nearly as loud as Myra Sue shrieking about getting a phone call.

Usually we celebrated Grandma's birthday by having a special family dinner and a cake. I don't think we ever had a full-blown party before.

"April Grace!" Mama said as Eli howled. She frowned blackly at me. "Go to your room right now, and do not come back down until you can be quieter."

"I'm sorry," I said, feeling it down to my toes. "I was just so excited about having a party for Grandma. A *surprise* party."

"I understand, honey, but you must remember that Eli is tiny. He needs to get lots of sleep so he can be healthy. When you or your sister yell out suddenly like that, you startle him."

"I'm sorry," I said again. "I'll be quiet. May I stay and help plan the party?"

Mama gave me a sad smile. "No, honey. Go to your room, think about ways to remind yourself not to be so noisy, and when you've done that, you may come back. Thirty minutes ought to be long enough. Now, run along. We have a lot to do and very little time to do it."

"Okay, Mama," I said with plenty of regret, 'cause I really, really wanted to be in on that planning business. "Grandma's birthday is next Friday. Are you gonna give her a party on her birthday day?"

"Yes. Now, run along." She turned to Isabel. "I do wish we'd thought of this earlier. We're going to have to hustle to get everything done."

Myra Sue was chattering on the phone and gave me a dark look when I passed her. If she thought I cared what she, Jessica, and Jennifer were going to wear to school on Monday, she needed to take her brain out and wash it.

Half an hour later, I went back downstairs. Mama and Isabel already had a guest list and a menu written down. Myra Sue sat at the table, but the way she squirmed, it seemed to me she wasn't enjoying herself as much as you might expect. She completely ignored me, which did not break my heart.

"You gonna decorate?" I asked as I sat down at the table.

"What do you think, Lily? Shall we decorate, at least in here?"

"I think you should put up a banner and streamers and have balloons," I put in eagerly. "And lots of candles on her cake. Lots of cake, Mama. And ice cream. And Pepsi. And chips."

"April Grace!" Mama said, laughing, holding up one hand. "Enough. I think if we fix the table real pretty, have some candles in the room and a *few* on the cake—"

"A few!" I almost hollered in protest, but caught myself in

time and turned it into a whisper-shout even though Eli was now sleeping in his crib in Daddy and Mama's bedroom. "You can't put just a *few* candles on her cake, Mama. Grandma is old. That cake'll need *lots* of candles!"

"Darling," Isabel said, kinda snooty but not as snooty as she has been in the past, "your grandmother is younger than her years, and we don't need to remind her of her age."

I frowned, not sure that made a lot of sense. And I didn't think Grandma was one of those kinds of women who cared about age anyway. But rather than risk being sent to my room To Think again, I chose not to argue.

"What can I do to help?" I said, trying to prove my dependableness.

"You may help us choose colors," Mama said, and Isabel nodded.

"Grandma loves pink. Rose pink and soft pink. She loves them together."

Isabel shmooshed up her nose a little bit at that. I reckon she does not like pink.

"Pink is for children," said Myra Sue Reilly, who has more pink T-shirts, socks, and undies than you can possibly imagine.

"Actually," Mama said, tapping the eraser end of her pencil against her chin, "I think that would be lovely. And I believe Mama Grace would be so pleased."

"Really?" Isabel said. Boy, oh boy, doubt was all over her face like a bad makeup job. "Well, if you say so, Lily. Pale pink and rose pink it is."

Myra Sue suddenly shoved back her chair and stood up fast. "Since April Grace is now here to help you, and you don't need me anymore, may I be excused?"

"Don't you want to help?" Isabel asked.

"I have *homework*."

Mama studied my sister for a moment, then said, "All right. Run along then." And the second we heard Myra shut her door upstairs, Mama added, "Myra is taking school so seriously this semester. She just studies all the time."

I figured her report card would prove how much she studied and how much of her time was spent slobbering over celebrity magazines.

"We'll have Nancy Agnes Greenleaf at the Grocerteria bakery make the cake," Mama said, getting back to the planning. "She does such a lovely job."

"*Nancy Agnes Greenleaf?*" Isabel echoed. "Goodness, where do people in this part of the world come up with names?"

I betcha ole Isabel wouldn't be so uppity if she ever was to see Nancy Agnes. That woman is beautiful like a movie star. Everyone says so.

"Will you make the punch, Mama?" I said. To Isabel I said, "She makes the best punch in the world."

"Lovely!" Isabel said, and wrote in her notebook. "And I shall prepare the hors d'oeuvres. Mini mushroom cap quiches, I think." She sighed, got a faraway look in her eyes, and continued, "Asparagus crostini and artichoke croquettes. Oh, and apricot-pecan brie tartlets."

I heard that list of crazy food with what you might call considerable consternation, which means all that peculiar-sounding stuff sounded pretty awful to me.

"Wow, Isabel, I didn't know you ever cooked *anything*."

"I shall consult cookbooks, of course. And this is gourmet cooking, not picnic food."

Oh brother. *Gourmet*. Gag me.

"Isabel," Mama said, smiling sweetly, "that sounds like a lot of work, and rather expensive."

"And I don't think anyone will want that stuff!" I added. "Why don't you fix them little pigs in a blanket? Maybe Mrs. Hobbs can make tiny little sausage biscuits, because they're so good and Grandma loves 'em. And chips and dip because what's a party without chips and dip? And nachos!"

Isabel looked horrified. "Absolutely not! This party will not be some kind of backcountry hoedown. Grace deserves to have an elegant, refined celebration."

I twisted my mouth.

"And what are we supposed to wear at this elegant celebration?" As if I didn't know the answer to that.

"Why, party clothes, of course. Men will wear suits, and women will be in dresses and heels. You girls should wear your very finest."

Good grief.

"That does not sound like fun, Isabel," I said, because I felt the woman needed to be educated. "In fact, it sounds boring. *Bor*-ing. Grandma doesn't want some dumb ole party where all you do is sit around eating food you can't pronounce and drinking punch with your pinky sticking out."

Isabel jerked like she'd been poked on the bottom with a sharp stick and blinked a dozen times.

"April," Mama said quietly, "there is a much nicer way of stating your opinions."

I sucked in a deep breath, remembering times when I've had to apologize for being truthful when it came out sounding rude. Sometimes, you know, the truth hurts. But I tried to reword my point.

"My grandma would rather have a fun party with fun food and nothing too elegant. She has *always* liked pigs in a blanket and stuff like that."

Isabel merely blinked at me. I was glad Myra Sue had gone upstairs and didn't hear all this because she might have pitched a fit to have asparagus dipsticks and crocheted artichoke hearts or whatever that stuff was Isabel had said.

"You know," Mama said thoughtfully, "I think Mama Grace might actually like a more formal affair. Some lovely, classical music on the tape player, pretty lighting, elegant food . . ."

Isabel smiled brightly while I felt like I was gonna choke just hearing such talk.

"Oh, Mama," I said, hoping the disappointment in my voice would cause her to reconsider such an awful notion.

"It'll be good for us all, in fact," she announced as if I hadn't said a single, solitary word on the subject.

"Yes," Isabel said, all sniffy, "I've said all along, this backwater pocket of the world needs some culture."

I gave her a look that fully illustrated exactly what I thought of her poor excuse for an observation. She did not even look at me to get the benefit of my expression, because she was in the throes of some sort of writing fit, scribbling away in her notebook like the ink in her pen was on fire. I heaved out a big sigh and got to my feet. Those two women were not gonna listen to me, and even if they did, they'd only listen long enough to shoot down any ideas for Actual Fun that I might offer. Poor Grandma. She was in for the most boringest surprise birthday ever thrown on Rough Creek Road.

I guess I should've been glad they weren't going to send me and Myra off to boarding school in South America. It sounded like about the same amount of fun.

Grandma's birthday was Friday, January 16, and it was a cold, sunny day. When I left for school that morning, Mama looked a little frazzled because she had a lot to get done before that evening. It was a good thing Isabel did not have classes on Friday. She showed up just as Myra Sue and I were walking down the driveway to wait for the bus.

Isabel pulled up in their pickup, stopped next to us, and cranked down the window. Boy, oh boy, if you'd met her just a few months ago, you would've thought that never in a million years would she drive an old pickup. Things sure do change.

"Darlings!" she said. "It is far too cold for you to stand here waiting for the bus. Jump in the pickup until the bus shows up."

You might have thought Myra Sue would have trampled me into pulp to get in first, but you'd be wrong. In fact, she cast a sneaky look toward the mailbox. At least it looked sneaky to me. Then she followed me around to the passenger-side door. I waited for her to get in first, but she gave me a little shove.

"Go *on*!" she growled. "Get *in*, April Grace! It's cold out here."

So I got in and scooted over, then she said, taking a step back and looking at the front tire on that side, "Oh, Isabel! I think you're getting a flat tire."

Isabel muttered something I will not write down. At least she muttered it instead of declaring it out loud like she used to do before she realized bad language is Totally Inappropriate. I tell you what, before she and Ian learned to tone down their cussing and hollering, Myra Sue and I got an education in words that we absolutely must not use, ever, in our entire lives, unless we want to be grounded forever. Sometimes I think ole Isabel never got grounded when she was a kid.

She got out of the truck and went to look.

"I'll check the other tires for you," Myra Sue hollered, and went running to the back. She made a big show of looking, but she also nipped over to the mailbox so fast my eyeballs crossed. She stuck something in there and made it back to the front of the truck before Isabel had time to notice.

"Myra darling, the tires on this side look just fine. Get in the truck, and I'll look on the other side."

When Myra darling got in the truck, she looked straight into my eyes, and I reckon she could tell that I knew she'd been a sneaky sneak.

Before I could utter a mumbling word, she pointed her

pointy finger in my face, about two inches from my nose, and snarled, "Don't you say a thing, missy! I was just checking to see if we had gotten any mail yet."

Now, she knows as well as I do that our mailman does not show up until midafternoon.

I opened my mouth to reply and she added, "If you say a word, April Grace, I will personally call J. H. Henry and tell him you are in love with him and want to marry him the minute you're old enough and that you want him to call you every single night until you elope!"

And she would, too. She's just that mean and rotten.

Isabel got back in the truck and grabbed her cigarettes. She stared down at that red-and-white package in her hand and chewed on her lower lip.

"Girls," she said quietly, "I'm trying to quit." She raised her head and looked at us. "I've only had one this morning."

"That's good, Isabel!" I said, grinning and encouraging, and gouging Myra Sue in the ribs so she'd do the same.

"Yes. That's wonderful." But the way she said it made it sound like it was the most boring thing she'd ever heard.

Isabel put the cigarette pack on the dashboard and looked at Myra Sue. She tilted her head a little to one side and sort of smiled.

"Myra, have I offended you in some way, darling? Because if I have, I'm certainly unaware of it," she asked.

Myra Sue looked at her all big-eyed and got a little teary before she blinked hard, once.

"No, ma'am. You haven't offended me at all."

I hoped she'd say more. She needed to say more, because

Isabel didn't understand, and Myra wasn't explaining her chilly behavior, and this just was not a positive situation at all. Myra looked out the window on her side. A frown chased across Isabel's face, and she thinned her lips until you couldn't see them.

"I'll tell you what's going on!" I blurted, wanting to put an end to this foolishness, though goodness knows Myra Sue was a big, fat pain when she was following Isabel around like a loyal hound dog and acting like she was Isabel the Second. I'm not sure why I wanted things to return to that awfulness, except I knew I didn't like the expression on Isabel's face. It's hard to see anyone get their feelings hurt.

But wouldn't you know, wouldn't you just *know*, that right then that big, stupid yellow school bus came roaring into view, and I couldn't say a blessed thing to bring some kind of stop to all that nonsense.

ELEVEN

In Times of Extreme Stress, You Can Sometimes Get Your Bible Verses Mixed Up

☆

When we got back to the house that afternoon, I expected to see things all elegant and fancy, but guess what? It wasn't that way at all. In fact, it looked just the same as always, and Mama looked more frazzled and worn-out than I'd seen her in a while. Isabel looked like she'd been pulled backward through a knothole, all brittle-faced and stiff. I'll tell you something else: I had daydreamed all day long about Nancy Agnes Greenleaf's special-made birthday cake, and it was nowhere to be seen.

And guess what? There sat Grandma, right at the kitchen table, as relaxed as anything, sipping coffee from her white "#1 Grandma" mug.

Boy, oh boy. Something was afoot.

"What's going on?" I blurted right out, because the guest of honor for a surprise party should not be sitting around chitchatting in the kitchen when her party was a few hours away and nothing had been done or decorated.

Grandma had the appearance of being all relaxed, but when she looked up, I could see plain as day she was upset. Uh-oh. Who spilled the beans about her party and spoiled the surprise?

"I did not say a single, solitary word to anyone!" I said stoutly before I got reamed out.

Grandma gave me the funniest look—funny odd, not funny ha-ha.

"What are you talking about, child?" she asked.

Isabel jumped up like a jack-in-the-box.

"April, dear, I need to talk to you!"

She grabbed my arm and none-too-delicately hauled me onto the service porch just off the kitchen. For once in my life, I could not speak. I just looked at Isabel as she hustled me into a corner. Daisy had been sleeping on her doggie blanket near the wall heater, but she woke up when we entered and lifted her head.

Isabel froze stiff, eyeballing Daisy like she thought that good old dog might bury her in the backyard, then dig her up later to eat with biscuits and gravy.

"What's goin' on?" I asked.

"Shh! I'll tell you." She kept her eye on Daisy as she talked. "Lily and I think Grace is upset because no one has mentioned her birthday."

"Didn't anybody even say 'Happy Birthday,' or sing to her, or anything? That's mean!"

"*Shh!* Keep your voice down. We aren't trying to be mean. We really want to surprise her. The thing is, she's been over here almost all day. She'd leave, and we'd barely start getting things ready, and she'd return. Then we'd rush around, hiding everything. Your mother and I are simply at our wits' ends trying to get her out of the house long enough for us to get anything done. Ian ran into town and picked up the cake this morning. It's *still* at our house because Grace simply must not see it yet."

Knowing my grandma had not even been wished a happy birthday the whole entire day stuck in my mind like a cocklebur. Someone could've at least said, "You're looking younger every year," or "Many happy returns."

"Poor Grandma!" I whisper-shouted, and Isabel hushed me again.

"Listen, April, you absolutely must help us. You must get her out of the house and keep her out of the house."

"For how long?" I gave her the stink-eye because I did not want to trick my grandmother who trusted me.

"Until the party."

"But that's not until seven o'clock! How am I supposed to keep her away for two whole hours when she wants to be here?"

Isabel huffed. "April, you always have the best ideas of anyone, and I'm sure you'll be able to come up with something. So you must do it, *ASAP!*"

Right about then Daisy got to her feet, shook off the sleep from her big, white body, then, waving her fluffy tail, ambled over to us. She butted her head against my thigh, begging to be petted, and that silly Isabel gave a little squeal, rearing back in full alarm.

"Oh, that vicious creature! Why do you people insist on keeping him?"

"Oh, good grief!" I hollered at that woman as I stroked Daisy's big, white head and rubbed her ears. "Daisy doesn't even hardly have any teeth! She's a million years old."

"What on earth is going on in here?" Grandma said, coming onto the service porch. "What're you girls looking for?"

Isabel's eyes got big, and she looked caught, but I turned right quick and pulled the box of washing powder off the shelf and handed it to her.

"And if you need the bleach, it's up there on that shelf." I told her, pointing to a shelf above the dryer.

Isabel gave me a big, grateful smile.

"Thank you, darling. I'll run into town tomorrow and get more detergent."

"Mercy! You doing the wash tonight, Isabel?" Grandma asked.

"Oh, Grace," Isabel said with what you might call a brittle laugh, "if I don't, Ian will have to wear the same shirt two days in a row."

"Oh my! Honey, I remember how hard it was, adjusting my housework around a work schedule when Voyne and I were young marrieds. 'Course, I didn't work very long in town. There was way too much to do on this farm, and his mother was a workhorse. I felt plumb lazy alongside her." She followed Isabel from the service porch and into the kitchen. I'm not sure what Mama thought when she saw Isabel carting out her big box of Tide and jug of Purex, but she never said a word.

When Grandma sighed big and loud and plunked herself down at the table, Isabel looked over Grandma's head and gave me the pleadingest look you can possibly imagine. Well, I could not let my grandma, who had gone all day long without a birthday wish, go without her party to make up for it, so I put my brain in gear.

"Grandma, you still got that video from Mack's Video Rental in Cedar Ridge?"

"You mean that oldie, the one with Katharine Hepburn?"

"Is that the one about the boat going down the river that we watched the other day?"

"*The African Queen*. Honey, that was a couple of weeks ago, and I already took it back. Why?"

"'Cause I was hoping we could go over to your house where it's nice and quiet and watch it again. You got any other videos you rented?"

"Not right now, but I can get something when I go after groceries on Tuesday. Mack runs a senior discount rental on Tuesdays. What would you like to see? He's starting to stock some good classics."

"Umm, I'm not sure what I'd like to see. Maybe we could go look at them now and I could pick out something."

Grandma just frowned and shook her head. "Not tonight."

I thought hard and fast for another way to get her out of our house. Oh boy. I came up with something that I did not want to do, not in a million years, but sometimes you just have to do what has to be done.

"Oh goodness!" I hollered suddenly, slapping my own personal forehead like I was a big dummy. "I need notebook paper." Which was true enough. I *always* need notebook paper. It's one of the hazards of going to school.

"Already?" Mama said, not looking up at me as she was digging in the cabinet, looking for who knows what. She pulled out two cans of tuna and a big can of crushed pineapple. I think she was desperately trying to make Grandma think she was getting ready to make supper. Tuna and crushed pineapple? Ick. "I'll run you into town tomorrow."

Mama obviously did not understand I was trying to Save the Situation. Isabel cleared her throat real loud and met Mama's eyes. Lucky for us, Grandma picked up that can of crushed pineapple and was studying the label.

"Oh dear," said Isabel. "You're out of paper? My goodness, that will never do! There are *all* those questions for my class you're supposed to copy and answer. You should get started tonight, but how can you if you have no paper?"

I gulped and said, "Grandma, would you please run me into town right now so I can buy some notebook paper? I got homework for Isabel's class, and I want to start writing stories for Mrs. Scrivner's class, and I got a really good one in my brain that I don't want to lose, and I just can't run out of paper!"

Grandma gave me a sharp look like maybe she suspected something, but I don't think she suspected a surprise birthday party. I think she suspected I had completely lost my mind.

She shot a look at the yellow clock on the wall.

"Law! It's 5:20, and the variety store is closed by now. But the pharmacy stays open till six, and I suspect Rob keeps notebook paper."

Rob Estes owns Estes Drugstore, but his store is more than just a drugstore. He carries everything from sour gumballs to grapefruit-flavored Squirt soda to pencil erasers to eyelash curlers. I figured he had notebook paper, too.

"You run upstairs, brush your hair, and wash your hands," Grandma said, "and I'll go get the car." She shrugged on her coat. "Don't dillydally, neither."

And out she went.

"My goodness!" Mama said. "April Grace, thank you for coming up with a good reason to go to town. And you must keep her occupied as long as possible, so whatever you do, don't come straight home from the store." She turned to Isabel. "Can we get it all done in less than an hour and a half?"

"We have to, Lily! We don't have a choice." Her eyes suddenly lit up, and she tapped her head. "And I know how to do it."

Off she trotted, out of the kitchen, and then we heard the clickety-click of her high heels on the stairs.

"If she thinks she's gonna get Myra Sue to do any work, she's in for a big surprise," I declared.

"We'll see," Mama said. "Now, get some money from my wallet to pay for your notebook paper."

As soon as I was all brushed and washed, I went into my bedroom and picked up my Bible. I opened it right up to the Lord's Prayer, read that, and then I read the Twenty-Third Psalm, then I read the Lord's Prayer again. And then I reread the part in the psalm about the valley of the shadow of death and how God walks with us everywhere, and I figured, scared as I was, God would be with me in that white Corolla while Grandma was at the wheel. I was still scared, but I felt better. Then I went downstairs, got two dollars from Mama's purse, and went outside to where Grandma had just pulled up into the driveway.

I got in her car and kept thinking the Lord's Prayer and the Twenty-Third Psalm.

You know what Grandma said to me as she backed out of our driveway and onto the road? Well, I'll tell you. She said,

"I sure do hope the deer stay in the woods tonight and stay off the highway. I can't see a blessed thing after dark."

"Lead us not into temptation through the valley of the shadow of death!" I hollered, without even realizing I said it.

"Mercy me, child," Grandma said mildly, driving along Rough Creek Road like she didn't mind the rocks, the ruts, the holes, and the dark. "You have done got your Bible verses whopperjawed."

I gripped the edge of the seat with both hands so tight, it would probably take the jaws of life to extract my fingernails from the vinyl.

"Yes'm," I said, swallowing hard. "And I'll watch for deer."

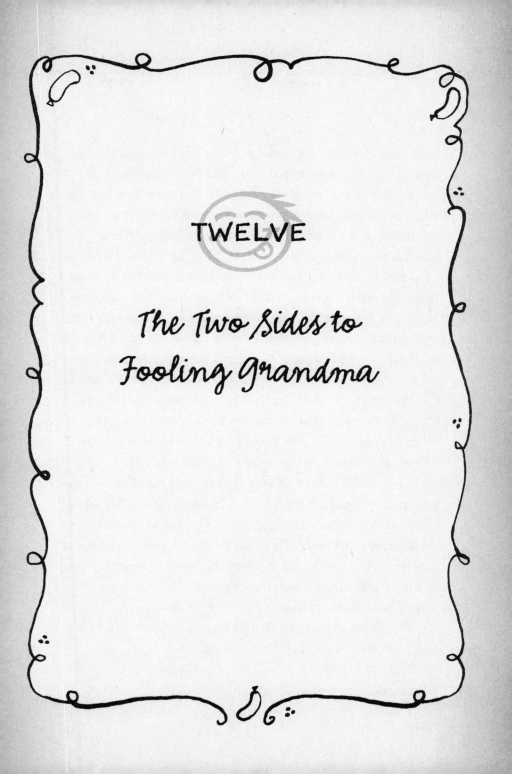

TWELVE

The Two Sides to
Fooling Grandma

As if I didn't have enough to fret about on that ride into town, a new thought popped up out of nowhere and scared me.

You know my grandma is *old*. I'm not sure how old, but underneath that tawny-colored hair, it's gray. And down below the makeup and lipstick and eye goop, she has wrinkles. She has always been in good health, and I've never known her to be sick with anything but a cold or the stomach flu or something like that. But here's what worried me. With Grandma being old, I wondered how smart it was for everyone to jump out and holler, "Surprise!" when we got back. At least I figured that's what would happen. I've never been to a surprise party, my own personal self, but in the ones I've seen on TV and in the movies, that's what they do. What if it surprised her so bad it gave her a heart attack right there at her very own party?

I prayed the Lord's Prayer again and silently added, "Please don't let everyone scare Grandma to death!"

I watched for deer on the highway and beside the highway, and I gritted my teeth when Grandma ran off the side of the road every time an oncoming car passed us, and I nearly made myself sick worrying about her having a heart attack at the party. And I also tried to figure out a way to make her stay in town longer than necessary when every blessed business in all of Cedar Ridge closed at 6:00 p.m., if not before.

We pulled up to Estes Drugstore on the square. It was the only business that had all the lights on.

Grandma squinted at her watch in the glow of the streetlight coming through the windshield.

"We got here in good time. Fifteen minutes yet. Why, we'll be home before you know it!"

The little bell above the door jingled as we walked in. Estes Drugstore is a nice, big store, with plenty of light so you can see everything on the shelves real good. It smells mostly like medicine, and I reckon since it's a drugstore, that's what it ought to smell like. There was music playing, too, the kind of faraway-sounding music that you never notice unless there is no one in the store but you and the clerks. Well, that night it was just Grandma, me, Judy Lawrence at the cash register, and Rob Estes, who is retired from the store, but I think he's there just about every day, anyhow. At least that's what Grandma said one time.

When we walked in, he stood near the front counter, straightening a display of magazines. He was all slicked up, too, in black slacks and a charcoal-gray jacket and a white shirt with a silvery satin tie. I betcha he'd just polished up his spiffy rimless glasses, too. Rob is tall and slim, with black-and-gray hair. Every time I see him, he looks real nice, but that night he looked extra slick. That's because he was going to Grandma's birthday party. And you know what? Ernie Beason and Reverend Jordan had been invited, too. I sure hoped we did not have an Awkward Situation like we did at the St. Jameses' housewarming party when Rob and Ernie both went off and left Grandma without a ride home. And that just goes to prove my theory: no one Grandma's age should have multiple boyfriends.

When Rob spotted us, his eyes kinda bugged out, but he put 'em back in right quick. I knew he wondered why we were

there at that time of day when we should've been home getting ready to surprise Grandma. But he did not say a word
about it. Instead, he approached us, smiling.

"Well, ladies!" he said. "What brings the two of you off
the farm and into the city at this time of day?"

Then he reached over to the candy display, picked up a
couple of Mint Dreams, and handed them to me with a grin.

"Thank you, sir!" I breathed gratefully, forgetting for a
moment my purpose in being in his store at almost closing time.

"April, run and get your notebook paper," Grandma said,
wandering over to the perfume counter. "We don't want to
keep these hard-working folks waiting when they want to go
home and get some supper." She sniffed a couple of testers,
then squirted her wrists.

"You know where the paper is, Miss April?" Rob asked.

"Yes, sir."

Now, I hated to keep those hard-working folks from their
supper, also, but I had to keep Grandma away from the house
as long as I possibly could. From the look in Rob's eye, and
his little nod, I think he fully understood my purpose.

The paper and pens and that sort of thing are on the far
wall of the store, about halfway back, so I ambled off in that
direction. And I mean *ambled*, like one of the cows does when
Daddy is trying to get her to move on and she doesn't want to,
so she pauses and looks around and takes a step or two, then
stops, noses the ground for a while, and takes another step.
Sometimes you can learn good life lessons from cows.

I stopped to look at a bottle of aspirin that was so big
it held a thousand tablets. Boy howdy, whoever needed to

buy that much aspirin must have had killer headaches. They probably lived with someone like Myra Sue, who is a built-in headache-making machine.

Then I moved on a bit and paused to eyeball a display of bunion pads. I don't know what bunions are or why they need to be padded.

A few steps more and I stopped to look at support hose. I even took a package of 'em off the shelf to look at 'em closer. They were denser and darker than Mama's sheer pantyhose that come out of big plastic eggs. What in the world do those stockings support, I'd like to know?

All of a sudden that package of support hose got snatched right out of my hand, just as rude and sudden as you please.

"April Grace Reilly, what on earth are you doing, lolly-gagging in the old-lady aisle?" Grandma asked, frowning like a bulldog. She put those hose back where they came from.

"Oh. Sorry, Grandma." I took a couple of steps and stopped. "Grandma?"

"Yes, hon?"

"Why are they called *corns*?" I pointed to the corn pads that were right next to pads for bunions.

Her mouth dropped open, and she looked at me like she thought I'd lost my ever-lovin' mind.

"Why, I don't know! For goodness' sake, April Grace, I never know what's going to come out of your mouth next. Now, let's march back to the paper and get you a pack."

Boy, oh boy, you have to be real creative when you're choosing notebook paper in the drugstore, because all that's there is narrow-ruled and wide-ruled. But I tried. I picked up a package of the narrow-ruled and stared hard at it. Every single teacher had told us at the beginning of the year, "No narrow-ruled paper. Wide only!" And they said it like it was a first-class felony to use it. I wondered if I bought it, and used it, and handed in homework on it, if ole Perry Mason on TV would come to Cedar Ridge and be my attorney.

Slow as molasses, I dragged myself up to the cash register with that paper.

"Mercy sakes, April," Grandma fussed at me. "Judy has done gone home, and Rob is wanting to close this place."

I glanced at the big, round clock on the wall above the register counter. 6:05. Oh brother. I laid that paper on the counter next to the cash register and dug out those two dollars from my jacket pocket.

Rob Estes, his own personal retired self, rang up the purchase, took my money, and gave me change. He put it in a sack, handed it over to me, and walked Grandma and me to the front door, where a key was in the lock. He turned that key and opened the door, and I started to step out into the cold night, but stopped so suddenly that Grandma ran right smack-dab into me.

"Wait!" I hollered. I pulled the paper from the bag and squinted at it like I'd never seen it before in my whole entire life. "I can't use this!"

"Why?" Grandma sputtered. "Whatever do you mean, child?"

"My teachers said no narrow-lined paper."

"Well then," Rob said, just as calm and kind as if we were the first customers of the day, "come back inside and get what you need. We sure can't have you handing in homework on paper your teachers don't want you to use."

I looked up at him, and he gave me a sly wink.

"Let's go back to the paper and find you what you need, April Grace," he said. To Grandma he said, "Grace, help yourself to a Mint Dream."

I followed him right to the paper, and he fiddled with every notebook back there, even the ones that were the kind secretaries scribble in.

"Does she know?" he asked from the corner of his mouth, like a gangster in an old movie.

I shook my head and replied out of the side of my mouth, "She was at the house all day and wouldn't go home, and they didn't get anything done, so I'm supposed to keep her busy for a while."

"I thought so."

He glanced over my head and handed me a big package of notebook paper. "Here you go, Miss April," he said loudly.

"Merciful goodness! Whatever are you two doing back here? Digging for treasure?" Grandma swooped down the aisle toward us.

"April and I were looking at the fine assortment of writing goods we stock in this store." He reached up, took a packet of mechanical pencils from a display peg, and handed them to me. "And with these you won't have to sharpen those wooden pencils. No charge because it's my contribution to the education of our youth."

"Thank you!" I breathed, hardly believing my good fortune. I loved mechanical pencils but had only had one in my whole entire life, and ole J. H. Henry "borrowed" it in the fifth grade, and when he gave it back, it was broken. Just one more reason that boy gets on my nerves, big-time.

"Why, thank you kindly, Rob. That's real nice of you." Grandma eyed the package of paper I held. "Do we owe anything more to change out that notebook paper?"

"Not a penny!" he said with a smile, then escorted us to the front. When we had almost reached the door, he said, "Oh, but there is something, though! Since this is an exchange, I have to fill out a little receipt. My bookkeeper gets his nose out of joint if there's the least little thing that isn't recorded . . ."

Grandma looked at him with a kind of suspicious expression. "I thought *you* were the bookkeeper since you retired."

He lifted one eyebrow. "Whatever gave you that idea?"

"I thought that's what you told me."

"Well, well," he replied, then did things on the cash register that involved punching buttons and eyeballing the receipt tape and writing things down. I appreciated that he took his own sweet time about it, too. Finally, he handed me a small receipt and said, "Sign that for me if you will, please, Miss April, to prove to my bookkeeper no one tried to get away with anything sneaky in this store tonight."

I like to have busted out laughing, because I knew he was making a joke about us keeping Grandma there as long as we possibly could. I gave him a serious, grown-up nod and wrote my name real slow and neat.

When I gave him back that piece of paper, he looked at it, then tilted his head to one side and studied me like he thought there might be a test on how many freckles I have.

"Actually," he said with a twinkle in his eyes, "I have far too much of this in the store, so do me a favor and take some of these off my hands." He reached right over into the candy display and scooped up a whole handful of chocolates and put them in a bag. He added the biggest candy bar I had ever seen in my whole entire life, then handed that bag to me.

"Wow," I said, taking the bag from him. "Thanks!"

"Mercy on us, Rob Estes!" Grandma gasped. "Whatever are you doing? April Grace, you do not need that much candy."

I'm telling you, I thought for sure she was gonna make me give all that chocolate wonderfulness back to him, but he frowned, shook his head, and made noises between his teeth.

"Tsk, tsk, Grace. Once food has been sold, there are no returns or exchanges."

"But we didn't buy—"

He held up one hand. "I'm sorry. The law's the law, and I can't go against the law."

"Yeah, Grandma, you don't want Rob to go to jail, do you?"

Her mouth flapped open and shut a couple of times. She looked at him, then me, then back to him, and finally she looked at the clock again.

"My word and honor! It's nearly a quarter till seven. Do you realize, child, how long you took buying that paper? We're gonna have to hustle."

He escorted us right to the door, fumbled way longer than he needed to with the key and the lock, and kept talking the whole time so Grandma didn't have an opportunity to get a word in edgewise.

"Good evening, ladies." He shook our hands warmly and

firmly, like we were in church. "I hope you have a wonderful evening."

"Thank you so much for everything," I said, full of happiness from the treasures he'd given me and how well he had piddled around slowly to keep us there longer.

Once we were back in the car, though, and ready for the drive back home, I sorta forgot about my good fortune. I fastened my seatbelt, silently recited the Lord's Prayer and the Twenty-Third Psalm one more time, and I even threw in a little bit of the Preamble to the Constitution as Grandma settled into the driver's seat.

"Grandma," I said, just as she started the engine, "I'm feeling queasy all of a sudden." That was sure enough the truth, and I knew the opportunity when I saw it. "Maybe we better not hustle. Maybe you better drive kinda slow."

"Oh?"

She gave me a look of concern and leaned toward me, peering into my eyes in the bluish light and shadow from the streetlights along the sidewalk.

"You gettin' sick, honey?"

She laid her soft palm along my forehead for a minute.

"No, ma'am. Not sick. Just a little queasy, probably 'cause we haven't had supper yet." As soon as I heard those words, I realized she might think we needed to hurry home so I could eat. "You better drive slow so I don't hurl in your car."

"All right, honey."

I want you to know we went home *slowly*. I mean, we went so slow it was like we were in a funeral procession and the corpse was doing the driving. Lots and lots of cars passed us.

Some of them honked like they were telling us off, but that was too bad for them. If it had been anyone but Grandma driving all slow and pokey that way, I would've gone plumb buggy because of it. But since we were way safer with her not zipping along like a race-car driver in the dark, I relaxed for the first time in I don't know how long with Grandma at the wheel. I got all tense again every time we met an oncoming car, 'cause she ran off on the shoulder, but at least she did it nice and slow. We were gonna be getting home later than seven o'clock, but at least we'd arrive in one piece.

Every little bit she asked me how I was feeling, and if we needed to stop. Every time I said, "I won't get carsick as long as you drive slow, Grandma." And that was the honest-to-goodness truth.

THIRTEEN

Well-Dressed Party Animals

♡

You know what? When we got home, there was not a single car there! Surely the party had not been called off.

The porch light was on, but the house wasn't all glowing bright like it would've been for a party. Boy, oh boy. Maybe I shouldn't have kept Grandma piddling around in the store so long, then creepy-crawling home so slowly.

"What time is it, Grandma?" I asked when she stopped the car.

She switched on the dome light to see her watch.

"Mercy me, it's a quarter after seven." She looked up. "How you feeling, hon? Still think you're gonna urp?"

"No. I think I'm fine."

"Good. Well, you run on in the house now and get you some supper, then get on that homework. You can get some of it done before bedtime, I'm thinking."

The car was still running, and she had her hand on the gearshift, as if she was getting ready to leave. Oh, good grief, I could not let that happen, even if there was no one at her party. Mama would at least have a celebration supper in there, or a cake, or something. Grandma could not go home all alone on her birthday without a single, solitary word of congratulation.

Right then I almost blurted out the whole sad story of how circumstances conspired to mess up Grandma's special day. A little voice in my head whispered for me not to do that.

"Aren't you coming inside?" I asked.

She sighed, and that sound held all the disappointment

you can imagine coming from someone at the end of their forgotten birthday.

"No, honey. I think I'll just go on home, take a nice, warm bath, maybe go to bed early. I'm a little tired."

Isn't that just the saddest thing you ever heard in your life?

"I wish you'd go in with me."

"Why? Are you afraid to walk up to the door by yourself?"

I gave her what I hoped was a pitiful look. If she thought I was afraid, she'd probably at least walk me as far as the door, and if we got to the door, she'd probably go inside.

"Yeah. Sorta."

"Goodness' sake!" she said, kinda snappish. "You are a big, grown-up girl, April Grace. There's no reason for you to be afraid of walking a few feet in the dark to your own door. The porch light is on!"

I crimped my mouth and thought as fast as my brain could churn. And then it did a cartwheel.

"I think you should come inside and at least explain why we're late," I said. "They might think I did something dumb to make us late or something." Which I did, of course, all that looking at old-lady feet stuff and piddling around buying the wrong paper, then having her drive slowly coming home.

She stared at me through the semidarkness inside of her Corolla, then blew out a big breath.

"Well, forevermore. Come on, then. Get your paper and chocolate. I'll tell your mama you were feeling poorly on the ride home. You won't get in trouble for feeling sick. Come on. Get out."

So I clutched my sack of notebook paper and chocolate and walked in that cold January wind beside Grandma toward the front porch. I could hear someone inside laughing, but Grandma's hearing isn't as sharp as mine, and she might not have heard.

We started up the porch steps, and I flew past her to the front door, hollering, "I'll get the door for you, Grandma!"

I hoped I yelled it loud enough for everybody inside to know we were there. I turned the knob and opened it a crack.

"You coming, Grandma?" I hollered.

"My stars, April Grace, why are you yelling?" she said as she got to the top step.

I pushed the door open all the way and shot a glance in. I saw what I needed to see, which was a houseful of people. I reckon they must've all parked around back, out of sight. I stepped aside so Grandma could go in first.

"Age before beauty," I told her grandly, and tried not to giggle.

"In that case, maybe you oughta go—"

She stepped across the threshold and I held my breath, praying to God that she wouldn't be so surprised that she'd have a heart attack right there on the spot.

Well, I tell you what. Instead of everyone leaping out of the shadows and corners and screaming, "Surprise!" they clapped very politely and started singing "Happy Birthday." It was a gentle surprise, after all, for which I am eternally grateful because I did not want to lose my grandmother at her very own birthday party.

All those candles Isabel had placed around the room gave

off the most beautiful glow you can imagine, like the air was full of gold dust. Grandma just stood there, her mouth about half-open, her eyes all wide, going from face to face to face as everyone sang. Folks from up and down the road were there, and so were lots of people from church, and all the ladies Grandma sat with during church services. Ernie, Rob, and Reverend Jordan were there, too, smiling and singing with everyone else. Rob caught my eye and gave me a wink, and you know what I did? I winked right back, grinning like a monkey.

"Law!" Grandma said, kinda squeaky. Then she said, "*Lawsy!* What in the world . . . Oh, for goodness' sake . . . Lily? Mike? What have you done?"

Daddy held up one hand and shook his head. "It wasn't me, Mom. It was Lily, Isabel, and the girls. Blame them!" He laughed heartily, and so did everyone else.

Grandma put a hand on both cheeks and gawked.

"Look at this house! Look at all those candles everywhere. Rose pink and pale pink. Oh, how pretty! And look at you folks, all dressed up like you're going to a revival meeting in the city."

Isabel, in her straight black dress, slicked-back dark hair, skinny high heels, and blood-red fingernails, stepped away from where she stood between Mama and Myra Sue to link her arm with Grandma's.

"Come with me," she said to her, then said in that voice that made everyone in our sixth-grade PE class tremble, "People!" Everyone hushed. "We shall return momentarily." She led Grandma off down the hallway, and they disappeared into Mama and Daddy's bedroom, at which point everyone started yakking and laughing again.

"You two were gone almost a couple of hours," Mama said, coming up to me and brushing a stray strand of hair back from my face. She looked real pretty in a dark-green velvet dress. "Was there a problem?"

"No, ma'am. I just did what Isabel told me and kept Grandma busy, and then just to make sure we wouldn't get back too early, I made sure she drove home real slow." I shot a glance down the hallway. "Why did Isabel take her off to your room?"

"To help Grandma get dressed up." She smiled at me. "I'm glad you did such a good job keeping Grandma busy. Isn't the house pretty? Myra Sue and Temple were a big help."

"Oh yeah?" I was surprised to hear that ole Myra Sue came out of her ivory tower to help. And it sure was nice of Temple to pitch right in, even though that fancy-schmancy stuff is not something she'd ever do.

"Yes. Temple won't touch the punch or the hors d'oeuvres, of course, because there's sugar in the punch and meat in the hors d'oeuvres, but she was a great hand in getting the roses arranged and the candles placed and lit." Mama cast a glance around at everything, and smiled. "Doesn't it all look lovely?"

"Yes'm. It looks real nice."

"Now, run upstairs and change into your party clothes."

♡

When I came back, I was wearing my nice dark-green, velvety dress that I got for the Christmas season and black patent-leather shoes, which I dearly hate because they're kinda pointy and they pinch my toes. Instead of my usual braid, I decided to let my hair hang loose. The air downstairs smelled like perfume and roses. Nice music played in the background, real soft and pretty. All those candles gave the house such a glow that it almost seemed like we were in a storybook. The ladies in their pretty dresses and men in dark suits visited with one another. They talked and laughed and moved around, and it was so pleasant and calm, you just couldn't help but enjoy yourself.

It seemed to me everyone who lived on Rough Creek Road and in Cedar Ridge must have been at our house that night, and they seemed to enjoy that fancy food Isabel had fixed. My baby brother would be in one set of arms, then a minute later someone else had him. The way he was passed around, that kid was gonna grow up thinking he was a box of candy.

At one point, some gray-haired old guy in a dark-blue suit with super narrow lapels was cuddling Eli and talking to him. When the man grinned, I nearly fell over 'cause I realized it was Forest Freebird holding my baby brother. His gray ponytail must've been tucked down in the collar of his suit, 'cause I didn't see it at all. Maybe he'd cut it off, but I doubted it. Let me tell you something: Forest Freebird has never worn anything but overalls and T-shirts while I've known him. That night he even wore shoes! And you should've seen Temple. Her hair was all loose and flowy and shiny, and her dark-blue, velvety dress had sparkles all over it. She even wore long silver earrings and slim, ballet slipper–looking shoes. You'd never believe in a million years either one could look like that unless you saw them for yourself.

I didn't have time to ponder Forest's and Temple's new images, though, because Isabel and Grandma came into the room right then.

"Our guest of honor is finally available for gifts and food!" Isabel announced in that snooty voice of hers, but she wasn't being snooty. She just sounds that way.

Everyone turned toward the two of them, of course, and you could see then why she'd hauled Grandma down the hall earlier. Isabel had fixed Grandma's hair in a poufy style and got her face all gussied up. Grandma wore a pretty dark-turquoise dress of some kind of shiny, satiny fabric with long gathered sleeves and lace on the collar, and a wide black belt. I was happy to see she was wearing nice black pumps, because sensible shoes with that dress might have made her look goofy. I did not want Grandma ever to look goofy.

Isabel led her to a chair next to a pile of gifts, and just as she sat down, Grandma spotted me.

"Tell me something, missy," she said, with her eyes narrowed. "Did you need that notebook paper?"

"I will someday."

Then everybody laughed because by then the story of how I'd fooled Grandma into making an emergency paper-buying trip into town had made the rounds at that party.

"I'm sorry I had to trick you, Grandma. We were desperate."

She nodded. "I forgive you." Then she grinned at me real big, and I knew she wasn't mad at all. She reached for her first present.

We all watched as she unwrapped gifts, everything from

a handmade cross-stitched apron to a wind-up music box to a couple of cookbooks. Ernie Beason gave her a gold-colored box of Godiva chocolates and a book of poetry. I didn't know Grandma liked poetry. Rob Estes gave her the biggest box of Russell Stover chocolates I have ever seen in my whole entire life and a bottle of some kind of expensive perfume. At least I figured it was expensive because Isabel went all nutsy over it, and the more expensive something is, the nutsier she tends to get. Reverend Trask Jordan gave her a medium-sized box of chocolates like you can buy at Wal-Mart and eighteen pink roses in a beautiful crystal vase.

I looked around to see what everybody thought of all this poetry, perfume, roses, and chocolate business, and they were all grinning and nudging one another. Now, don't get me wrong. As you know, I love chocolate as much as, if not more than, Grandma does, and I figured I'd be helping her eat all that candy. But I'll let you in on a little secret. If those men were trying to outshine each other by getting Grandma something romantic, they should have thought of something more original than all that chocolate-covered baloney. They should've thought of something like a trip to Spain, or a cruise to some island, or even a car ride up to Branson to have dinner and see a music show.

Right about then I noticed something: Myra Sue was nowhere to be seen. She'd been in the room when Grandma and I first got home, and she'd been in on the singing of "Happy Birthday." Mama said she had helped get things decorated. So where was she now? I'd bet my piece of birthday cake she was upstairs in her room, looking at herself in the mirror, winking and making kissy faces because she thinks she's so all-fired gorgeous.

Boy, oh boy. Sometimes that girl has less sense than a fried egg.

Ian and Daddy carried the biggest cake I'd ever seen into the living room. The icing was pale pink with lots of Barbie-pink roses. That whole entire cake had not one candle on it, which I thought was a grand disappointment. But I reckon candles would've taken the place of those roses made out of frosting, and that would've been a pure shame. Following Ian and Daddy came Mama, bearing a single pink cupcake glowing with as many lit candles as could possibly be stuck into the top of a cupcake.

Grandma's face was flushed and pretty, and the light of all the candles everywhere shone in her eyes. Everyone sang "Happy Birthday" for the second time, and she blew out the cupcake candles. That was one of those moments that I wanted to hang on to inside my head and remember all my life.

She took those little candles out of her cupcake and sucked the frosting off of each one, grinning while she did it. I figured Isabel would curl up her nose at such a stunt, but she was laughing as much as anyone else. Isabel surely was being one of the family that night. You'd never know she could be such an all-fired pain in the patootie sometimes.

From where I stood near the archway between the hall and living room, I saw Forest Freebird open the front door. I reckon he heard a knock the rest of us couldn't hear.

Cold air rushed in from outside, sending shivers over my skin. All the candle flames flickered and laid low like they wanted to go out. Pastor Ross was standing not far from me, and that cold breeze stirred his dark hair. I don't know why, but right about then those words from his sermon from a couple of weeks ago echoed into my head: "Things are gonna change."

I'm not sure how I knew it, but right then, I knew that Big Change I had been dreading had something to do with whoever or whatever had come sweeping through our front door. Something in my stomach rolled over and clenched tight at what I saw, and I shivered and scuttled across the room to my daddy and mama.

FOURTEEN

A Real, Live
Screamin' Mimi

❀

"Hooooweee! Now, that's what I call *cold*!"

The frog-croak voice and the mule-bray laugh that followed reached us before we saw the speaker.

Forest led the person toward the living room. She stopped right smack-dab in the middle of the arched doorway. Voices fell away as we all gawked at her. That woman was a sight, and here's just a few reasons why. Number one: She wore a cowboy hat, and ever since that Event last summer with Jeffrey Rance, who tried to hoodwink my grandma out of her house and our farm with romance and lies, I have no love for cowboy hats. Number two: Beneath that purple cowboy hat, her hair was a color I have never seen on a real human person. (Think Heinz ketchup stirred up with Welch's grape jelly.) Number three: Her face was as wrinkled and crispy as wadded-up sandpaper, and her orangey-red lipstick gave me chills. And number four: I believe if you're a million years old, you should not wear miniskirts, even if you're wearing a frontier jacket with a long fringe on it that comes past the skirt's hem. A fringe does *not* cover up bony white knees, let me tell you.

Did I forget to mention she was wearing bright-red cowboy boots?

"Have I interrupted something?" she asked, then brayed that donkey laugh again. She broke into a disgusting cough that sounded like Grandma's cat, Queenie, when she hacks up a fur ball.

I guess because Forest was the one who'd let her inside the house, he thought he should be the spokesperson, especially as Daddy and Mama stared at her like everyone else and didn't move or say a word.

"It's a surprise party," he told her in his soft, sad-sounding voice when she quit coughing.

"Oh?" She looked around, then flung out her arms and laughed again. "Well, surprise!"

Good gravy, but that laugh was enough to make the wax dribble right out of my ears.

Then she finally seemed to notice Grandma sitting in the special chair with crumpled gift wrap around her and presents at her side and the birthday cupcake in her hand. The strange person looked right at my grandma and grinned, showing the grossest brown teeth you can possibly imagine. It was like something from a horror movie. I am not supposed to watch horror movies, but I did once at 2:00 a.m. at Melissa Kay Carlyle's house when her mama had already gone to sleep and did not know we watched it or that we stayed up the rest of the night with the lights on because we did watch it.

"Why, Grace Reilly! I almost didn't recognize you, woman! You got old!"

She laughed again, a wheezing cackle this time. Grinning like a goon with her hands on her bony hips, she ran her gaze all over the room until she found Mama standing beside Daddy on the other side of the room. She gawked at her for a minute.

"Well, my stars, Lily!" she croaked out. "Seeing you is like looking in a mirror thirty years ago." When no one said a word, she continued, "Don't you even recognize me, Sandra Kay Moore, your own dear mother? I haven't changed that much, have I?"

Beside me, Mama gasped and kinda sagged against Daddy. Grandma dropped her special cupcake, frosting-side down. It hit the floor with a splat.

You know what? That old woman acted like she didn't even notice. Her gaze found me. She eyed me up and down. Then she gave me that brown grin. I shuddered a little. At least I think I did, but maybe we had an earthquake right then.

"Would you look at that? Goodness, you are the spittin' image of me when I was a little girl. Come here, Sunshine, and give your mimi a great big kiss." And she hunkered down a little with arms wide open again as if she thought I'd fly on wings of joy to kiss her wrinkly ole face.

I stared at her and felt my eyeballs about ready to pop free of my skull. I prayed for someone, anyone, to please, *please*, tell me this "Mimi" woman was not my other grandma.

When I did not fly into her arms as she seemed to expect, she straightened and looked at Mama again.

"Well, Lily, I came all this way to see you. Don't you have anything at all to say?"

Mama made a funny noise, like she wanted to laugh and cry and scream all at the same time, then she ran out of the room, right past that woman and down the hall. Daddy took off after her. I would've followed, but if I did that, I'd have to pass that awful old lady, and I did not want to be snared in her arms and kissed by those orangey-red lips. Instead, I edged over to Grandma's chair and clasped her shoulder, just to make sure I was connected with her. When she stood up, I hung on to her arm.

"Sandra Moore, what are you doin' here?" She spoke as if

there was no one else in that room. I guess maybe she'd forgotten everybody because they were all silent as rocks. They stared at that woman like they thought she was something out of a scary movie.

Boy, oh boy, it takes someone with no couth to crash a birthday party!

"Grandma," I whispered, "that isn't really her, is it? That's not really Mama's mama, is it?"

"'Fraid so, honey," she whispered back. Without looking at me, she patted my hand. To that old woman, she said aloud, "I don't see where you find your nerve, Sandra."

"Don't take that uppity tone with me, Myra Grace Reilly. I have every right in the world to be here. In case you've forgotten, Lily is *my* daughter."

Grandma raised one eyebrow. "I haven't forgotten that, but I figured you had."

That woman narrowed her eyes at Grandma like she was gonna charge across the room and slug her a good one. Of course no one in the room, including yours very truly, would've let her. Then she changed. Just like that. Her face went from mad to slack. She looked at me again and smiled.

"Little redheaded princess," she said, coming toward me with her hands stretched out. Let me tell you a couple of things. Number one: If that woman thought I was a princess, she needed to be taken to the hospital in Blue Reed to get her brains examined. And number two: Those hands were as bony as chicken claws and white as chalk, except for liver spots and the tip of her index finger, which were browner than all get-out, like her teeth, and I figured if she touched me, I'd probably just rot away. I edged even closer to Grandma, who put one arm around me, all comforting and strong.

"Won't you even say 'Hi, Mimi'?" she said. "You know you *gotta* call me Mimi and not Granny or Grandma, don't cha? Because I'm not old enough to be your grandmother."

Was she kiddin' me? She looked old enough to be Methuselah's great-grandmother. I'll tell you something else. There was just *no way, José* that she could be less than two million years old.

Then she broke into the worst fit of coughing you ever heard. I thought she was gonna hack up her lungs, her liver, and maybe half of her toenails—which were probably long and yellow. I shuddered again. I wondered if she had a disease. Then I remembered how Mr. Dreyfuss, the grade-school janitor, used to cough just like that, and everyone said it was because he smoked three packs of cigarettes a day. That was probably true. Every time I saw him, he was outside puffing and smoking like one of those old trains you see on western movies. This Mimi-person looked like a three-pack-a-day smoker to me.

"You're shy, aren't you, princess? Just like your mimi when I was your age. Here, since you're such a bashful little thing, let's just shake hands." She stuck out her right hand. Now, let me tell you, I did not want to shake hands, but with everyone in that room staring, I figured I had to.

I braced myself to look her in the eye like it is right and proper to do when you shake hands, but I could not force myself to look higher than the brown-stained tip of her nose. Actually, I wanted to hide my own face against Grandma like

I used to do when I was little and I'd see something awful or scary. Slowly, like molasses being poured on a frozen pond in January, I put out my hand.

You know what that sneaky old woman did? I'll tell you. She grabbed my hand and yanked me hard against her.

"Ha!" she crowed. "Tricked you so I could get some sugar, didn't I?"

Then she kissed me all over my face until I thought I'd die from toxic-waste lips. And then she laughed and coughed about two inches from my nose. Boy, oh boy, her breath stunk like an ashtray. I clawed my way to freedom in the most unprincess-like way you can possibly imagine, grunting and squirming like crazy. I think I might have wiped my face with my sleeve, but I'm not sure. When you're traumatized, you just don't remember every little detail.

"I'm gonna go see about my mama," I choked out, and fled from that room faster than you can believe. That yucky old woman could not possibly be related to my beautiful, sweet, clean mama.

I wanted to run outside and suck in fresh air, which I dearly needed, or run upstairs and take a hot shower, which I planned to do, believe me. You know what? If one of Temple's concoctions had been sitting somewhere within reach, I'd probably have grabbed it and stuck my nose right in it, just to clear my nose holes. But right then I needed to see if Mama was all right. I rushed into the kitchen. It was empty, but I thought I heard my daddy's voice and followed the sound right through to the service porch and on outside. The moonlight was soft and silvery as the night stretched away, frozen and dark and secretive, like it had completely forgotten that sunlight would fill up the sky in a few hours and reveal all the night's hidden places.

"Mama? Daddy?" I said when I saw them a few feet away in the windy, cold shadows of the house. My breath fogged around my face.

There was a short silence, then Daddy said, "Go back to the party, April Grace."

I did not budge an inch. Instead I asked, "Is Mama all right?" and the scared feeling I had in my insides sort of made me feel nervous, like last fall when Mama was really sick and I didn't know she was pregnant. This time, though, I knew what was going on, and I wasn't so much worried as concerned that that old Mimi-person had upset her into being ill.

I heard the soft murmurings of their voices, and I waited because I'd been taught better than to barge right over and interrupt.

"Come here, punkin," Daddy said at last, softly.

In that murky moonlight, Mama's face was whiter than the sheets on wash day. Her eyes were swollen. She held her arms out to me, and I ran to them. She wrapped me in a hug so tight I could hardly breathe. Then she kissed me all over my face, like I'd been gone a thousand years. She kissed the places that Mimi-person had kissed, erasing them completely. I surely hoped Mama did not catch any Mimi-germs.

Daddy stroked my hair as I put one hand on either side of her face and looked right into her eyes.

"Are you all right?" I asked.

"Sure, honey," she said, smiling at me as she caught both

my hands in hers and squeezed them gently. "Just . . . shocked."

I took in a deep breath and let it out. Daddy stroked my head again, 'cause I'm sure he knew I was upset. It felt good to be close to him and Mama, to know we loved each other.

"Mama, is that woman really your mother?"

She hesitated, then nodded. "Yes, honey."

She scrubbed at her eyes like they were itching her to pieces.

"Why?"

She stopped rubbing and gave me a funny look.

"Why what, honey?"

"Why is that woman here, on Rough Creek Road, in our house?"

A cold breeze shot across us. Mama rubbed her bare arms, and Daddy pulled her close into the circle of one arm and me into the circle of the other. Not one of us was wearing a coat, and the wind whipped our bodies like it was trying to get our attention. I snuggled in closer.

"I don't know why she's here," Mama said to me. "I guess she wants something."

"What do you reckon she wants?"

"I don't know," she said again, like she was tired.

"Do you think she's gonna stay long?"

"Oh goodness, I hope not!" And then she bit her lip as if she shouldn't have said that.

I didn't say anything for just a second, then I said, "You never talk about her, Mama."

"I know."

Again it was quiet, but I'm not much of one to let things

stay silent for long, if there are things going on that create drama in our house.

"You gonna tell her to leave?"

Daddy cleared his throat, and I looked up at him.

"April Grace," he said, "we've never told anyone to leave our house."

Well, that was true enough. Ian and Isabel lived with us for what seemed like forever last year, and they were regular pills, and not once did Mama or Daddy say to either one of them, "I think you ought to get out now, 'cause you have done worn out your welcome."

"My own personal self, I don't want that woman here," I said, because someone needed to say it.

"She's my mother, April Grace," Mama said sadly.

"But Mama, there is something . . . scary about her."

"I know, honey. She's different."

I looked at Daddy, and he gave me a gentle smile I could see in that moonlight. His smile seemed to say, "It'll be all right."

"She'll probably leave soon," Mama added. "As far as I know, she's never stayed in one place for very long." She said nothing for a minute, like she was praying or seeking guidance or something, but then she took a deep, shuddering breath and turned to Daddy and blurted almost the same thing I'd asked her. "Mike, why is she here? After all these years, why now?"

He hugged Mama up to him, kinda rocking her in his arms a little.

"I wish I had some answers for you, sweetheart," he told her. "Maybe she's . . . oh, I don't know . . . lonely and needs someone around."

"Then where has she been all this time?" I asked. "If she was lonely, why didn't she show up before?"

I stood there, hoping Mama would confide some details about that old woman. You see, I knew a few secrets about Sandra Moore. Secrets that Grandma shared with me last summer about stuff I wasn't supposed to know. She told me that Sandra Moore had abandoned Mama and given her to a mean old great-aunt who starved and mistreated her. Grandma had shared this with me only because she felt I needed an example of doing good things even when life has kicked you in the teeth. You see, Mama forgave her mean ole aunt and took care of her until she died. Grandma said Mama had never allowed her Unfortunate Circumstances to turn her into a bitter, rotten person.

Mama never wanted to discuss these events, so I have never, not even once, hinted that I knew anything.

"I don't know where she's been. I haven't heard from her in years and years. You see, April Grace," Mama said, lifting her head and straightening her back as if gathering courage, "my mother left me behind when I was just a baby."

"And you were raised by Aunt Maxie." That much was common knowledge in our family.

"Yes. Great-Aunt Maxie did her best to take care of me, but she was old and never in the best of health. She wasn't always kind," Mama said, then she went on to tell me some of those things I already knew, like how Aunt Maxie didn't always feed her very much or make sure she had the right kinds of clothes for whatever the weather was.

"Sandra came for me once and took me with her. I'm not

sure what happened, but she brought me back after a year or two and gave me to Aunt Maxie again. By then, Maxie was getting sick, she had a very small, fixed income, and she did not want me. But Sandra didn't care. She left me there anyway."

"And this is the first time you've seen her since then?" I asked.

Mama nodded. "I thought she'd probably died long ago."

I sucked in a lungful of that cold night air and nearly froze my sinuses.

"I don't think she should get to stay here in your nice, clean, warm house and eat your good food and kiss your very own daughter with her nasty lips and act like she's related to me, or that I should love her, because I don't!"

"Well, honey, I never said I wanted her to stay here. In fact, I don't expect her to stay. Let's just take it one step at a time, okay?"

The back door opened, and I squinted into the darkness and made out the skinny form of Isabel St. James. She stood for a time, peering around, but when she spotted us, she came trotting over in her high heels. Have you ever seen a tall, skinny woman trot in high heels and a slim, straight skirt? Well, most of the time it's funny. Right then, though, I was too worried to snicker at Isabel's tottering approach.

"Reillys, is that you?"

"It's us, Isabel," Daddy said. "Well, it's some of us. Myra Sue isn't here."

She stopped near our little huddled mass and wrapped her arms around herself. At least she had long sleeves.

"Lily, dear, Grace sent me to find you and see if you were all right."

"I'm fine," Mama said in a strong voice. If you'd been standing in the dark and not able to see her very well, and if you hadn't been in on the conversation, you'd have thought everything was hunky-dory and we were all just hanging around outside because getting our noses froze off is so much fun.

"In fact," Mama continued, "we're just going back inside."

"You sure you're okay?" Daddy asked her as she started to move away.

"Positively," she said, and I could hear the reassuring smile in her voice. "I was just surprised, that's all."

"Well, Lily," Isabel said, her voice as snooty as I've ever heard it, "I don't mean to hurt your feelings, but your mother is perfectly dreadful, and no one would blame you if you simply went somewhere else until she left. I'd be happy to give you the keys to our house, if you'd like to take sanctuary there. A moment ago she lit a cigarette, and when I told her you absolutely did not allow smoking in your home or around your children, she nearly blew smoke in my face as if I were a nuisance and said, 'Oh, is that a fact?' As if she did not believe me! Well, I mean to say, forgive me, my dear, but she is completely unrefined. Are you sure she's your mother?"

"I'm sure."

Hmm. See? I wasn't the only one who found it hard to believe those two women were related.

Isabel cleared her throat in the most serious, disapproving manner.

"I directed her to the front porch," she said, "but it took

Ian and Temple backing me up to get her to go. I know you would never ask her to leave the party, but if you want to slip off to our house, I'm sure everyone would understand."

"Thank you, Isabel. That's very kind of you." She sighed deeply, as if gathering in strength. "But I have to deal with Sandra at some point."

"But, honey, you shouldn't have to deal with her at a party," Daddy said.

"Mike makes a perfect point, Lily. Bursting in the way she did, crashing Grace's party . . ." She paused, then asked, "You weren't *expecting* her, were you?"

Mama shook her head vigorously. "No! And I can't imagine why she's come back after all these years. My mother never was one to take life seriously. For her to just show up this way, unannounced, unexpected . . ."

A dim image flashed in my head of ole Myra Sue huddled over the mailbox and whispering on the telephone when she thought no one was around. Then a little light seemed to come on in my brain, and I let it shine there for a while as I looked more closely at the mental image of my sister. That girl had been secretive and sneaky and sulky for the last couple of weeks. Daddy had thought she had a boyfriend. Mama, Isabel, Grandma, and nearly everyone else thought she was going through a teenage phase. But maybe it had been something more awful than anyone could have guessed: maybe Myra had invited that awful screaming Mimi into our house!

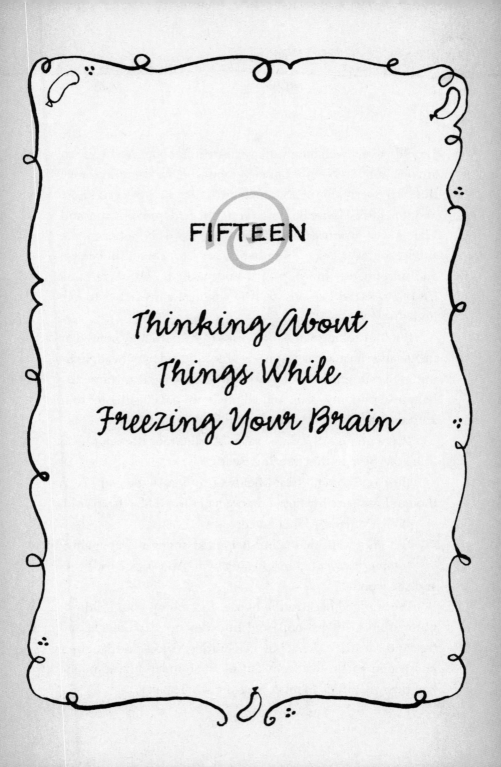

FIFTEEN

Thinking About Things While Freezing Your Brain

I couldn't very well mention my suspicions about Myra Sue to anyone just yet. Number one: Why would my sister do something so purely dumb? Number two: She did not even know about Sandra Moore because Grandma had told only me, and I had never, ever breathed a mumbling word about her to one single, solitary person. Number three: That smelly, unkempt, and unrefined Mimi-person would never be on Myra Sue's list of Preferred Persons, so why would she invite her to our house?

But I'm telling you something right here and now: that image and those ideas just hung around inside my head, itching my brain until I nearly wanted to claw right through my hair, my scalp, my skull, and all my brain guts just to get to it and scratch.

"Let's go inside," Mama said. "April Grace does not need to be out here in this freezing weather."

"Just one thing," I said before I took a single step, even though I was sure my lips and nose had turned blue from cold.

"What's that?" Mama asked.

"I do not want that Mimi-person kissing me ever again."

"Don't worry, punkin," Daddy said. "You stick beside me, and she won't."

We trudged back to the house. I'm telling you, I did not want to go in there, but I did not want to stay outside and freeze to death, either. The celebrating voices and laughter had begun again, but from outside it sounded like someone had thrown a thick blanket over the whole party.

In the living room, I grabbed hold of Daddy's hand. The candles still burned, but not as brightly as before. A lot of that cake had been cut and eaten, but it sure didn't look as yummy as it had thirty minutes ago. Grandma was chatting and smiling with Pastor Ross, but she seemed less happy. You know something? It looked to me like all the fun had gone right out of Grandma's party, and maybe right out of Grandma.

You know how Isabel said that old woman had gone out to the front porch to smoke? Well, she wasn't there. No, sirree! Instead, she was standing inside, all close to Mr. Brett, twirling a strand of her awful red hair with one finger and talking to him. Oh brother. Do you suppose that icky Mimi-person was flirting with Mr. Brett, who was about three hundred years younger than her? He wasn't flirting back, I'll tell you for sure. In fact, he darted his eyes all around the room like he was looking for an escape hatch. Of course, Mr. Brett was too polite to run off and find one. Lucky for him, Forest Freebird and Ian came to the rescue. That Mimi-person looked a little surprised at their interruption and kinda aggravated as he got all involved in conversation with them.

"You know, I haven't seen Myra Sue for a while," Mama said, glancing around.

"Maybe she's taking care of Eli," Daddy suggested.

"No. Mrs. Hopper has Eli now. See? She's rocking him in Mama Grace's rocker." Mama frowned slightly. "I was so busy getting this party ready, and then after everyone came, I told her to take care of Eli for me, so I didn't worry about it, but . . . actually, Mike, I haven't seen Myra Sue much at all tonight."

"If that girl has been on the telephone this whole night—" Daddy said.

"I think she's in her room. I'll go check," I said.

"Okay, honey," Mama said. "Tell her I said for her to stay off the phone, and that I said to come downstairs. She's expected to be at Grandma's party."

I figured my sister was up in her room. Besides, I wanted to explore the notion that she was in cahoots with Mimi. Which still seemed dumb to me. If she had been, wouldn't she be there, hanging around That Woman? Unless, of course, she didn't want anyone to know she'd cooked up such a hare-brained scheme . . . and even if she had, it still did not make a lick of sense. In fact, I could hardly believe my imagination even came up with the idea.

I edged past that Mimi-person, who was now all wrapped up in conversation with Ernie Beason. He was smiling politely at her. Maybe he did not smell her stinky breath or notice her brown teeth. I shot a glance at Grandma to see if she'd noticed this new development. She had. She was glowering good and proper at Ernie. Or at Mimi. Or both. I skittered right out of the room, unnoticed.

My sister was not on the telephone in the hallway, so I tore off up the stairs and went straight to her bedroom. I knew she was there 'cause I heard Michael Jackson's shrill voice piping out from the other side of that door.

"Hey, Myra Sue!"

"Go away," she hollered.

"I can't. Mama sent me up here."

There was a bit of time before she opened the door slightly and eyeballed me out of the inch-wide crack.

"Why?"

"Because it's Grandma's birthday!" Any dunce would know that without even being told.

She huffed at me.

"Grandma has a birthday every year."

Sometimes I wanted to smack that girl.

"Yeah, well, so do you. How'd you like it if no one went to your party?"

She bugged her eyes out at me like she thought I was stupid.

"I don't want a bunch of old people at my party," she said, all snippy. "Besides, there's a whole houseful of people down there. She is not going to miss *me*. As if she would, anyway. This entire family is going to regret how they've treated me when I'm famous."

Oh brother. Sometimes Myra tried to act like she was all pitiful and neglected, and that "when I'm famous" bit was enough to sour my stomach. But I had to persuade her to come downstairs, no matter how big a drip she was.

"Of course Grandma misses you. Mama and Daddy miss you, and they said for you to come down."

She crimped her mouth all prissy and put-out.

"I have things to do."

"Like what?"

"Homework, if you must know."

"Oh, I'm so sure! Myra Sue, you have never been a

homework hound before in your whole entire life. Why are you so all-fired obsessed about doing it now?"

She slammed the door right in my face. You know what I did? I'll tell you. I opened it right up and walked in. I thought she was gonna whomp me, but I got out of the way in time. Wearing her best blue dress and shiny black flats, she ended up falling over a pile of dirty laundry in the middle of the floor.

"Get out!" she screamed at me. "You are such an intruding . . . intruding *intruder*."

I ignored her and looked around that filthy room. "Aren't you afraid you're gonna catch the bubonic plague?" I asked my goofy, messy sister.

"Be quiet!" She kicked and scrambled, trying to get loose from all those dirty socks and underwear and shirts and jeans and stuff.

"How can someone as prissy as you be such a slob? You reckon something is gonna come crawling out of all this trash someday and carry you off?"

"Turn blue, April Grace Reilly! And get out of my room!" She finally stood up.

She looked like she was gonna throttle me, so I skittered to the other side of the room. Well, as best as I could skitter through magazines, crumpled notebook pages, a history book, a math book, a science book, and an English book scattered across the floor like she'd thrown them away for all time.

I would have dearly loved to confront her about that weird little list I found, and tell her I knew she was up to No Good, but in her current state of mind, I knew if she knew

I had it, she'd rip my gizzard right out. For the time being I shoved all thoughts of the list out of my head.

I stopped that girl dead in her tracks when I said, "Did you invite that awful ole Mimi-person to Grandma's party?"

She looked genuinely surprised.

"What? What's a *Mimi-person*?"

"Sandra Moore."

"Who?"

"Did you invite her?"

She huffed at me and stomped her foot. "I did not invite anyone to that party! Why would I invite anyone to a boring old party full of old people, especially someone I've never heard of?"

"So you're saying you didn't invite our other grandmother to this party?"

Her eyes got bigger than two full moons.

"Our other grandmother?"

"Do you mean to tell me you weren't down there when they brought out Grandma's cake?"

She narrowed her eyes at me. "What do you mean *our other grandmother?"*

Suddenly I knew how to fix that Myra Sue so she'd never run out on a party for Grandma again.

I grabbed her arm and said, "Come with me."

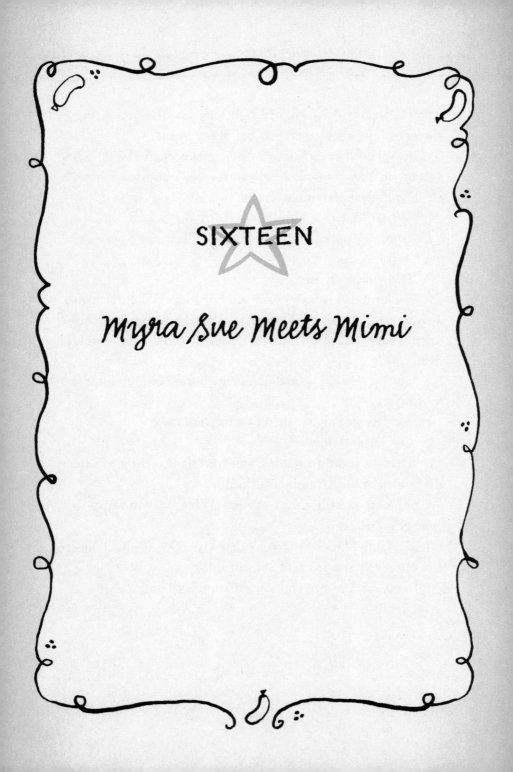

SIXTEEN

Myra Sue Meets Mimi

☆

"There's Myra!" Mama said as we got to the bottom of the steps.

Mama stood nearby, holding the baby, and I figured that by the way he was squirming like a little worm, she was gonna go feed him. That kid eats about every two hours. I wondered how much he'd eat when he was as old as me. Daddy would probably have to get an extra job in town just to buy extra groceries for Eli.

"Honey, where have you been?" she asked my sister.

"I have homework, Mother," Myra said, all prissy.

Mama gave her a Look, and I wanted so bad to holler, "Oh brother, I'm so sure!" but I didn't. One thing Mama did not need right then was to worry about something dumb my dumb sister was doing. Didn't she have enough to worry about with that old woman who'd barged in?

"April Grace said 'our other grandmother' is here. What's she talking about? We don't have another grandmother."

Mama looked upset, but Eli started squalling so loud, all she said was, "Go let Grandma know you're helping her celebrate her birthday, Myra Sue. Then come to the bedroom and I'll explain the rest to you. "

Myra Sue shoved out a sigh like you can't believe, but she said, "All right. But if I fail history for attending a party, don't blame me."

Boy, oh boy, I reckon I got a big mouth sometimes, and I stick my foot right in there, shoes, socks, and all, but my sister did not have a Single Clue about when to keep her yap shut.

Eli was screaming fit to be tied, so Mama pinned a hard look on ole Myra, and I knew there was gonna be consequences if my sister kept being all snitty and snooty.

While Mama hurried off toward her bedroom to feed the baby, Myra Sue grabbed my arm so hard, I yelped like a pup and yanked myself free.

"Did you drag me down here just to get me in trouble, you big, fat brat?" she snarled.

At that remark, I got all uppity my own self. "I did not get you in trouble, Miss Smarty Pants. You got yourself in trouble because you have a big mouth and no couth. And anyway, you aren't doing homework, and you know it, and I know it, and you know I know it, and I know you know I know it, so just drop it."

She looked confused for a minute. That girl cannot think when she's standing, because all the blood that should be supplying her brain has drained clear down to the far edge of her pinky toe. Then she squinted her eyes at me, but I did not give her a chance to slap, pinch, or grab.

"Let's go in the other room and get some cake before you get in more trouble," I said to her, as if I cared whether or not she got grounded until she was forty-two years old, or if she had to scrub the service porch with her very own personal toothbrush, which Mama would never suggest, but it would serve that girl right.

She did not budge.

"I want to know about *our other grandma*!"

"Mama just said she'll tell you about it."

"You tell me now, you brat!"

Boy howdy, that girl could be unreasonable. If she did not want to wait until Mama explained it to her, then so be it.

"Come with me," I said, "and you'll see for yourself."

She shmooshed up her lips, but she did not do the Isabel-blinking business. Instead she looked at me like she was examining my brain for worms and/or warts, but she followed me into the other room.

Grandma was surrounded by some of our guests, but she noticed when Myra and I walked in. She smiled, kinda tight and forced, but I was glad she saw my sister had made An Effort. She and Myra waved to each other, then Myra said, "Okay, so now Grandma knows I'm here. Show me this other grandmother."

I glanced around and saw that Mimi-person eating cake and sitting on the sofa with her bony, white legs crossed. One foot wiggled back and forth like crazy in its red boot.

"Follow me," I said to Myra, and believe it or not, she did.

We stopped near That Woman. In one hand, she balanced the biggest hunk of birthday cake you ever saw, and in the other hand she had a cup of Mama's good cloud punch. She was guzzling it down like she'd been in the Gobi desert for the last thirteen decades and hadn't had a drop to drink in all that time. When she lowered the cup, she spotted me. She had a foamy, red mustache and she wiped it right off with her sleeve as if she had no manners, which she did not, I'm pretty sure.

"Well, there's my little carbon copy!" she said, grinning at me and showing those stained teeth.

I did not shudder this time, at least not right out where

you could see me do it. I'll tell you one thing right now: if I was gonna look like her when I got old, I think I'd shave my head and move to the moon.

"Ma'am," I said, polite as all get-out, "this is my sister. She's fourteen." Then I turned and said to Myra, "This is Sandra Moore. She's Mama's mother." Please take note that I did not say she was our grandmother. Somehow I just could not hack out those words in an introduction.

You know what? I think I turned invisible right then, because that woman did not look at me again. She stared and stared at Myra Sue, then she grinned real big.

"Well, my goodness, I did not know I had a glamour girl for a granddaughter. Precious thing, you are a regular little princess, aren't you? My word, you look just like Princess Di!"

I nearly choked when she said that, and Myra just stood there, gawking at her.

"What's the matter, princess? Cat got your tongue?"

"No, ma'am," Myra Sue squeaked out.

I wasn't sure if she was so tongue-tied because that Mimi-person was just so awful, or if she actually believed she looked like Princess Diana and was grateful someone finally noticed. If ole Myra Sue took the woman's words seriously and started acting like she was some kind of Royal Person, I figured sooner or later someone would have to lock her up in a princess tower somewhere because there would be no living with her.

"Come to me, darlin' girl. What's your name?"

Myra Sue just stood there as if she really had lost her tongue somewhere.

"Her name is Myra Sue Reilly," I said. "Me and Myra are named after our *grandmother*."

"Oh?" Still staring at Myra, she said, "Neither of you has a *Sandra* or a *Kay* in your name?" She sounded kinda miffed.

"No, ma'am."

"Well, I don't think that's very nice." She put her cake plate on the floor, caught my sister's hand, and pulled her closer. Then she started grinning again and studied Myra some more. "I b'lieve you've got your Grandpa Earl Joe's eyes. His were bluer than the summer sky, too. He was a handsome feller."

Who in the world was Grandpa Earl Joe? I had never heard of him in my whole entire life.

"She got her blue eyes from her own daddy," Grandma said, right behind us. She had one hand on my shoulder and one on Myra's. I was purely glad to feel it there, too.

Sandra-Mimi glanced at Grandma and kinda narrowed her eyes.

"Don't get all uppity with me, Grace Reilly. I'm these girls' grandma just as much as you are."

"You might be their grandmother, but you ain't their grandma, not like I am."

Mimi uncrossed her legs and sat up like she was fixin' to stand.

"Hoooweee! Don't get your drawers in a knot just because I didn't want to hang around in this one-horse neck of the woods my entire life."

"I know you went off because you thought you were gonna be some kind of big star!" Grandma shot right back at her. "But I don't remember seeing your name in lights anywhere."

Whoa. Ole Myra Sue wants to see her name in lights, too. Could it be she got all that dreaming of being a famous actress from this weird grandma? It's worth thinking about, I tell you.

Right about then I noticed the room was real quiet around us, and I peeked over my shoulder. Folks were leaving, unsmiling and perplexed, silent as egg-sucking dogs skulking out of the hen house. A glance at the hallway showed Isabel and Temple handing coats to people and telling them good-bye in hushed voices. Daddy, Ian, and Forest shook hands and murmured to people as they left. It made me think of scenes from funerals I'd seen on TV.

Grandma and Mimi were so busy glowering at each other, they did not even notice. Just after the last guest left our house, Mama came into the room, carrying Eli.

"What happened?" Mama asked, looking at the empty chairs, the cake and punch remains, and paper napkins scattered around. "Where'd everyone go?"

"The guests left," Isabel said. "We had something of an upset in here."

We all looked at Sandra Moore, who was happily smacking down her cake again and ignoring Grandma.

"More cake for the rest of us!" she sang out. "And it's been a long time since I've had cake this good."

She shoved in a bite so big, it could have squooshed right out her eyeballs and ears. Now, that was just plain tacky, and it nearly made me never want to eat cake again. She looked around, and her chewing slowed. For the first time, that woman seemed to realize she was the only one who was having herself a jolly old time. She slugged down the rest of her punch, shoved the cup at me, and said, "Fill 'er up, wouldja, Sunshine?"

Well, I was more than glad to get away from her, so I went off to get her more to drink.

"Seems to me folks don't know how to have fun around here!" I heard her say. Boy, oh boy. She did not know we had been having fun just fine until she showed up.

"Can I hold that baby?" she asked about the time I was handing her over her refill. As yet, she had not really said much to Mama or Daddy. In fact, what seemed weird to me was how she came parading into our home as if she was a regular visitor, and we should all be happy to have her there.

Mama's eyes got kinda big, and you could see plainer than day she did not want to hand teeny little Eli over to that loud, frowzy woman. Isabel came from across the room to the rescue, her high heels clicking like a frenzied woodpecker on the hard floor.

"Oh goodness!" she said, curling up her nose. "That child has a dirty diaper. Let me take him, Lily, and I'll clean him up." She took Eli from Mama and glanced at my sister. "Come with me, Myra darling. You can hand me the moist towelettes. April dear, you can get the baby oil."

"Huh?" Myra said, like she didn't know anything at all. Grandma grabbed her hand and steered her out of the room.

"I'm coming," I said as soon as that woman took her cup of punch from my fingers. In the background, quiet as mice, Ian, Forest, and Temple started cleaning up.

"There's no need for a whole delegation of y'uns to go change a diaper," Mimi said. "You sit here, Sunshine, and talk to your mimi." She grabbed my arm and yanked me down beside her. You might think a scrawny old woman like her would have no strength, but I reckon she lifted special weights for her fingers or something because she held on to my arm and I could not get free.

I figured if I'd yelled, "Let go of me, you old kook!" I'd probably get in trouble, so I sat there like a statue, and the only things I moved were my eyes. I looked at my mama and my daddy. Mama hurried to the sofa and sat down on my other side. She pulled me close to her and kissed the top of my head. I liked the feeling of my mama on one side of me, but I did not like the feeling of that Mimi-person on the other side. And you know what? She still had hold of my arm.

"Well, Sandra?" Mama said.

"Well what, Lily?" she said, crossing her skinny ole legs again. "You don't act very happy to see me."

I glanced up at Mama, who seemed to be searching real hard for the right thing to say.

"I'm stunned," she said. "I never expected to see you again in my life."

"Yeah," I piped up, turning to the old woman. "We all thought you were dead a long time ago."

You know what? Mama let that comment go. But only for just a bit, then she said, "April," like she was reprimanding me because she thought she should, but not because she really meant it.

That old woman eyeballed Mama for a few seconds, then she looked at me.

"Did your mama tell you that I died?"

"No, ma'am."

"Oh? What did she tell you?"

"She never talked about you at all."

It was like her face froze. She didn't even blink.

"Your mama never talked about me?"

"No, ma'am."

She twisted her mouth and squinted her eyes and wiggled her left foot like crazy. She let go of my arm, finally, and I was grateful like you couldn't believe.

"Well, your mimi has a lot to tell you then!" She picked up her cup and gulped it all down. "Yes, sirree," she said when she finished, "we got lots to catch up on around here." She grinned at all of us like catching up was going to be more fun than going to Disney World.

"For now, though," she said, "I'm tired. Where's my room, Lily?"

Mama blinked, then she and Daddy looked at each other, kinda horrified.

"We don't have an extra room," Daddy said when Mama seemed unable to speak.

"That's right," Mama murmured.

Well, you could have knocked me over with a dried-up, old Q-tip because I never thought I would hear such words come from the mouth of either one of them. I guess Mama heard my eyes get big, because she turned to me.

"Time for you to go to bed, honey. Scoot on up to your room now."

Now, here's the thing: most of the time I want to hang around and listen and chime in, but in this case, I just wanted to get away from Mimi and her smell and her brown grin and that whole business. I was purely happy to trot off upstairs and hit the hay. And let me tell you, I *ran* out of that room before she could grab me and kiss me good night. Urp.

SEVENTEEN

Who's Been Sleeping in My Bed? Not Me!

☺

It didn't take long to shower, brush my teeth, and put on my pj's. I fluffed my pillows, got into bed, and arranged the covers all snuggly and comfy around me, then I picked up my book. I eyeballed my door, hoping that old lady didn't get a wild notion to come in and kiss me good night.

It took me a good while to get involved in my story because the night's events—everything from tricking Grandma to escaping from that Mimi-person—flickered around in my mind like an irritating moth. I was just about ready to forget about reading that night when Mama knocked on my door and called out softly, "April, honey?"

Let me tell you something about door knocking and my mama. She always knocks and she never goes busting into your room like some mothers do, like Melissa Kay Carlyle's mother, for instance, who just opens the door without warning, even if you're standing there in your *underwear* trying to get dressed.

"Come in, Mama." I hoped that old woman was not lurking around behind her.

Mama entered with some clean, folded sheets on her arm. She looked frazzled and weary and a little pale. She was alone.

"You okay, Mama?" I asked, sitting up straight.

"I'm fine, honey. Listen, I want you to get up and help me change the bed linens, then I want you to go sleep in Myra Sue's room."

"What?" I squawked.

"Don't give me a hard time now," she said. "Come on. Get up."

Boy, oh boy. I crawled as slowly as possible out of my very own comfortable, warm bed in my nice, clean room.

"You aren't putting that woman in here, are you?" I asked.

Mama handed me both pillows from the bed. "Change the pillow slips, honey. And yes, I am. She needs a place to sleep."

Well, wouldn't you just know it. Mama was trying to do the Right Thing, just like she always did. This time, though, I wished she hadn't decided the Right Thing was putting Mimi in my room.

"Well, then why can't she sleep in Myra Sue's room?"

Mama had taken off the blankets and the top quilt. She started removing the sheets, but paused to look at me straight.

"Because it would take too long to get Myra's room clean, that's why. Besides," she said as she went back to her work, "Myra Sue had to give up her room for a long time when Ian and Isabel stayed with us, then later when Grandma stayed here. So it's your turn."

I frowned so hard that my forehead actually ached. As a rule I try not to be a selfish person, but this had nothing to do with being generous. Number one: No one in her right mind would want to sleep in Myra Sue's rat's nest. Number two: She slept with that dumb radio on. Number three: I did not want that Mimi-person stinking up my room or my bed.

"Don't give me any trouble about this, April Grace," Mama said sternly. She was giving me the Look again.

I knew there was absolutely no hope in arguing or even pleading my case. So I said, "Do you think you can at least have Myra clear a path between the bed and door?"

Mama handed me one side of the sheet, and I helped her fit it on the mattress. She gave me a quick, gentle smile.

"I think we can arrange that. In fact, you finish putting on these clean sheets, and I'll go speak to her about it."

"Mama?"

"Yes?" She was at the door, but turned to look at me.

"Do I have to call her Mimi?"

"Would you rather call her Grandma?"

"*No.*"

She started to go through the door.

"Mama?"

"What is it, April?"

"You called her Sandra."

"Yes. I did."

We just looked at each other for a bit. I thought she was going to say something else, but then it seemed like she was lost in thought for a bit. She gave me a sad, little smile and left me to finish changing the sheets on my bed. I should've known better than to think ole Mimi would stay anywhere other than right here. I should've known Mama and Daddy would let her stay because they've never turned away anybody. They always say if you're gonna be a Christian, then you need to act like Christ.

Myra Sue wasn't any happier than I was about sharing her room. In fact, she glowered and grumped at me like everything was all my fault. Then after a little while she quit saying anything at all. I don't even think she said her prayers. And you know what else? She slept with her notebook all cuddled up. I guess she thought I'd snoop in it and read all her secret "homework" papers. You know what? Just between me and you, I would've, if I could've got hold of it, because I really, *really* wanted to know what was so interesting and all-fired important that she had to sleep with it.

☺

The next morning when I woke up, my throat and eyes were a little scratchy, and I figured I'd probably developed an allergy to that Mimi-person.

I went downstairs and there she sat. She was a sight. Without that dumb purple cowboy hat, you could see, plain as day, about an inch and a half of grayish-white hair growing between her scalp and that awful red color. Also, it was stringy, like it needed a good wash. Her face still wore whatever makeup was left on there from last night, so I knew she had not washed *that*.

She had her smokes and her lighter right next to her plate just like Isabel did when she was living with us. She also sat on her backside and watched Mama cook, just like Isabel used to. In fact, if you squinched up your eyes into teeny tiny slits and stared at her, you might think Mimi actually was Isabel dressed up like an old lady. Boy, oh boy, two of 'em within a half-mile of each other right here on Rough Creek Road. Not that they were completely alike or anything, but you could just look at both of them and know they could mess everything up if they took a notion to do so.

"Well, good morning, Sunshine," she croaked at me, then had a fit of coughing like you wouldn't believe. When she finished, she slurped her coffee. "Lily, I sure taught you how to make a fine cup of coffee. Guess you learned a little something from me, didn't you?"

Mama did not answer that directly. Instead, she brought the coffeepot over to the table, filled Mimi's cup, and said, "I'll have your breakfast ready soon." She glanced at me. "Good morning, April Grace."

"Mornin', Mama," I said, sitting at that table as far from Mimi as I could.

"Not gonna say good morning to me?" Mimi asked.

Well, I'd hardly had the opportunity, given that she'd coughed out her lungs and then started talking right afterward.

"Good morning," I said, as pleasantly as possible without encouraging any kind of hug or kiss. I looked around for Grandma because she always comes over every morning about that time.

"Is Grandma here?"

"I'm right here!" Mimi said with a laugh that sounded like she gargled with Rice Krispies.

"I mean my *real* grandma."

Before Mimi could respond to that, Mama said, "She's not been over yet. She probably slept late." She did not even scold me for being snotty. In fact, she asked, "How'd you sleep, honey?"

I sighed, then I coughed.

"Ole Myra hogs the bed and the covers," I said. I cut a sideways glance at Mimi but decided not to mention how I'd worried about her sleeping on my bed. I'll tell you something. I had to hold in another shudder when I thought about it.

Mama turned to the stove to stir the eggs, and Mimi shook out a cigarette.

"Well, I slept like a little baby in your room, Sunshine," she said, even though no one asked her. "You've got a mighty comfortable bed and a sweet little room there, all neat and pretty."

She picked up her lighter, and I piped up, "Speaking of little babies, you can't smoke in our house. All that smoke is not good for Eli."

Mama looked over her shoulder.

"No smoking in the house, Sandra," she said, not even pretending to smile.

Mimi let the flame go out of her lighter and tapped her cigarette against the table. "It's cold outside, Lily. Are you really gonna make me go out there?" She tipped her head to one side and batted her lashes, like she thought she was a cute little girl. I wondered if that was how she got her way when she was a little kid. It seems to me Myra Sue gets her way when she does that "cute and helpless" thing. It sure is easy to see now where my sister got a lot of her worst characteristics.

Just imagine. Fifty years from now, Myra Sue might look and act just like Mimi.

Mama just stared at her, and Mimi finally got up, sighing like a martyr. Now, that right there was enough to tell me she was deeply related to Myra Sue.

"Your breakfast is ready," Mama told her.

"I'll just have a couple of puffs, then." Mimi went toward the back door. "Is a couple of puffs too much for inside?"

"Yes." The word fell out of Mama's mouth like a rock.

Mimi must've puffed quicker than you count, because it seemed she went outside and turned around and came back in about five seconds. But when she sat at the table again, I could smell the cigarette odor, so I guess there'd been enough time.

"Is there anything else you need, Sandra?" Mama asked as she set a plate in front of her.

Mimi looked at her bacon, scrambled eggs, and grits, reached for the saltshaker, and without looking up from her shaking, said, "I need you to sit down and have breakfast with me. It's been a long time since we had a meal together, daughter."

She put down the saltshaker and looked up.

"I need to take care of Eli," Mama told her, and off she went, leaving me alone at the breakfast table with Mimi. I reckon she figured Mimi wasn't any kind of threat, other than to my very own eyes when I looked at her and my nose when I smelled her and my ears when I heard her.

That old woman shoved in a forkful of eggs, and while she chewed, she buttered her toast. I kept my eyes on my own plate. If Mama could give her the cold shoulder, so could I.

"You don't talk much, do you, Sunshine?" she asked.

Boy, oh boy. If she only knew. But I just kind of shrugged and didn't say a blessed word. If I wasn't so hungry, I'd have left most of my food right there on my plate and trekked out of that kitchen before she could get wound up talking to me.

"What grade you in, sugar?"

"Sixth."

"You like school?"

"It's okay." I did not want to get involved in telling her about the awful trials and tribulations of Cedar Ridge Junior High. I coughed.

"You make good grades?"

I nodded.

"Good! You not only inherited your mimi's looks. You inherited her smarts, too."

Well, I nearly gagged on my grits, which would have been a pure shame because we were eating cheese grits that morning, and they're my favorite. Did Mimi really look like me when she was a kid? For a crazy minute, a vision of my future self floated in front of my eyes, when I'd be old and scrawny with stringy white-and-purply-red hair, nicotine-stained teeth, and short skirts showing my bony, old knees. And her smarts? How smart does a person have to be to go out in public looking like that? I prayed the fastest prayer I have ever prayed in my life, begging God not to let me be that dumb or that ugly. Which naturally led to my next thought.

"Smarts, eh?" I said, before I could stop myself. "How smart do you have to be to abandon your own kid twice?"

I guess Mimi did not expect that remark to come shooting out of my little sunshine mouth, because she looked downright shocked.

"I thought you said your mama never said anything about me."

"She didn't." And I shut my yap tighter than a rusted lid on a mason jar.

She chewed on her lower lip while she stared at me. I think maybe she thought if she stared at me hard enough I'd crack like a suspect on one of those TV cop shows. But I didn't. I slathered some jelly on my toast and munched it, meeting her eyes mildly.

She sat back in her chair and tapped the tabletop with her long, dingy fingernails. Boy, oh boy, Isabel would have a spell if and when she ever saw 'em. I wondered if she'd announce to Mimi that "nails are a decoration, not a tool, dahling," like she told my sister last year. Which, if you haven't noticed, is one reason why Myra does as little housework as she can get away with.

"So I have some notoriety on Rough Creek Road, eh?" Mimi said. She kinda grinned, almost like she *wanted* to be known for being a rotten person.

Boy, oh boy, I was gladder than you can believe that Melissa Kay Carlyle was coming to spend the day with me. This woman had to be seen to be believed.

EIGHTEEN

Melissa's Tale of Woe

＊

At midmorning, an ugly, brown minivan pulled into our driveway, and Melissa jumped out. She came running up to the house like she couldn't get away fast enough from that thing. I threw open the front door and she hurried in, her eyes wide, her short, dark hair windblown and messy.

"Is that your mom's boyfriend's van?" I said, eyeballing it. I wasn't too impressed since it looked like something an alien from the planet Mergatroid might drive. I guess it was better than the little rust bucket Ms. Carlyle drove, though. About half the time, that old car wouldn't even start.

We watched the van disappear down Rough Creek Road, and Melissa sighed from the pits of her very soul.

"Yeah, he showed up this morning before we were even up," she said with all the mournfulness you can imagine. "Man, oh man, April Grace, do I need to talk to you."

"Boy, oh boy, do I need to talk to you, too! And you might as well keep your coat on, because there is no place in the house where we can talk."

Her round eyes got rounder. "Why not?"

I could hear Mimi hacking and coughing, so I figured it was just a matter of time before she came out of the kitchen and spotted us.

"Wait for me outside," I hissed at Melissa, then I galloped up the steps, yanked my coat out of the closet, and flew back downstairs and out the front door faster than you can turn around twice.

Melissa stood shivering and confused on the porch, right

by the front door. I grabbed her hand and whisper-shouted, "Come on!"

Our feet pounded the frozen ground as we jetted across the hayfield toward Grandma's house, and when we arrived, breathless and sweaty under our clothes, Grandma was sitting in her nice, soft armchair, sipping coffee.

"Mercy on us, girls!" she said, spilling coffee down her front as we burst inside. "Is the house on fire?"

"No," I panted out, shutting the door and leaning back against it to catch my breath. "But *our* house might as well be, from the smell of that ole lady's breath!" I pushed off the door to stand on my own two personal feet and felt a little dizzy. Normally, dashing across the field to Grandma's would not wear me out like this, but this day was not normal. Number one: It was colder than an icicle outside. Number two: I was wearing a heavy coat, a heavy sweater, thick socks, and winter boots. Number three: I was completely stressed-out. Number four: I was catching a cold, and when you run while catching a cold, you feel like an army is marching through your sinuses and setting up camp around your uvula, which is that little hangy-down thing in the back of your throat. Those four things combined like a thick stew of aggravation.

"Mimi took over my room," I said. Then I sneezed about five times. That crazy cat Queenie, who was lying along the back of Grandma's chair, hissed at me, then streaked out of the room like she thought my sneezing might get on her precious fur. She has sneezed plenty of times, and I didn't go running. Dumb old cat.

Grandma set down her cup and saucer with a clink on the

little table next to her chair and handed me the box of tissues she kept there. I used about 593 Kleenexes to blow my nose and wipe my eyes.

"Good morning, girls," she said, with all the good manners I had not bothered to use. "Melissa, how are you today, honey? I missed you at the party last night."

"Good morning, ma'am. I wanted to go, but my mom had other plans for us. I hope you had a happy birthday."

"I see. And I did. Thank you, honey." Grandma smiled at her, then turned to me. "You say Sandra has taken over your room?"

"Yes! And I had to spend the night in Myra Sue's gross, old bedroom, and just in case you were wondering, she still hogs the covers, and her bedroom is dirtier than a two-edged sword."

Grandma was silent for a minute then she shook her head.

"I was afraid of something like that. It's not like your folks to turn someone away," she said.

"I know!" I said with considerable distress. "Even if it's that creepy Mimi-person."

Melissa followed our conversation, looking from Grandma to me and back again like she was watching a tennis match.

"Who's Mimi?" she asked.

I sucked in a deep breath. "She's Mama's mother."

Melissa put her hands on her hips. "I didn't know your mama had a mother."

"Well, she does," I said glumly, coughing a few times.

She grinned. "So you have two grandmas! That's so cool, April Grace."

I gawked at that girl like she had lost her mind, but all her grandparents had passed away before she was born, so I reckon I understood why she wanted a couple of grandmas all her own. But believe you me, she would not want Mimi.

"Girls, take off your coats," Grandma said as she got up, "I'll make us some biscuits and chocolate gravy."

"Oh boy!" Melissa and I said together, forgetting about Mimi for a little bit.

I'd had breakfast not long ago, but I imagined poor ole Melissa was hungry. Ms. Carlyle is a lousy cook. Besides, you don't need to be hungry to enjoy chocolate gravy and hot biscuits.

We carried our coats into Grandma's bedroom and laid them on her bed. I loved that room. It was full of framed photographs of Daddy when he was little and of Mama and Daddy way back when they were young, and all the school pictures of me and my sister. One of my most favorite pictures is of Grandma and her husband, Voyne Ray Reilly, back when they were first married. I never knew my grandfather, and the only vision I have of him is from this very picture, when he was a handsome young man in an army uniform from World War II. I picked up that photo in its old brass curlicued frame and eyeballed it hard.

You see, even though I have red hair, green eyes, fair skin, and freckles like Mama, I sometimes think I look a little like Grandma, too. And now here comes this Mimi-person who says I look like *her*. I stared at that image of my grandma.

Melissa stood so close, she was breathing on my neck as

we looked at that photo. Her breath was kinda stinky, like she'd eaten a banana not long ago.

"Do you think I look like her?" I asked, tapping Grandma's young, smiling face.

Melissa tipped her head to one side, then to the other as she studied that picture.

"Yeah, kinda. When you smile. And the shape of your face. And your nose. And your eyes kinda look like that. It would help if this picture was in color instead of black-and-white."

"They didn't have color back then," I declared. "Okay, so my eyes look like hers, and my nose looks like hers, and my mouth looks like hers, and my face is shaped like hers, so yeah, I guess I look like my grandma. Right?"

She squinted and eyeballed me, then the photo, then me again, and finally nodded. "Right!"

I grinned real big and put that picture back on its special doily on the dresser.

"That crazy Mimi tried to make me believe I look like *her*, which I would never want to do in a thousand million years."

Melissa trailed me back into the living room, and we flopped onto the sofa. I picked up the old photo album Grandma kept on the coffee table and started looking through it, taking special note of all my relatives, which are few in number. My mama and daddy, grandma, sister, and one aunt. No cousins or uncles. No grandpa, either, 'cause Grandma's husband died a long time ago, and I'd never heard of Grandpa Earl Joe, who I reckon was my other grandpa. I reckon he died, too. In fact, after looking at that photo album and thinking about relatives, I was kinda curious about him. What kind of man would want someone like Mimi?

Next to me, Melissa sighed real loud and kinda slouched down like she was feeling poorly.

"You catching a cold, too?" I asked her.

"No. But I need to talk to you."

Then I remembered Melissa had a problem, too. My problems were bad enough, but I wasn't the only one in that room. I snapped shut the photo album, put it aside, and grabbed a few more tissues out of the box. Facing my friend, I pulled my legs up under me and rested my elbows on my thighs.

"What's going on, M. K.?" I sniffed back my runny-nose stuff.

She imitated how I sat, and we faced each other.

"That man, Lester Purdy? The guy my mom likes?"

I nodded. "Yeah?"

"He's got kids."

"I didn't know that!"

"Yeah, me neither, until he came to pick us up last night in that awful van thing he drives and brought them with him. He's got four kids, and they live in Brixey, so they don't go to school in Cedar Ridge."

"Four kids! Wow!" I thought about that for a bit. "Did your mom know about them before last night?"

She shrugged. "Maybe. Anyway, he has three boys and a girl, and they are awful. Jeremy is thirteen; Jason is twelve. Paul is eight and DeeDee is seven. They are so noisy and they fight all the time, and he just lets them. Last night at McDonald's—"

"You went to Blue Reed last night?" I guessed this because the closest McDonald's to Rough Creek Road is in Blue Reed.

"Yeah. He was going to take us to Red Lobster, but his kids threw a hissy fit for McDonald's. I was kinda disappointed because Mom and I don't go out for meals very much, and both of us were looking forward to a nice place, especially as we had to miss the birthday party. Mom even bought herself a new outfit. Well, those dumb kids of Lester's acted like the Tinker twins, only worse."

Oh, that was not good.

"They used fries like slingshots to hurl ketchup all over the place, and they ruined Mom's new dress. And they made fun of my hair, and they made fun of our house and how small it is and how old our furniture is."

"Golly," I sighed in sympathy. "And your mom likes this guy?"

She sighed, too, and looked down at her hands as she picked at a cuticle.

"I guess. I mean, she never goes out with anyone, and now all of sudden when she does, it's with this guy and his four bratty kids."

"Do you like *him*?"

She shrugged. "He's kind of a dork. I mean, he says things like, 'Hey, Melissa, did you have a rad day at school?' Or like last night, he said, 'This Big Mac is totally awesome.'"

"Ugh." I said. There is nothing worse than a grown-up trying to be cool. If they're cool, it's because they don't even know they're cool. They just are. If they aren't, there is no amount of "cool" talk that's gonna make them cool.

"Have you told your mom how you feel?" I asked, sniffing. I thought for a minute I was gonna sneeze, but I didn't. Instead my eyes watered like tiny little spigots.

"No. I mean, there's not been much of an opportunity. Lester and his kids hung around until late last night, and they showed up way early this morning. So I haven't really been alone with my mama." She sighed and gazed out the window for a few seconds, then bit on that cuticle, just like Myra does when she's nervous and upset.

"Me and my mom aren't like you and your mom, April Grace," she said. "We don't visit and talk much. She's always so tired and stressed-out when she gets home from work, and she just wants peace and quiet. At least that's what she's always telling me."

Boy, oh boy. How sad would that be if you couldn't talk to your very own mother? I wanted to make Melissa feel better.

"Your mom is really nice," I said, and she nodded. "It's real obvious that she loves you."

"Yeah. She does." She smiled. "We have a little tea party every Tuesday."

"You do?" I wasn't sure Melissa had ever told me that.

"Yeah, she makes a pot of tea, and we have buttered toast and cups of tea, then we watch *Who's the Boss?* and *Growing Pains*."

I grinned, seeing an image of them sitting at the table, having tea and toast. "That sounds like fun."

"It's real nice. But if she and Lester get together . . ." She shuddered.

I thought about it for a minute then I said, "You know

what? If I were you, at the next tea party, I'd tell her how I felt about Lester and all his kids."

"Really?"

"Sure!" Then I coughed a bunch of times.

"But what would I say? April Grace, my mom does not like for me to talk about serious things. When I do, she says I'm stressing her out, and she gets grumpy. And you know she gets grumpy a lot."

I knew that. Boy, did I know that. Ms. Carlyle was not the most patient person in the world. But, maybe, if Melissa approached her gently . . .

"Just be honest," I suggested, "but don't blurt it out like I'd probably do and ruin everything. Your mom is really nice, even if she gets grumpy a lot. She'll listen."

"Yeah. Maybe."

Then something occurred to me that nearly made me fall off the couch.

"Hey! You know what?"

She looked about half-alarmed, and when Melissa gets alarmed, her eyes look like saucers.

"I just thought of something! Your mom is tired and stressed-out most of the time, and all she wants is peace and quiet. Right?"

"Right. Of course. You know that, April Grace! So?"

I sneezed twice, wiped my eyes, and blew my nose.

"So she's not gonna get any peace and quiet with those four kids of his running around, squirting ketchup and stuff," I said.

She stared at me, and then it was like the sun came up in her brain.

"You are so right, April Grace! Those kids would drive my mom right up the wall. Sometimes she won't even let me have the television on because the sound gets on her nerves."

"If she's all starry-eyed over Lester, she might not have even thought about it her own personal self. Tuesday evening, at your tea party, just tell her that."

Light and hope dawned on her face. Melissa clasped her hands to her chest and closed her eyes like she was praying.

"Oh, thank you!" she breathed.

I wasn't sure who she was thanking with her eyes closed that way, me or God. Who knows? Maybe she was praying. Maybe she'd asked God to help her find a way out of a bad situation and He'd used me to answer her prayer.

I grinned all over myself, even though my cold symptoms were getting worse.

NINETEEN

Plans Made over Chocolate Gravy

✿

"Girls, the biscuits and chocolate gravy are on the table," Grandma called from the kitchen. "Come help yourselves."

Now, I'll tell you something. Mama makes wonderful biscuits, but I think Grandma's are every bit as good. They are tall and light and flaky. You put soft butter on one while it's hot, and that butter will sink into the tenderness of that biscuit, then you bite down through the crunchy outside and into the soft, buttery middle, and you will think you're eating a biscuit made in heaven. But if you spoon that sweet, silky-smooth chocolate sauce over those hot, buttery biscuits . . . yum.

It was nice in Grandma's cozy, warm kitchen, and normally I would enjoy eating that magnificent treat and drinking tall glasses of cold, fresh milk, but today it tasted only okay, not as good as usual. It hurt a little to swallow, but I would never mention that right out loud in case someone decided I should not eat if it hurt.

"Tell me about Mimi," Melissa said, and spoiled the whole atmosphere. Of course, she did not know she was spoiling it, so I did not get aggravated at her.

So I told her about Mimi, and how she was so pushy.

"You should see her, Melissa," I said. "She's as skinny as Isabel and has stringy purply-red hair and thick, blue eye shadow and red boots."

"Wow."

"Well, you know you're going to have to spend time with her, honey," Grandma said, surprising me. She had brought her knitting to the table, and while we ate, she sat there click-ing her needles together faster than you can blink.

"Actually, Grandma," I said, "I was hoping I could just stay here with you until she goes away."

Grandma did not say a word, and I waited, polite as all get-out, because I thought she was counting stitches. But she had time to count 586 stitches, and she still did not respond.

"Grandma?"

"That will be up to your mother," she said finally.

"She'll say no," I sighed. "And in the meantime, that old woman has taken over my whole entire room, and I have to stay in Myra Sue's. It's like living with Oscar the Grouch. Only he's neater. And friendlier."

Grandma held up the thing she knitted, and I saw she was working on a large, brown sweater the color of oak leaves in the fall.

"Well," she said, examining her work critically, "Sandra Moore has never been known to stay in one place long. Likely, she'll be moving on soon."

That made me feel a little better. Grandma lowered the sweater to her lap and met my eyes.

"How's your mama taking to Sandra being there?"

"She's none too friendly. She sure isn't making that Mimi-person feel all cozy and welcome like she did Ian and Isabel."

"That does not sound like Lily at all."

"I know."

The phone rang, and when Grandma hung up, she said, "That was your mama. She said you and Melissa Kay could stay over here as long as you wanted today, but she sounded pretty tense. In fact, I think we should go over there. Your daddy and Ian had to go somewhere, Myra Sue's busy with her homework, and your mama is having to deal with Sandra all by herself."

"Uh-oh."

I didn't cherish the thought of being around that old woman any more than was absolutely necessary, but the mere thought of my mama being completely alone with her made my being there Absolutely Necessary. However, I still needed to talk to Melissa, so I said, "We'll go over, but is it okay if we [   ] the chocolate gravy?"

[M]ercy, child," she said, putting her knitting into a blue-[y]ellow quilted tote bag. "I made a pot full of it, but if [th]ink you can hold that much, go ahead. There are more [bit]s in the oven."

[Sh]e went to get her coat, and when she came back into the [   ] she gave me a kiss on the forehead.

[Y]ou feel okay?" she asked, peering into my eyes. "Looks like you might be catching a cold."

[I c]rimped my lips. "I think being around Mimi has made [me alle]rgic."

[Sh]e laughed a little at that.

[It']s gonna be all right, honey. I promise you. Stay warm, [do]n't get overheated. Drink some orange juice. There's [in] the fridge." Then she smiled at Melissa and kissed [her for]ehead, too, before she went out the front door, toting [the] bag.

[Li]sten, Melissa," I said as soon as the door shut behind [Gran]na. "I gotta talk to you."

"About Mimi?"

"No. We've done talked about her all I can stomach. I need to talk to you about my dumb sister."

Melissa slurped down the last of her milk and got up to fill her glass.

"What about her? Did you catch her making kissy-faces at herself in the mirror again?" she asked, snickering. You see, Melissa thinks the things Myra Sue says and does are funny, while I think they are dumb and highly annoying.

"She does that all the time. But that's not what I want to talk about. I think she's up to something sneaky."

Melissa's eyes got rounder.

"What?" she breathed, leaning forward.

"First off, you should see her around that mailbox. You'd think she was gonna win the Publishers Clearing House Sweepstakes—"

"Wouldn't that be cool? Wow, A. G., just think of all the awesome things you could buy and places you could go—"

"We are not talking about the sweepstakes!" I snapped. Boy, oh boy, try to talk to some people and they get side-tracked. "I'm trying to tell you that my dumb sister is hiding something in the mailbox."

"You think she's hiding money?"

I stared at that girl.

"*Money?* Now, where in the world would Myra Sue get money to hide?" She opened her mouth to reply, and I said, "So help me, if you mention that Publishers Clearing House business again, I'm gonna scream."

Melissa huffed at me and folded her arms across her chest.

"I was going to ask if she's been doing extra chores or babysitting or something, but if you're gonna be all snotty and hateful, April Grace Reilly, I'm not going to talk to you! I'm already upset enough without my best friend being mean to me."

She was plenty mad, and I didn't blame her, I guess.

"I'm sorry," I said, and meant it. "I'm upset, too, and I reckon I just got carried away with everything. Let's start over, all right?"

She narrowed her eyes at me and twisted her mouth like she was thinking about it. Little by little, her face relaxed and she looked away like she was tired of seeing me.

"All right, I guess. But"—she turned her eyes to me again—"if you're hateful to me like that again today, I'm calling my mom to come pick me up."

"Don't do that! I need you."

"Now," she said, scrooching a little bit in her chair, "tell me about Myra Sue."

So I told her all about the mailbox, and Myra staying in her room, and writing all those papers, and sleeping with her notebook, and how she hardly participated in Grandma's birthday party, and how she's been so distant from Isabel St. James, who had been her ultimate role model for months.

Then I pulled out of my pocket what Isabel might call the *pièce de résistance*—which means, "Boy, oh boy, you can't top this." I unfolded that paper with all the drama you can imagine and smoothed it fifty times because it was getting pretty battered by then, I'd looked at it so often.

"Listen to this, Melissa: 'Midnight Cruise. Treehouse Rendezvous. Never on Sunday. Cream Cheese in Florida.'"

Melissa did not say a word until I was finished.

I sat back and said, "What do you think?"

"Well, maybe she's writing to her boyfriend."

"*Boyfriend?* Myra Sue Reilly with a *boyfriend*?"

"She's one of the prettiest girls in Cedar Ridge High School. Why wouldn't she have a boyfriend?"

"Because my daddy will not let her have a boyfriend yet."

"Oh," she said, looking disappointed, but I wasn't going to let myself get sidetracked by this.

"What do you think of this list?" I said, waving it around.

"I dunno. And that list sounds like . . . like . . . I don't know what that list sounds like."

Well, good grief. I reckon Melissa has little to no imagination. I was hoping she'd come up with something I hadn't thought of.

"So what are we gonna do?" she asked.

I leaned forward and said in a low voice, even though there was no one to hear me, "We're going to find out what she's up to."

"How're we gonna do that?" Melissa whispered.

"I don't know, exactly, but we're gonna snoop."

She grinned. We both loved to snoop.

TWENTY

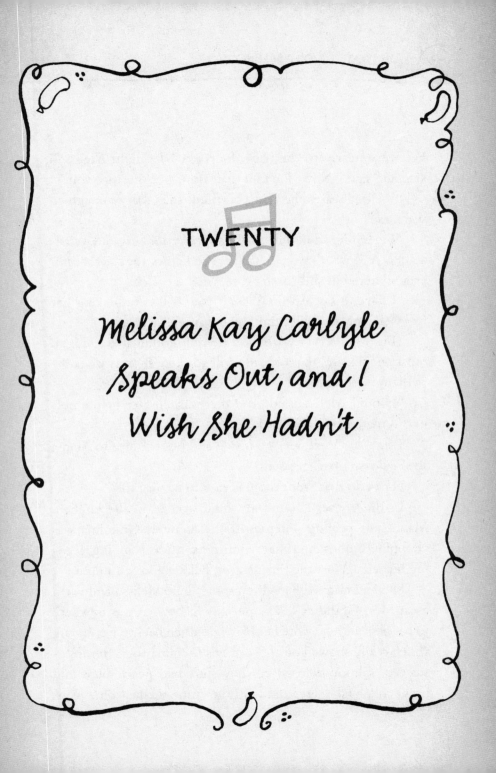

Melissa Kay Carlyle Speaks Out, and I Wish She Hadn't

♫

We were nearly to the back door when I caught Melissa's arm and said, "Now, don't let that Mimi-person scare you."

"Well, it scares me that you think she's scary enough to scare me."

"I'm telling you, Melissa, she's spooky-looking and weird-acting. And what's worse, it's like she knows she's *not wanted* around here but she doesn't care."

"I have to say, April Grace, if your folks are making her feel welcome, she will think she *is* wanted."

"But Mama isn't warm and friendly to her like she is to most people, and that old lady still acts like she's as welcome as the flowers in May."

"Hmm," Melissa said. And that was all. Her helpfulness in this matter was sadly lacking.

I sighed. "Well, let's go inside and be real nice to Mama so she doesn't feel stressed."

"I can do that. Your mom is easy to be nice to."

In the house, I found all three women in the kitchen. Mama was peeling potatoes at the counter, Grandma was chopping onions, and that Mimi-person was standing, leaning herself against the refrigerator, talking a mile a minute.

She had cleaned herself up some since Melissa and I had escaped to Grandma's. The purple cowboy hat was nowhere to be seen, and she wore her hair smoothed back in a ponytail, which really showed off those grayish-white roots. Her long-sleeved, salmon-colored cowboy shirt had pearl snaps and brass collar tabs. Her tight-fitting, stone-washed blue jeans looked like something the girls in high school wore. And guess what? She had on those dumb red cowboy boots again.

"She looks funny," Melissa whispered, "but she doesn't look scary or like a bad person."

I stared at that silly Melissa, then dragged her out of the room and back into the hall before Mimi spotted us.

"Anyone who did what she did to my mama is not a nice person, Melissa Kay Carlyle!"

"I'm just saying she doesn't look as bad as you said."

I narrowed my eyes at that girl. "What? Are you saying I'm *lying*?"

She sort of shrugged, but before she could say anything, the telephone rang.

"I'll get it!" screamed Myra Sue as she flung open her bedroom door.

"I've already got it," I said, picking up the receiver, which was about two feet away from where I was standing. "Hello?"

"Is that April?" said a refined voice.

"Hi, Isabel. Yes, it's April Grace."

"Is it for me? Is it for me?" Myra Sue galloped down the stairs and tried to grab the receiver. "Give me that phone!"

"Get away from me!" I barked at her with my hand over the mouthpiece.

"My dear, how is your mother doing?" Isabel's voice said in my ear. "Is that dreadful woman still at your house?"

"She's still here, and I guess Mama's all right, but I think that Mimi-person has her all in a knot."

"I was afraid of that when I saw how things went last night. Shall I come and lend my support?"

Now, I had to think about that for a minute. Isabel's talent for being a giant pain in her own special way could cause plenty of stress and trouble on its own. On the other hand, she genuinely loved Mama, and I knew she had her best interests at heart.

"You know what, Isabel . . . I think . . . Excuse me, just a minute, please." I turned to Myra Sue, who continued to be a Gigantic Drip by prancing and jiggling and grabbing. "Get away from me and this telephone, Myra Sue Reilly! This call is *not* for you, or about you."

"I happen to know Isabel prefers talking to a person of intelligence," she said, and grabbed at the phone. I turned sharply.

"Then she doesn't want to talk to *you*."

Melissa stood a few feet away, watching this circus. I sent her a pleading look, and she gave me a nod because *she* is a person of intelligence. At least most of the time.

"Myra Sue," she said, "I really like your nail polish. What's it called?"

Boy, oh boy, was that the best she could do? But it worked because my dumb sister stopped grabbing for the phone immediately, smiled all bright, and held out both hands like she was fixing to play Beethoven's "Moonlight Sonata" in a concert hall.

"It's 'Strawberry Kisses,'" she said while Melissa oohed and aahed over it.

"I think Mama would like you to be here," I said in the mouthpiece to Isabel.

"Then I'm on my way, dear."

I hung up and announced, "I'm off the phone now, Myra Sue, you grabby-pants-of-the-universe."

"I'm expecting an important call," she said with such drama, I nearly choked. "I might have missed it!"

"Oh yeah, I'm so sure," I said, rolling my eyes. "Who from? Bon Jovi? The Reverend Billy Graham? Or maybe the Queen of England?"

Then I thought of something. If Myra Sue was busy on the telephone, yakking with some of her dingbatty friends, she'd be oblivious to the rest of the world. Maybe Melissa and I could trundle through that clutter and figure out what her big, fat secret was.

"Actually, I'm sorry, Myra Sue. Maybe someone *did* try to call you while I was on the phone just now," I said reasonably.

"Duh, April Grace!" she screeched. "That's what I tried to tell you!" She grabbed up the receiver and started dialing like her fingers were on fire.

I bit my lips to keep from grinning, then jerked my head toward the stairs for Melissa to follow me up there.

"Whoa!" she said, stopping on the threshold of Myra's bedroom. "Are you kidding me? Your mom lets you guys keep your room like this?"

I whirled around. "You know *this* is not my room! And Mama lets us keep our rooms however we want to because she says everyone should have their own space because it helps us to learn a little independence and responsibility." I looked around. "But ole Myra could look up both of those words in the dictionary, and she'd still be a slob."

"My mom would come unglued," Melissa declared, stepping over a pile of Myra's dirty jeans.

"It's worse since she's gotten all sneaky," I said, pointing to a pile of papers on the bed. "And I hate sleeping in here. It's like all this junk makes noise."

Melissa blinked at me. "Really?"

"Well, not literally. But sorta, yeah."

She stepped over a purse and a squashed box of Kleenex and three *People* magazines to get to Myra Sue's dresser.

"Would you look at all this nail polish and perfume?"

I scrunched my mouth. "That part of the mess is all from Isabel St. James. There's some makeup somewhere, too. Isabel called it a mercy kit when she gave it to Myra." I shook my head in pure disgust and sneezed three times. "She needs to give her a vacuum cleaner and a mop and call it a disaster repair kit."

Instead of helping me, that silly Melissa started piddling with all those bottles.

"April," she said in a funny tone of voice. "What's on that list again?"

I sighed. "You need to help me with these papers, not be over there playing with—"

"Wasn't one of them Cream Cheese in Florida? And wasn't another Never on Sunday, except it should have been spelled s-u-n-d-a-e?"

I clomped across a bunch of junk to get to her and grabbed up one of the nail polish bottles she held out. It was cherry red.

"Never on Sundae!" I read the label aloud. Then I grabbed up all those nail polish bottles and read every single label, and guess what? Every item on that list was a color. "Cream Cheese in Florida" was a light, toasty brown; "Treehouse Rendezvous" was kinda odd with a little green or something mixed in. Eww. Midnight Cruise was dark, dark red.

"Well, I am purely put-out!" I declared, clunking those bottles back down on top of the dresser. "That list is nothing more than a rotten ole shopping list."

Melissa heaved a sigh and shrugged like it was No Big Deal. Except it was to me. I heaved a sigh bigger than Melissa's.

"What do you want me to do, April?"

I sneezed, then coughed, then blew my nose on three separate tissues.

"Let's go through these papers, 'cause ole Myra is always huddled over these notebooks. She tells Mama she's doing homework, but I know better than that. Myra Sue is not a homework kind of girl. See if you can find that notebook she sleeps with it like it's a teddy bear."

Melissa joined me at the bed, and we had just picked up a mess of those papers when the door crashed open.

"Get out of my room!" Myra Sue honked at us like a barnyard goose. She charged across the room like a goose, too. A mad goose. "Get away from my private papers! You awful, nasty, creepy, cootie brats." She yanked the pages out of our hands, tearing some of them, then she threw them on the floor and shoved us both out the door. *"Get out!"*

Boy howdy, when Myra Sue slams a door, it makes all your mucus membranes vibrate.

"Girls! What on earth is going on up there?" Mama called from downstairs.

I had time to tell Melissa, "Don't say a word about this," before Mama appeared in the upstairs hallway. She gave me a funny look.

"Myra Sue won't let us be in her room."

"Well, I'll see about that!" Mama said. "You girls have to share while Sandra is staying with us." Mama went right past me and opened Myra Sue's door without knocking, which showed just how mad she was because, like I said before, Mama *always* knocks.

"Young lady, you will allow your sister and her friend to be in this room, and you will get along with them. Do you hear me?"

"But they were in my things!"

We crept toward the door and looked in. Mama stood in the middle of the room, her arms straight down at her sides, her fists curling and uncurling.

"How could anyone not help but be in your things?" she said. "Your things are everywhere! Clean this room, Myra Sue Reilly. Clean it right now."

"But I have homework—"

"Clean this room right now!" Mama pivoted and stalked out. She brushed past Melissa and me like she didn't even see us.

Myra Sue glared at us. I figured I'd discover her secret a lot easier once her room was clean.

"You have to help," she said to Melissa and me, all snippy and mad.

Now, if I thought helping her clean her room would solve this mystery of her secret life, I'd do it. But I knew as well as

I know my own name that she'd land on me like a buzzard on roadkill if I got within a foot of whatever she was hiding. There was no way I was gonna help that girl pick up her own dirty laundry and used tissues and damp towels.

"We ain't doing a blessed thing. This is not our mess, Myra Sue." I coughed.

"OH!" she screamed and stomped her foot. "You're gonna regret this, missy! If you hadn't been snooping in my stuff, Mama would not have come up here."

"La-di-da!" I said airily. "Come on, Melissa. Let's go see what's on TV."

At the top of the steps, Melissa stopped and said, "If you're so concerned about Myra Sue having a secret, why don't you tell your mom?"

"Because I have learned from experience not to tell anyone anything until I have solid proof. Whatever Myra's doing is probably so dumb, it's not worth mentioning to any of the grown-ups right now. I want to keep my eye on her."

"Well, if it's that dumb, why do you care anyway?"

I bugged my itchy eyes at the girl.

"Because. I'm curious. And maybe she's doing something more serious than it seems."

"Oh," she said, almost tired-sounding, like she thought my notions were lame. "I'm just glad to be away from Lester Purdy's dumb kids for the day."

"Yeah. Let's go downstairs. When ole Myra has the room clean, we'll take another look."

Before we were all the way down the steps, there was a knock on the front door.

I opened it and Isabel stepped inside. Without saying so much as a howdy-do, she tugged off her tight black gloves.

"Where's your mother?" She shed her coat and handed it to me like I was a maid.

"Hi, Isabel," I said, hoping to remind her of Good Manners and Proper Greeting. "She's in the kitchen."

"That woman in there with her?"

"Yep. And Grandma, too."

"Hmph!" And off she marched, her high heels clicking against the wood.

I wondered if she was gonna put Mimi in her place. Lots of times, Isabel just blurts things out. Hmm. Sometimes I think Isabel and me are a lot alike, except I know when to say hello to people, and when not to be rude.

Melissa and I sort of slinked along behind her to see what, if anything, was gonna happen in the kitchen.

You know what we saw when we peeked in there? I'll tell you. Grandma, Mama, and Mimi were sitting at the table, and Isabel was just standing there, eyeing them. A big pot of soup was simmering on the stove, and the kitchen was warm and steamy from it.

"Get you some coffee, honey," Grandma said to Isabel, "then have a seat."

Mimi sat sideways in her chair, legs crossed, swinging one foot back and forth. She eyed Isabel up and down and sideways while Isabel filled a cup.

"You don't look like you belong here," Mimi said, then she slurped her coffee, making the ickiest, slurpiest sound you have ever heard.

Isabel straightened her straight spine like someone had poked her with a sharp stick. She looked down her long, pointed nose at the woman. Boy, oh boy, I've seen that look before.

"I beg your pardon?" she said. I knew as well as I know my name she wasn't begging any pardon. Mimi must've known it, too, 'cause she kinda snickered and sneered and drank her coffee some more.

"Isabel's pretty much part of our family now, so *she* belongs here," I said from the doorway, surprising everyone, most especially my own personal self. Isabel gave me a smile and a wink.

"Thank you for saying so, April, dear." She sat down and turned to Mama. "Lily, how are you doing?" We all knew what she meant, so she might as well have just said, right out loud: *How are you holding up since this dreadful plague of a woman crashed into your world?*

Mama gave her a smile. Well, what else would you expect from my mama?

"I'm fine, thank you, Isabel. And thank you so much for all your hard work yesterday."

Mimi eyeballed Isabel's fancy manicure, her slicked-back hairdo, and her elegant, long-sleeved blouse. Isabel ignored her.

"Darling, it was worth the hard work to give Grace a surprise birthday party. Thank goodness April Grace came along to get her out of the house, as she simply would not leave and stay away long enough for us to get anything done!"

Grandma plucked her knitting out of the tote bag and got busy with her needles and yarn. "Well, I didn't know you were trying to plan a party. I thought everyone had forgotten about my birthday and was feeling kinda low about it."

"I'm sorry you had to make that trip into town," Mama said, "but we had to get rid of you somehow."

"Yeah, and it was a real experience, let me tell you," I said without thinking, and that drew the attention of all of them.

"Hey, Sunshine," Mimi said. "You gonna introduce us to the little sunbeam you've brought along with you?"

She peered at Melissa from eyes that were blue all over, and by that I mean from just below the painted-on eyebrows down to the thick, blue liner all around the eyelashes, top and bottom. I do believe that old lady wore about three pairs of false eyelashes.

We took a couple of steps into the kitchen.

"This is my friend, Melissa." I dipped my head toward the woman and said, "That's Sandra Moore."

"I'm *Mimi!*" she declared loudly, with that crusty laugh. "You might as well call me Mimi, too, Sunbeam."

Melissa actually grinned at her. "How do, ma'am. Mimi." I thought she was gonna curtsy, for crying out loud. I gave her a dirty look, but she ignored me. "I like your boots," she added.

Ole Mimi grinned like a monkey at that and stuck out one foot, waving it around.

Well, I tell you what. I wanted to smack that Melissa. In fact, I grabbed her hand and pulled her out of the kitchen for the second time that day, saying to the grown-ups, "We're gonna go look at Eli."

"What's the matter with you?" I hissed as I herded her down the hallway toward Mama and Daddy's room.

She yanked her hand free, frowning at me.

"Nothing! Why?"

"Why are you being all nice and friendly to that woman when you know how I feel?"

Her mouth flew open, and she stared at me like *she* wanted to smack *me*.

"I have a right to be nice and friendly to anyone I choose, April Grace. I think Mimi looks interesting, and I think you should be nicer."

I bugged out my eyes and coughed.

"Are you kiddin'?" I said when I quit hacking. "That woman went off and left my mama when she was just a little kid."

"That was a long time ago, April. Maybe she's changed."

I crimped my mouth because that was not what I wanted to hear, even though way back in a tiny part of my mind and deep down in my heart, I knew Melissa had a point.

"Maybe so, but being the child of a child-abandoner caused my mama to have a hard life!"

Melissa studied me like she was trying to read my whole entire mind.

"Sometimes, April Grace Reilly, you can be completely unreasonable, and when you are, you're downright unlikable."

She delivered those words in the same tone of voice that she might say, "It is a sunny day outside," and I was purely offended to my gills.

I wanted to stomp my foot and holler, but my throat

blocked and the words refused to form. That girl just kept talking.

"I don't have a grandma," she said stoutly, "not even *one*, and you have *two* of them sitting in there right this minute, and you don't even appreciate it."

"Grandma is my *only* grandma," I said fiercely when the block finally shrunk from my throat. "That Mimi-person only came around because she wants something. My mama said so!"

"April Grace, I love your mama to pieces, and I'm sorry for what happened to her when she was a girl. But maybe, just maybe, your mimi is sorry, and now she wants to be a part of the family."

"How can you say that?" I asked, aghast. Then that stupid little voice in my head said my best friend might be right. But I did not want to hear it or think about it. Instead, I shoved that little voice into a dark closet in my mind and slammed the door.

One thing I realized, though, was that if we didn't come to a truce, my friend would be calling her mom to come pick her up, and that would be the end of us spending the day together. In spite of her making me feel mad right down to my toenails just then, I still wanted to hang out and have fun. And we definitely had not discovered anything about Myra's secret yet.

I gulped in some air to chase out my anger.

"Let's check on Eli. If he's awake, you can hold him if you want to."

Melissa gave me a funny look from the corner of her eye, but then she nodded. "Okay. I'd like that."

When best friends fight and they can't agree, it seems to me the best thing to do is not get carried away. Letting things cool off had kept me and Melissa Kay Carlyle from slugging each other more than a few times—which is more than I can say for me and Myra Sue.

TWENTY-ONE

That Thievin' Mimi

☺

We crept into the bedroom, quiet as anything, and right up to Eli's little crib. He was making a funny face, like he either smelled something or saw something icky in his dreams, then one little fist batted the air.

"I think he's waking up," I whispered. "He's the hungriest kid I've ever seen in my whole entire life. He eats about every two minutes."

Melissa stood there and grinned at him.

"Look at his nose. It's the ittiest, bittiest nose I ever saw."

I glanced at her nose. "I bet you had the ittiest bittiest nose on any baby ever born in the whole United States, 'cause yours is still little and cute."

She wrinkled it, and the freckles that paraded along it curled right up.

"I'd like to have a Roman nose," she said, staring straight ahead and making an air picture in the middle of her face.

"No, you don't. Isabel St. James has a Roman nose."

"Really? I just thought she had a big ole honker. I didn't know she was Roman."

Now, that right there was a comment worthy of someone as dumb as my sister, not someone as smart as my best friend, but then I noticed she was grinning, and it was all a big joke. I guess it was her way of breaking the tension that had been between us.

Eli bleated out a little cry that sounded just like a baby lamb. His face was so scrunched that it made me think of a dried-up potato.

"He's gonna set up to bawling any second," I told Melissa. "Go ahead and pick him up 'cause he's awake."

Even though she had held him a few times before, I still watched like a hawk, ready to rescue that boy in case she handled him like a bowling ball or something. She had him all cuddled up, and he was twisting his mouth around, a sure sign he was hungry. He whimpered again.

"Here, let me have him."

She turned away.

"No! You have a cold. You'll give it to him."

She had a point.

"Well, if you'll just pat his back and bottom real gentle, he likes that."

He grunted and wriggled in her arms, and for a minute I thought he'd gone back to sleep, but then came that squinched-up face and flying fists, and he began howling.

"Guess we better take him to Mama," I said, but just as we turned to go out of the room, in swooped Mimi, her long, skinny arms stretched out and her bony fingers reaching like the witch in *The Wizard of Oz*. She took that boy right out of Melissa's arms like we weren't even there.

"Now, now," she said, soft as anything, "here's Mimi's good boy. Yes, he is." She kept murmuring as she stroked his cheek and touched the tip of his nose, and I was amazed at how sweet that old woman was right then. He hushed and did not make another peep, though he was looking at her in that unfocused way babies look at people. I do believe Eli liked her. You know who else liked her? Good ole Daisy, that's who. Right then she came into the bedroom and nosed

Mimi, then wagged her tail like she totally approved of the whole scene.

"Well, hi there, doggie," Mimi said. "You are one beautiful dog, you know."

I was starting to warm up to her, and I didn't want to do that, so I said, "I think Eli's hungry."

"You're probably right, Sunshine. Want to run and get his bottle?"

"He doesn't have a bottle. He has Mama."

She glanced at me.

"I see. Well, shall I take him to her, or will she come and get him?"

Mama rushed in right then, like she'd been called.

"Did I hear the baby?" She gave Mimi a worried look, like she thought Mimi might offer Eli a cigarette or something.

Mimi handed him over just as slick and gentle as you please. Just like she'd handled lots of babies in her life, though I don't hardly see how someone who'd abandon her very own daughter twice would have the heart to take care of babies. But as much as I hate to admit it, I've been wrong before.

"Thank you, Sandra. If you and the girls will go back to the kitchen, I'll join you directly."

I followed Mimi, watching her red-and-white ponytail swing back and forth as she walked. From the back, if it weren't for all that white hair merging into that purply-red, you'd never know she was an old lady.

Grandma and Isabel were whispering when we walked in, but they hushed immediately. Mimi picked up her cigarettes and lighter off the table.

"Lily won't let me smoke in the house, so I'll brave the cold." She eyed Isabel. "You're a smoker. You want to join me?"

Isabel's expression turned all uppity.

"How do *you* know I smoke, pray tell?"

"'Cause you got the look, lady." She pulled on her coat.

Isabel jerked.

"The look? What look?"

"Like me. My look. But I don't look so bad, do I?" She laughed that crusty laugh, showing her brown teeth.

Isabel's eyes got bigger than I have ever seen them in my life, and for a minute there, I thought she was gonna hurl.

"You comin'?" Mimi persisted. "I'll even give you one of my smokes."

"No, thank you," Isabel croaked out.

Mimi shrugged and sashayed through the kitchen and service porch and on out the back door.

"I look like *that*?" she asked, staring in alarm at the back door.

No one said anything for a minute, then Grandma said, "Of course not! Don't listen to that woman."

"Yeah, but you know what, Isabel?" I said because I couldn't help myself. "If you keep smoking, you might end up with brown teeth and brown fingers and a discolored tip on your nose, not to mention brown lungs." She blinked about twenty times, then I added, "If you live long enough. Have you heard Mimi cough? And I don't think she has a cold."

Isabel was quiet for the longest time, just staring at that back door. Then she brought herself back to the rest of us with a shudder.

"I have an announcement," she said, looking around as if she was speaking to an audience of five hundred instead of just us. "I am going to quit smoking. If I have to go to a doctor and get shots or patches or that awful nicotine gum, I'm going to do it. I absolutely *refuse* to look like that woman in a few years."

"Isabel, I think that's wonderful!" I said, clapping my hands.

"Yes, honey," Grandma added, grinning. "It will be so good for your health if you'd stop smoking, and I know Ian will give you all the support he can."

"She was just trying to be nice," Melissa said suddenly.

Grandma stopped knitting, and Isabel paused with her cup midway to her mouth.

"What's that?" Grandma said.

"Mimi invited you outside, and she even offered you one of her cigarettes," she said to Isabel. "She was trying to be friendly."

Isabel set her cup down with a clunk, and Grandma thunked down her knitting. They both stared at that girl. *I* stared at that girl, but given what she'd said earlier, I wasn't as surprised as Grandma and Isabel.

"She's not someone with whom I choose to associate," Isabel sniffed.

"Me, either!" Grandma said.

Melissa just sat there, looking kinda lost. Now, I readily admit I agreed with Grandma and Isabel, but I didn't like seeing my friend look uncomfortable in my very own house. I spoke up.

"Melissa says that just because Mimi was a rotten person years ago, it doesn't mean she's still rotten."

The two women kept looking at Melissa, then Grandma picked up her knitting and made a few stitches.

"A leopard doesn't change its spots," she said finally.

"No, indeed," Isabel murmured, and sipped her coffee.

And no one else said another word. But I'm telling you there was something inside me that shifted and turned in my stomach. There had been some major spot-changing going on from those two women sitting right there at that table. And if those spots could change, so could other spots.

Mama came into the kitchen with Eli. He was all bright-eyed and content.

"Oh, give him to his Auntie Isabel!" Isabel said, grinning all over herself as Mama placed the baby in her arms. Eli belched like a long-haul trucker. Boy, oh boy.

The phone rang, and Mama, who was wiping off her shirt where Eli had spit up a little, said, "Get the phone, will you, April honey?"

I reached the phone a split-second before Myra Sue landed on the bottom step. I reckon her feet must've sprouted wings to get there that fast without breaking her neck on the trip down, but I still beat her.

I picked up the receiver, and we went through a second episode of that grabbing and dodging business. I reckon we'd go through it ten thousand more times or until Myra Sue got smart. The ten thousand seemed more likely.

"Hello?"

"Let me talk to Myra Sue," said Jennifer Cleland. Or maybe it was Jessica. Those girls sound just alike to my ears. Whoever it was, she was snotty and bossy.

"Hang on," I said, then covered up the mouthpiece and told Myra Sue, "You should tell your friends to learn telephone etiquette. Here."

She yanked the receiver right out of my hand and gave me a dirty look, then she turned her back on me. That girl and her friends were all so rude, it's a wonder their toenails didn't curl backward and grow fur.

"Come have your lunch, girls," Mama called from the kitchen. "The potato soup is done."

Right then, all thoughts of Myra Sue's rudeness and Mimi's weirdness and Melissa's soft-hearted comments went flying right out of my head because even though I was still full from all the biscuits and chocolate gravy I ate at Grandma's, Mama's potato soup is the best ever, and I wanted some of it. The chunks of potatoes are soft and tasty, and the soup part is thick, flavored with plenty of melted cheese and crumbled, smoked bacon. Onions and garlic give it plenty of kick.

Melissa and I settled down at the table, and Grandma ladled generous helpings into everyone's soup bowl, even Mimi's.

"Too bad Mike and Ian aren't here for lunch," Grandma said. "Lily has the knack when it comes to potato soup."

Mama poured milk for Melissa and me as Mimi walked back into the kitchen and sat down at the table.

"Who was on the phone, April?" Mama asked.

"Jessica, or maybe Jennifer."

"I should have known." She sat down. "Myra Sue gets more phone calls in a week than the rest of us do in a month."

"Popular girl, eh?" said Mimi. "Well, can't blame the boys for calling her."

There was a little silence, which I broke by saying, "Any boy who's dumb enough to call Myra Sue deserves to talk to her."

"Why, forevermore!" Grandma said, frowning at me.

"April," Mama said, giving me a Look, then she went to get Myra, who came back with her, looking madder than a wet hornet for having had her conversation halted.

"There's our little Princess Di," Mimi said, grinning all over her face. Hearing that, it seemed to me ole Myra Sue didn't know if she should get all smiley and sweet or if she should stay all sour and mad. Apparently sour and mad won out, because she flopped down in her chair and glared at her soup like she wanted to throw it against the wall.

"I'm sure the darling girl will have more boyfriends than she knows what to do with one of these days," Isabel said, giving that soured-up darling girl a smile.

"You mean multiple boyfriends like Grandma?" That question just slipped out of my mouth like it had been greased up and ready to go. There was a Big Silence as everyone looked at me like they could not believe I said that, right out loud, even though it was a true statement.

I ate a mouthful of that delicious soup. "Yum," I said, ignoring all those eyes and frowns.

"You have a lot of beaux, do you, Grace?" Mimi said with a smirky little grin. The tone of her voice said she didn't believe for one minute that any man would be interested in my grandma.

Grandma shifted in her chair just a wee bit, and I figured if I valued the opportunity to finish my soup, the smartest thing for me to do was to keep my yap shut.

"Grace has several gentlemen callers," Isabel said, delicately dabbing her lips with her napkin. "The fellows in our part of the world know a good thing when they see it."

"Ha!" Mimi barked. "I've been here less than twenty-four hours, and I already got me a date for tonight."

Now, I do believe everyone was probably just as curious as I was, but no one wanted to let her know we were the least bit interested. Except Myra Sue, who wanted to keep sulking, and Melissa, who had taken a shine to Mimi.

"Wow!" Melissa said. "Who you got a date with, Mimi?"

That woman made a big production of slurping a great big spoonful of soup.

"Fellow by the name of Ernie Beason. I met him at the party last night. You know him?"

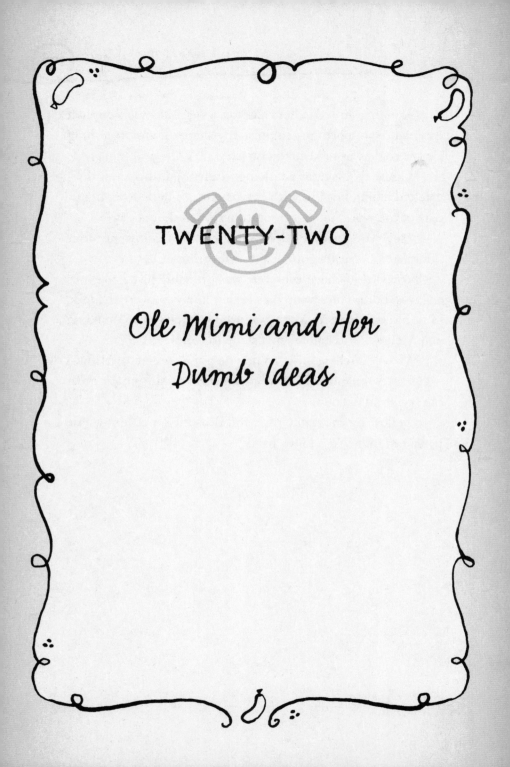

TWENTY-TWO

Ole Mimi and Her Dumb Ideas

I want you to know we all stared at that old woman like she had just grown big, hairy toes out of her forehead.

"You have a date with Ernie?" I finally gasped out.

"You betcha!" She grinned real big and winked with all those fake eyelashes.

Well, I'll tell you what. We just sat there gawking at her. There was not a single sound in our whole entire kitchen except for the ticking of the yellow clock on the wall and Mimi slurping her soup. One thing about it, if she and Ernie went out for dinner, he'd probably never in a million years go out with her a second time because she had such foul table manners.

"I just can't believe it," Grandma said finally, faintly sitting back in her chair like someone had unplugged her bones. "Ernie? *My* Ernie?"

Mimi raised her penciled-in eyebrows.

"Whatya mean, *your* Ernie? You're not married to 'im. I don't reckon you're even going steady or engaged to 'im, are you?"

"I can't believe . . ." Grandma let her voice trail while she shook her head. She looked about half-sick.

"Why on earth would Ernie Beason ask you out when he and Grace are an item?" Isabel asked.

"An item, are you?" Mimi asked Grandma in a tone that said she didn't believe it.

"But April Grace just said Grandma Grace has more than one boyfriend," my best friend Melissa Kay Carlyle said like the Big Mouth she sometimes is. "Why can't Ernie have more than one girlfriend?"

Oh, brother. Oh, good grief. Oh, good gravy. I just wanted to crawl under the table. Melissa had a point, but the only two who weren't Totally and Completely Embarrassed by that question were her and Mimi.

"Well, Gracie," Mimi said, laughing a little, "not only have you lost weight and dyed your hair, you're as popular as you were in high school when you stole ever' boyfriend I ever had."

This was such a revelation to me, and I reckon to the rest of us, that I was all set to ask a thousand questions. But then Mimi started coughing. She coughed so hard I thought she was gonna bust her lungs and pass right out, but she didn't. When she finished, her face was redder than raw liver. She sat there and gasped for a million years while we all gawked at her in considerable alarm. I did not like the woman, but I certainly did not want her to gasp to death at the kitchen table.

Mama jumped up and got her a glass of water.

"Shall I call an ambulance?" she asked, concern pouring out of her eyes.

"No ambulance," Mimi wheezed, eyeing the water but not touching it. "It's just my bronchitis acting up."

Bronchitis, my foot.

"I am definitely going to quit smoking!" Isabel declared grandly.

Mimi finally drank her water. She set down the glass and looked straight at Grandma, and neither one of them said a blessed word, but you could almost hear the tension grinding away, getting ready to spew into some big mess at any second.

Isabel broke the spell and changed the subject by saying, "Lily, have you had any more of those frightening phone calls? Every time my phone rings now, I simply dread to pick it up."

She had changed the subject, all right, but this change was no improvement over the rivalry between Grandma and Mimi. All that unease I'd felt before when I thought about those phone calls churned around inside my stomach again.

"Has someone been calling you and hanging up, Isabel?" I asked.

"No, but I expect it any day."

"No, we haven't received any more of those calls," Mama said. "In fact, Mike says it was the storm that sent power surges through the line and caused the phone to ring when no one was calling." Then Mama smiled a little. "No one around here has a chance to answer the telephone when Myra Sue's in the house, anyway."

Myra Sue pooched out her lower lip and gave a big-eyed blink, as if she were posing for the poster child of the most pathetic and mistreated creature on the face of the earth.

"I haven't had any calls," Grandma said. She had turned from Mimi and was now acting like the woman was invisible.

"Sometimes people call our house, but they've dialed the wrong number," Melissa put in. "They always say, 'Sorry, I must have a wrong number.' Nobody's called us and then just hung up."

"That's good, honey," Mama said. "I'm glad no one is bothering you." She looked at Myra Sue. "We've not had any more hang-ups, have we, Myra?"

Before that girl could respond, though, Mimi spoke up.

"Guilty!" she sang out, with one hand in the air like she had just hollered, "Hallelujah!" instead.

"What do you mean, guilty?" Grandma said, slamming her gaze back to Mimi and frowning so hard she nearly turned her face inside out.

Mimi dropped her hand to the table. She fiddled a bit with the handle of her spoon, then, without looking up, she said in a very quiet voice, "It was me."

Nobody uttered a mumbling word. She breathed deep and blew it out softly. Before she could say more, the back door opened, and Daddy came in with Ian right behind him. They were laughing and brought in plenty of cold, fresh air with them.

"Well, hello, lovely ladies of Rough Creek Road," Daddy greeted, smiling as he unbuttoned his coat.

"You should see the herd of goats we just saw," Ian added, oozing with excitement. "Amazing! I'm hoping we'll have a herd like that in a few years."

Isabel blinked at him about five hundred times, then she gave him the stink-eye. Either he was getting to where her dirty looks ceased to bother him, or he just didn't notice the red that was rising on her face and in her eyeballs.

"No goats, Ian!" she declared.

"Yes, goats, Isabel. Now that Mike and I have the shed nearly built, I'll be buying some nannies and a billy in a couple of weeks."

You should've seen her face. Isabel seemed mad about those goats, but I guess she knew Ian was gonna get his way this time, no matter what she said.

"What's going on here?" Daddy said as he poured coffee for himself and Ian. His smile had faded considerably in the last minute or so. In fact, he fixed his gaze squarely on Mimi just like he knew she had stirred up something. She looked away immediately.

Mama got the men some soup bowls and spoons from the cabinet.

"Sandra Moore was fixin' to enlighten us on something important, I b'lieve," Grandma said. Her voice was chilly, and she did not wear a hint of a smile. She stared a hole through that other old woman.

"Oh?" Daddy said. "Go ahead, Sandra."

He leaned back against the counter and took a sip of coffee. Ian stood just a couple of steps inside the doorway. His feet were wide apart, like he had planted himself there to stop anyone from running out the back door. Everyone in that kitchen was staring at Mimi.

She was all pink in the face, which made her blue eye makeup look like the mask for a cat burglar. I reckon she was completely embarrassed to have the whole entire clan gawking at her.

"Those phone calls," she said, looking down at her cup and fiddling with the handle of it. "Those hang-ups. I did that."

"How's that?" Daddy said in that real quiet voice he uses sometimes, and believe me, it's worse than if he yelled, because it means his coals have been stirred.

"I got scared and hung up," she said, still nervously playing with her cup handle. "See, I thought if I called you, Lily"— she looked up long enough to glance at Mama, then

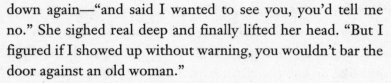

down again—"and said I wanted to see you, you'd tell me no." She sighed real deep and finally lifted her head. "But I figured if I showed up without warning, you wouldn't bar the door against an old woman."

The kitchen clock ticked louder than ever, and no one said anything because we were waiting for her to finish.

"It was only two or three times, and I lost my nerve every time. I didn't mean to upset anyone. I figured you'd just think it was a wrong number."

"Well forevermore!" Grandma looked as sour as Myra Sue.

"Well, people go and dial wrong numbers all the time!" Mimi said.

"Yeah," Melissa piped up, like a big, fat dope. "Somebody called our house just the other day, and it was the wrong number."

"You just said no one called and hung up—"

"That's right!" she snapped. "No one has called and simply hung up like a rude person. We get *wrong numbers* sometimes, April Grace. Weren't you even *listening* to me?" She bugged out her bright eyes and glared at me.

I glared back. I tell you what. Maybe it was because I was feeling rotten with a runny nose and sore throat and a cough that had a mind of its own that Melissa was getting on my nerves. Maybe she was getting sick, too, and I was getting on her nerves, but one thing was for sure: I was about ready to call her mother myself to come take that girl away if she didn't stop sticking up for Mimi. When she did that, I felt like she was taking sides against me and Grandma and Mama.

"Do you realize the discomfort you've caused these people?"

Isabel said, shooting fiery darts at Mimi from her eyes. "Even *I* have been terrified that some awful backwoods baboon might be lurking about, stalking residents along this road, just looking for someone to rob or assault." She looked around at the rest of us and added, "I have even considered getting a *dog*."

"What kind of dog would you get, Isabel?" I asked because curiosity was eating me in great big, hungry bites.

She blinked at me a dozen times. "Well, I don't know. A Chihuahua, maybe."

I hooted at that, but hushed right quick because I knew this was not the time and place to be laughing at Isabel's crazy ideas.

Mimi pursed her lips and looked around.

"Well." That's all she said, then she pushed back her chair. "Excuse me." She grabbed up her cigarettes and went outside.

"Forevermore!" Grandma said. "Imagine, all this time it was just Sandra Moore playing tricks on the telephone."

Mama looked about half-sick.

"You know what?" she said. "If she had asked me over the phone if she could come here . . ." She swallowed hard. "I would have told her to stay away."

There was just the tiniest silence. I think we were all surprised Mama would say that.

"Well, Lily, no one would blame you," Isabel said.

"Of course not, honey!" Daddy added.

"Absolutely!" Grandma agreed, nodding.

"But she's my mother!" Mama passed her gaze over all of us. "All those things she did . . . that was all long ago. I should no longer feel this deep resentment, and yet I do. Excuse me, please." She scooted back her chair real fast and left the kitchen. A few seconds later, her bedroom door closed softly.

I wasn't sure if the awfulness I felt inside my body was from the creeping crud or whatever was making me sneeze and cough, or if it was because I felt so bad for Mama. Maybe it was all those things combined in one big, fat feeling of rottenness.

"No one could possibly blame her for feeling that way," Isabel echoed her own words.

All of us agreed out loud, except for Melissa, who usually keeps her mouth shut when she thinks she should, and Myra Sue, who rarely has anything intelligent to add to any conversation. Both of them just sat there like a couple of rocks. If ole Melissa was gonna stand up for Mimi, she ought to at least have extra sympathy for my mama.

From my itchy, watery eyes, I glared at Myra Sue, who rolled her own eyes at me in return, and then I glared at Melissa, and she just looked at me like I was a brick in the wall, as if she didn't care that I was feeling sick. I sniffed good and hard, then coughed up half my lungs, and she didn't even blink.

As soon as I finished my soup, I very politely stood up, and because Mama wasn't there to stop me, I left the room without inviting Melissa to go with me. A minute later I heard her voice and realized she was talking on the phone, telling her mom to come and pick her up.

Out on the service porch, Daisy was a far better and understanding companion than my best friend, anyway. So there.

TWENTY-THREE

The Ways Spies Spy
When Wind Blows in
Their Eyes

⁎

Melissa went home not long after I left the table. She went right out the front door without saying a single, solitary word of good-bye to me, and I peeked through the curtains just in time to see her get into that brown van.

Now, I have to admit I felt sorry for Melissa having to go back into that noisy mess with those Purdy people, but she got on my last nerve by sticking up for Mimi instead of Mama. I had hoped she'd help me scavenge around the mailbox area, maybe see something I'd missed in my quest to uncover my sister's secret, but now it was too late. Well, she could just go on home and put up with her maybe-future stepfamily.

I sighed and turned from the window, wishing we'd not fought. Then I coughed and hacked into a Kleenex and felt even worse.

A bit later Myra Sue went upstairs, but soon she came scurrying down again, pulling on her coat.

"Where are you going?" I asked.

"I really don't see how where I'm going or what I'm doing is any of your business," she said, so uppity your liver would clabber like old milk if it had the chance. Then she ran out the door without even buttoning her coat or putting on her hat.

I sneezed a bunch of times, then coughed like crazy as I watched her go prancing down the drive toward the mailbox. Of course! How could I forget that the mail just ran? And I for sure never really did believe that crazy story about ordering gifts, especially as Grandma's birthday was over and she did not get anything special from my dumb sister.

I started to turn away, but movement in the trees on the other side of the road caught my eye. No one could mistake that purple cowboy hat and that weird red hair. She walked right up to Myra Sue while my sister pilfered through the mail. The two of them talked for a bit, then—would you believe it?—they turned and ambled off down the road. Mimi had one arm around Myra Sue's shoulders, and Myra didn't shove it off or anything.

Now, I have to tell you, this was a weird situation. Myra Sue hates the cold, she is very particular about the people she talks to, walks with, or hangs around, and Mimi had been griping about having to go outside to smoke like she might freeze to death before she could light her nasty old cigarette. I found it strange that, number one, both of them were out in the cold, and number two, Myra was walking along with Mimi, as if she liked her.

I threw on my coat as fast as possible, and lucky for me, my gloves were in the pockets. Unlucky for me, my good, warm hat was upstairs, but I wasn't about to waste time going up there to get it. I did not feel like going outside, but it's what I did, because how else was I gonna find out what was going on if I didn't snoop?

You know what? Things sure would be easier if people would just stop keeping secrets and acting mysterious.

I stepped out into the cold, brittle daylight that made my eyes ache and water even more. Now, you should know that along Rough Creek Road, we have fields, we have hills and hollers, and we have trees. Of course, I was not going to go trotting along behind Myra and Mimi in the middle of the road where they could see me. How in the world could I find out secrets if I was right out in the open that way? I trailed after them. The trees and their shadows hid me as I passed through the wooded parts. I hunkered down like I had the bends as I crept along the open spaces.

Their voices rose and fell, but the wind blew in my ears so much, I hardly heard a blessed word. How in the world was I supposed to find out what my sister was up to, or if that Mimi-person was in cahoots with her about it? I regretted even more that Melissa went home, because maybe she would've been able to hear what those two were chatting about so intently. My ears were beginning to ache way down deep inside where all those funny-looking, little hearing doohickeys are located. And when I sneezed or coughed—which I was now doing pretty often—I did it into my coat. Yes, I know that's gross, but what would you do? Sneeze and hack right out loud where they'd hear you and spoil everything?

Those two females stopped all of a sudden and turned. I dropped to the cold, hard ground so fast, I like to have broken every bone in my body, plus my face. I reckon I stayed out of their sight, because they walked right past me, right back the way they'd come, murmuring quietly like two best friends telling secrets, like they thought someone might overhear right out there in the middle of nowhere. As if a soul in Zachary County cared . . . well, except me, I guess.

Once they were out of sight, I sat up and stared glumly at the ground. I had not learned a single, solitary thing, but I was cold. My ears ached. My head felt dizzy and pained. Finally, I got up and walked back to the house, completely depressed.

"Where have you been?" Mama said the very second I walked in the back door. She was refilling the sugar bowl at the kitchen counter.

"Takin' a walk," I said, sniffling, wiping, and blowing just like anyone does when they've been outside in the middle of winter.

"In that cold wind, and without your hat? And where's Melissa?" she said, putting the sugar bowl on the table.

"She got kinda mad and I got kinda mad, and she went home. Can I have some hot chocolate?"

Mama narrowed her eyes and put one hand on her hip. "What did you girls fight about?"

I glanced around, saw no one else was in the kitchen, and said quietly, "Mimi."

"Oh, mercy. Well, that's nothing to fight about."

She started making a fresh pot of coffee, and I watched for a little bit, then I said, "Mama? Myra Sue and Mimi were walking along the road together like they were buddies. Do you think Myra invited Mimi to come here?"

Mama's mouth flew open, and she looked at me like I'd lost my mind.

"Now, how on earth could she have done that? Your sister never knew a thing about Mimi."

"You never told her anything at all?"

"Never! I didn't think you girls needed to hear about her and . . . well, about how she is . . . or how she was."

That made sense to me. Daddy would have never uttered a mumbling word if Mama asked him not to. So that only left one person who might've said something, even though I doubted Grandma would have mentioned Sandra Moore to Myra Sue. You better believe I was gonna ask her anyway. But not right then.

"Mama? I don't feel so good."

She lost her irritated expression and looked at my face real close. She laid her hand against my forehead.

"Oh, honey, you're feverish. Run upstairs, take a nice, warm bath, and put on your warmest jammies and robe. I'll fix you some hot tea."

"I was kinda hoping for hot chocolate 'cause chocolate always makes me feel better." In fact, my grandma always says, "Chocolate is always good for what ails you," to which I always respond with a strong "Amen!"

"Tea's better for you. Now, scoot."

When I came back downstairs, Mama looked at me and said, "Back upstairs with you, honey, and crawl into bed. I can see you're sick."

Now, I have to admit I felt almighty rotten from the top of my head right down to my toenails. But no matter how sick I was, I did not want to lie in bed in Myra Sue's rat's nest of a room.

"In my own bed?" I asked with all the hope in the world.

"No. In Myra's bed, and Myra will have to bunk down with Sandra. We don't want your sister catching whatever you're coming down with."

"You really think I can recover in that awful bedroom?"

"Yes," Mama said firmly. She put a hand on my shoulder and gently steered me toward the stairs. "Up you go." Then she followed me up, one hand lightly on my back, like she thought I might fall over backward or something. I wasn't *that* sick, but having her hand there made me feel better.

"My goodness," Mama said, looking around Myra's cleaned-up room with a smile. "That girl's been busy."

"Hmm," I said. My throat was getting sorer, and I wasn't going to waste what little bit still felt good by talking about the most aggravating girl who ever lived.

Mama pulled back the quilts and sheets, fluffed the pillows, then beckoned to me.

"Hop in, sweetie, and snuggle down. I'll bring you some hot tea."

I could not believe what I was about to ask, but I asked it as I crawled into bed while the sun shone in the afternoon sky.

"Will you call Temple?"

"Oh?"

I nodded.

"Her special tea. It tastes purely awful, but when I got sick winter before last, it made me feel better. Remember?"

"Well," Mama said, smiling and tucking the covers around me, "we'll see how you feel a little later. I'll call her, though." She kissed my forehead with her soft, cool lips, then she left me alone in that room that hardly resembled Myra Sue's bedroom at all.

I could hardly believe my goofy sister had cleaned her room this well in such a short amount of time. I mean, it seemed to me an entire crew of cleaners might have to work for at least twelve years just to clear a path between her dresser and her closet. Thinking about it hurt my brain, but some things are stronger than pain, and for me at that moment, curiosity won out. I hung my head over the side of the bed, lifted the bed-skirt, and looked. Well, there you go. Every blessed thing she had scattered everywhere had been shoved under that bed. It looked like a landfill.

I pulled myself back into the bed and laid down flat. For a while, it seemed my thumping head would never return to normal. If I opened my eyes, the room spun like crazy. Not only that, I thought I might barf. So much for curiosity. For the time being, I planned to lie there and not move so much as an eyelash.

You want to know the bright side of being sicker than a dog? If it lasts long enough, you get to miss school, that's what.

TWENTY-FOUR

Almost a Civil War in Our Very Own Kitchen

I was going to have to stay in bed until Mama decided I wasn't infectious. When you're coughing and sneezing, rubbing your eyes, being hot one minute and cold the next, and your hair aches, and your teeth itch, being infectious is just bound to happen.

Every single adult in our family, including Mimi, came right into my room to lay a hand on my forehead and ask how I was feeling. Even the St. Jameses and the Freebirds popped in. Well, you knew good old Temple was bound to pop in with her natural cures. I was glad to see her and that awful tea, which tastes and looks like axle grease and toadstools boiled in stump water. I slept really well after I slugged down a cup of that stuff, even though she would not let me add sugar to it. When I woke up, my head did not hurt so badly.

I surely felt cut off from the rest of the world, even though Mimi insisted on being in the room with me some, and thought she ought to Read Out Loud to me, like I was unable to read for myself. I practically begged her not to, but she just smiled her brown smile and read to me anyway. Little kid books. Oh brother.

Grandma visited as much as she could, and so did Daddy and all the rest, except Myra Sue, but nobody got very close or stayed very long because they did not want to carry germs to Eli. Which I understood. I did not want that boy to feel as rotten as I did. Mimi had the good sense to sit across the room from me so I did not breathe on her—or her on me—while she read.

At one point, while Grandma was smoothing my covers, I croaked out, "Grandma?"

"Yes, hon?"

"Did you ever tell Myra Sue about Mimi?"

She frowned and shook her head.

"Why, no. Rise up and let me plump up your pillows. Why would you ask me such a thing?"

While I was sitting up, I took a minute to blow my sore nose. "Because she's been hanging around the mailbox and the telephone a lot, and it seems to me that she might have been writing letters or calling Mimi and inviting her here. Especially as they seem to be such pals."

Grandma plumped my pillows then put them behind my head again, and it took me a little scrunching around to get all comfortable again.

"April Grace," she said, sighing loudly, "I declare, you have got the wildest imagination. If your sister is 'pals' with Sandra, I don't see it. And if she talks a lot on the phone, it's because she's at that age. And as for writing letters . . . I don't know anything about that. Have you *seen* any letters?"

"No, ma'am, but it just seems like—"

"It just seems like to me you need to quit fretting about things that don't concern you and concentrate on feeling better. You can't get over being sick if you're worrying. Get you some sleep now."

And with that, she gave me a kiss on my forehead, patted my shoulder, and left the room.

Boy, oh boy. Even when you're sick they don't take you seriously.

The next day was Monday, and that morning, Myra Sue stood in the doorway and glared at me.

"I need some socks," she said as if she thought I should rise up out of my sickbed like Lazarus from the grave and hand her over a pair of socks, or maybe even put them on her lily-white tootsies.

"Help yourself," I said, then coughed for about five minutes. Temple's tea had not helped my coughing in the least.

"Do not cough your germs all over me," my sister said, as uncompassionate as a rotten egg. Then she tiptoed in, yanked a pair of pink socks from her drawer, and ran back out like she thought I was gonna blast her with cooties and germs.

"You are the biggest wimp in the entire known universe, if not beyond," I croaked.

She flounced off and slammed the door to my very own private bedroom, which she was sharing with Mimi. Boy, oh boy, I dreaded going into my room again when those two vacated it for good. Just the thought of the smell and the mess discouraged me right to the bone and nearly made me feel sick all over again.

Monday at about noontime, Mama came into the room with a bowl of broccoli-and-cheese soup, a peanut butter sandwich, a glass of orange juice, and a cup of hot tea—her own regular kind of tea with sugar this time, not Temple's tea. On that tray, Mama also brought in my schoolbooks and pencils.

"I called the school and got your homework assignments for today."

Since Mimi had wasted so much of my time reading me *Goodnight Moon* and *The Berenstain Bears*, I really planned to read the last bit of *Rebecca* while I had the chance. Well, I guess I'd just have to wait to find out what was gonna happen with Mrs. de Winter and Mrs. Danvers. Do you know in that whole entire book, you never do find out the first name of the character who tells the story?

I felt good enough on Tuesday to go downstairs, and I could have probably gone to school, but I was awfully tired and weak.

"You're still a little peaked," Mama said. "I want you to stay home one more day."

Let me tell you, I did not argue with her. She called the school again and got Tuesday's homework assignments from the teachers' assistants, and I sat at the dining room table that morning while Mama mopped and vacuumed, and Mimi piddled around with a dust cloth.

At ten o'clock, she said, "Come on, Sunshine, let's watch *The Price Is Right*."

"I'd like to finish this homework," I said. I wanted to get it over and done with so I could spend the rest of the day reading the last of *Rebecca*.

"Oh, come on," she said, grinning at me. "Betcha I can win every game."

"Every single one?"

"Yep. Every single one."

Well, now. I doubted anyone was clever enough to win every single one of those games on that show. I figured she'd bug me like crazy until I agreed.

"All right," I said. "Prove it. Every game."

So we sat side by side on the couch, and she hollered out bids with the contestants. Mama came into the room about halfway through the show. She sat in Grandma's rocking chair and watched it with us. You know what? Mimi came closest to the actual retail price without going over *every single time*. And she would've won the showcase, too.

"My goodness, Sandra!" Mama said, almost smiling. "You know your stuff!"

"Thank you, honey," Mimi said, smiling at her, as if she was glad Mama had noticed she was good at something, even if it was just knowing the prices on a TV game show.

"Wow!" I said. "You woulda won a lot of prizes if you'd been on that program."

Mimi nodded energetically.

"Yep. And maybe someday, when you're all grown up, you can take your mimi to California and she can be on *The Price Is Right* and meet Bob Barker." She hollered this like she thought it was an actual possibility and she was already on contestant's row.

I wanted to say, "Don't count on it," but I didn't.

"I'm gonna finish my homework now," I told her, polite as you could hope for when talking to a screaming mimi, and went back into the dining room before we could do any more of that bonding business I've heard people talk about.

I'll let you in on a little something: I liked Mimi more right then than I had liked her the whole entire time since she'd walked in our door. Maybe something Melissa said on Saturday had worn off on me. I thought that maybe, just maybe, Mimi might actually be sorry for the things she did and was trying to be a good person, and maybe . . . Well, I shoved all those thoughts right out of my mind, because I did not want to be disloyal to my mama and grandma. Of course, it seemed to me like things weren't as tense and ugly as they had been. I mean, Mimi jumped right in and helped in the house, and she did a good job of it, too. I think Mama appreciated that, because she'd always thank Mimi for whatever she had done. Plus, she was a good cook.

I was almost finished with my history questions about the War Between the States when Grandma came in the back door. You could see she was almost bursting with something to tell us, and when she saw Mimi frying pork chops at the stove, she pointed at her. Now, I was taught pointing was impolite, but I guess Grandma forgot her manners right then.

"Well, Sandra Moore, just about the time I think you've sunk as low as you can go, you just sink even lower."

Mimi raised her penciled-on, dark-red eyebrows.

"Oh? I always thought cooking pork chops was a good thing."

Well, now. I forgot all about the Battle of Bull Run right then, because I thought we might be getting our very own personal Civil War right in our very own kitchen.

"I go into Cedar Ridge every Tuesday and do my week's shopping," Grandma told Mimi.

"Good for you," Mimi said. "Did you buy me anything?"

Grandma narrowed her eyes. "I do all my grocery buying at Ernie's Grocerteria."

Mimi grinned her brown-tooth smile. "How is Ernie,

anyway? We had such a good time on our date. That man is—"

"Knock it off, Sandra!" Grandma said, almost yelling. I have never heard such a thing in my life as my very own grandmother yelling because she was mad. In fact, Grandma doesn't *get* real mad—at least she didn't until Sandra Moore came on the scene.

Mama came into the kitchen holding the handle of the dust mop like she'd forgotten she was sweeping. Her eyes were large with surprise and, like me, she did not say a word.

"Ernie called me back into his office, and he told me a few things."

Oh, wow. I wriggled in my chair because this sounded important.

"He told me he most definitely did *not* ask you out on a date."

Mimi just stood there, half-smiling while the pork chops sizzled. "We went out, Grace. What would you call it, if not a date?"

"I'd call it a dirty trick. You told him you needed a ride to the bus station and he thought he was taking you there so you could catch a ride back to Omaha. That's what you told him."

Mimi shrugged one shoulder and turned back to the stove.

"I wanted to check the bus schedules. Ernie and I had a good time," she said.

"That's not what he told me—"

"Oh, really, Grace Reilly," Mimi whirled around, holding up the fork she'd been using to prod those chops. "He wouldn't tell *you* he had a good time, because he knew you'd get jealous. You're an *old woman* who needs to *grow up*."

"Don't you call me old. You are older than I am, Sandra Moore!"

"By four months! And I have kept my figure, and my looks."

"You haven't kept anything, and you need to quit trying to take what isn't yours."

"Now, you listen to me! If your boyfriend, or boy*friends*, find me more appealing than they find you, that's too bad for you—"

"Okay, that's enough!" Mama said. "I will not have the two of you shouting at each other in my house in front of my children. See? You've woke up the baby with all this yelling."

Wow. I nearly swallowed my aching tonsils. They must have really gotten on Mama's last nerve, because she hardly ever snapped at people.

Mimi's mouth flew open, but she did not say anything. Mama marched out of the kitchen.

There was so much silence in that kitchen between those two grandmothers that my ears nearly melted.

"I think it's time you left," Grandma finally told Mimi. "You have done wore out your welcome."

Mimi put the pork chops on a platter and set about making gravy in the skillet.

"And I think you should mind your own business, Grace. If Lily wants me to leave, she'll tell me to."

Oh brother. If we waited for Mama to get rid of that old woman, I'd be staying in Myra Sue's room until Myra Sue became a rocket scientist or the world came to end, which-ever came first.

"I'll tell you one thing," Grandma said, and her eyes were hard as flint rocks, "you stay away from Ernie Beason. He's a nice man and he don't need the likes of you ruinin' his reputation."

"Doo-dah, doo-dah," Mimi sang, like she didn't care a lick what Grandma had to say. She turned back to the stove and started stirring that gravy, but I could see by the look on her face that she cared more than she was letting on.

Grandma looked fit to be tied, and then she just walked right out the door without saying so much as a "howdy-do" or "see ya later" to me. I don't think she even saw me, although I was standing right there as big as life.

I slipped out of the kitchen and found Mama in her bed-room, folding Eli's baby clothes. I mean to tell you, she was folding them like she was in a fold-'em-fast contest where the prize was eight million dollars in gold. Her face was pink and her eyes were teary.

"Mama?" I said softly.

She glanced at me and kept folding.

"Are you okay?"

"I'm fine. You need to finish your homework, honey."

"I'm almost done." I reached over and picked up a soft, little towel. When I sniffed it, it smelled all sweet and cuddly, just like my baby brother. "Mama, isn't it hard on you, having Mimi here?"

She didn't say anything for a minute, then said, "Not exactly. She's not in the way. She's helping around the house.

She's good with you children. What I'm having trouble with, April Grace, is my feelings toward her."

"Oh?" I felt almost grown-up, hearing Mama say such a serious, personal thing to me.

She folded the last little sleeper, then took the towel from my hand and folded it. She put it on the stack of clean clothes, then she pulled me into her arms and gave me a nice hug and kiss.

"Don't you worry about things, sweetie. I'll work it out. I'm trusting God because that's the best thing I can do right now."

"Does it bother you when the two grandmas fight?"

She gave me a slight smile. "They were rivals a long time ago, and I guess some things never change." She let go of me and stepped back. "Now, you. Scoot back into the other room and finish your homework." She felt my forehead. "Who knows? Maybe tomorrow you'll feel good enough to go to school."

Oh goody.

When Myra Sue ran in that afternoon, she was all grins and eye-sparkles, and she practically flew up the stairs. I had been sitting in Grandma's little rocker in the living room when she whooshed by, and I wanted to tell somebody about Mimi and Grandma's fight. My sister was not my first choice at all, but Melissa Kay Carlyle was not someone with whom I wished to discuss this event until she apologized for being such a dipstick and taking Mimi's side against the rest of us. Honest to goodness, though, I had to talk to someone before I burst like a carnival balloon.

"Get out of here, you creep!" Myra Sue screamed at me the very second I walked into the room.

She was rummaging through her dresser drawers, and I saw some jewelry I'd never seen before.

"Well, now it's my room, too." I took a step closer so I could look at that sparkly stuff, but she shoved everything in the drawer and slammed it closed.

She narrowed her eyes at me and kinda pranced like she had ants in her pants.

"Well then, you can have it! I hate this room, anyway."

"You're not getting *my* room, Myra Sue Reilly! As soon as ole Mimi hits the road, I'm moving back in and you can have this room back. But you're not taking over my nice, clean, very own bedroom. Where'd you get those fancy earrings big enough to choke two starving mules?"

I plunked my backside right down on the bed where I'd been recuperating for the last three and a half days. She snarled at me like a rabid poodle.

"I don't have any earrings—"

"I just saw 'em, Myra! Right there in that drawer." I pointed at it. "So where'd you get 'em? Are you some kind of jewel thief?"

"What? No! You don't know what you're talking about."

"Is that why you've been skulking around, acting weird? You've become a thief and you steal ugly jewelry? Where you gonna wear it, Myra Sue? No one around here wears gaudy stuff like that. Just on soap operas, and those people—"

"If you tell me one more time that those people aren't real, I'm gonna . . . uh . . . I'm gonna . . . I don't know what I'm gonna do, but I'm gonna do it, and you won't like it!"

"So then tell me where you got those earrings, and maybe Mama won't find out you got 'em hidden in your underwear drawer."

She glared at me while her brain processed this information with all the speed of a three-toed sloth.

"Leave me alone! I have . . . I want . . . I'm going to change out of my school clothes. I have homework and stuff to do."

"Go ahead and change your clothes. I've seen you in your drawers, and believe me, you ain't much to see," I informed that goofy girl. "But I'm not leaving just yet. I want to tell you something first."

She put one hand on her hip and gave me a look of complete eye-rolling boredom.

"I can't think of anything you'd have to say that might be important," she sniffed.

"It's about Grandma and Mimi."

"So?"

"So since you're so buddy-buddy with Mimi, I thought you might be interested in their fight."

Now both hands rested on her hips like she was one of the lunch ladies in the cafeteria when boys are throwing peas at each other.

"What do you mean *buddy-buddy*, pray tell?"

Even though she hadn't been following Isabel around like a pup lately, that woman's way of speaking had rubbed off on Myra Sue like a black-walnut stain in the fall of the year.

"I mean that I saw you and her going down Rough Creek Road the other day, whispering like two big, fat gossip machines."

"I don't know what you're talking about! We did not go off down Rough Creek Road, and we were *not* whispering!"

I just stood there, waiting for her to realize what she just said. That girl is so dense, she can't even catch her own fibs unless someone points them out to her. I didn't bother.

"If you're not interested in what's going on, then I won't tell you," I said, all lofty and mysterious. I expected her to get nosy, but she didn't.

Instead she said, "Good! I have too many things to do without having to listen to your childish stories. I will be so glad to get away from here."

Oh brother.

"Fine, but you're stuck here for a few more years," I said, still feeling the need to talk and hoping she'd turn human, but she didn't, and I wasn't about to bare my soul to someone who is so all-fired uppity and prissy and uninterested.

"Not soon enough," she said, pulling a pair of jeans from a drawer. "Now, get off my bed and out of my room."

I am the first to admit that Isabel St. James would not always be my first choice of Someone to Talk To, but in this case, I figured she'd be better than anyone else, especially as she dearly loved Grandma and Myra Sue, and did not like Mimi, and all three of those people had me in a dither. I decided to go see Isabel.

I grabbed my coat, making sure I had my warm hat and gloves. I sneaked downstairs quiet as anything, because I knew if anyone saw me going outside, they'd have a hissy fit and make me stay in. I was sick and tired of being sick, I can tell you that.

You know what happened? I'll tell you. I met Isabel St. James coming up the steps just as I was going out the door, and I was purely glad to see her. I thought maybe she was here to save the day.

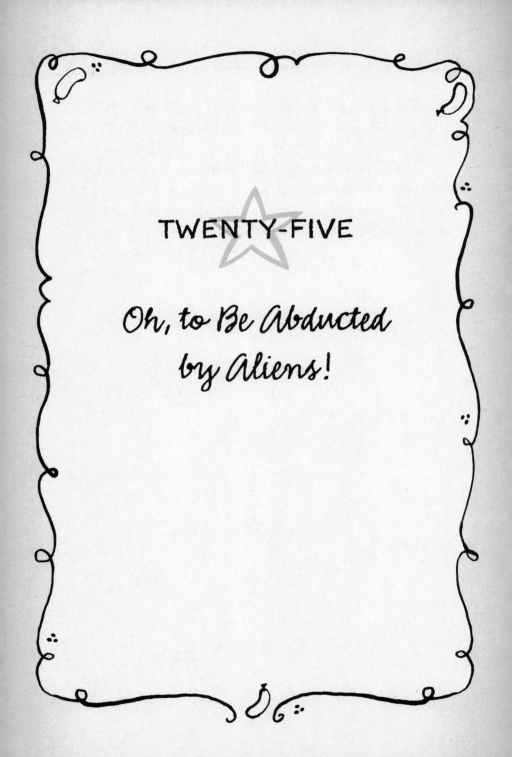

TWENTY-FIVE

Oh, to Be Abducted by Aliens!

☆

Isabel St. James came trotting up the porch steps in those high heels of hers, but when she saw me, she stopped like she'd run into a brick wall.

"Oh! Hello, April. How are you feeling?" she asked, then she pulled a tissue from her pocket and held it over her nose and mouth as if I were contagious, infectious, *and* radioactive. She is the Biggest Hypochondriac you could ever hope to meet, but I was happy to see her.

"Much better!" I said, cheery as all get-out, even if my voice still sounded rough as sandpaper.

"Good! Then you'll feel up to studying for the test next Tuesday. These are today's handouts."

She handed me a stack of papers that seemed to me as thick as the Holy Bible itself. I eyeballed those papers full of dates and names and terms and wondered if I could get sick all over again. This was an assignment Mama hadn't gotten from the teachers' assistants when she called. After all, Isabel does not have an assistant. If Melissa Kay Carlyle had been any kind of a friend, she woulda called me as soon as she got home from school and told me about this development.

"Boy, oh boy," I said grimly. "Thanks a heap."

"Should you be outside in this cold?" Isabel said, pulling her coat closer around her.

"Probably not, but I gotta talk to someone, and I was coming to see you."

Now, I'm the first to admit that Isabel and I have never been the best of pals, but over the months we've developed an understanding of each other, and I like her pretty good sometimes. Other times, like when she gets uppity or snooty, I just want to stick a stamp on her backside and mail her right back to California where she came from. But it's been a while since I felt that way.

"Oh?" She looked surprised. "Why did you want to come and see me?"

"Mimi. She is causing trouble."

"Oh, that dreadful woman! What has she done?" But before I could say a word, she said, "We must get you out of this freezing cold. Is she inside?"

I nodded.

"Well then," she said, tucking a couple more tissues even closer around her nose and mouth. "Let's sit in the pickup. It's still warm from my drive here."

We hurried to the truck and got inside. That tissue around her breathing holes distracted me and drove me so crazy that I had to say, "Isabel, I'm not infectious. And besides, you're teaching now, so you're gonna be exposed to more sneezing, coughing, and puking germs than you can shake a stick at."

She nearly turned green when I said that.

"Be sure you take plenty of vitamins," I encouraged comfortingly. Before she could talk herself into having double pneumonia, I plunged right into the situation about Mimi and Grandma. I did not leave out a single, solitary detail of their encounter, either—not even the smell of the pork chops as they were frying.

"I'm plenty worried that Mimi is going to turn everything

so upside down here that we will never get back to normal," I declared in conclusion.

"Oh, that horrible, *horrendous* woman!" Isabel said, one scrawny hand spread across her chest. "I simply can't *bear* that she's trying to ruin Grace's social life." She closed her eyes and rested the back of her head against the seat. "What can we *do*, April? There must be *something* to stop this hideous creature from wreaking such havoc."

"If Mama would tell her to, 'Hit the road, Jack,' we'd all be better off."

"Of course we would, but your mother would never do such a thing."

Isabel shmooshed up her lips and her eyebrows dipped.

"Hmm," she said, like she was thinking and she had to make ugly faces to get the thought processes churning.

I did not have to go through any such exercise. A good idea rolled right into my brain.

"For some reason, Mimi thinks she's now a major part of our family. She acts like she belongs with us, like she's been here forever. Here's the thing, Isabel: if she were to come and stay at *your* house, she might decide to go away."

Both of Isabel's eyes popped open, and she lifted her head to give me the most panicked look you can imagine.

"That woman in my *home*? My dear, you can't possibly be serious!"

I warmed right up to the subject.

"Don't you see, Isabel? Mimi is hanging around because she thinks she has a right to, just because she's Mama's mama. But she was such a rotten person that she wasn't really any kind of a mama to speak of—so she shouldn't be surprised that we don't want her messing up our family."

"Yes, I fully realize how completely dreadful that woman is. Lily shared with me about her sad childhood not long ago, before Eli was born."

I felt my eyes get big.

"*She did?* Mama *never* talks about that."

"One day we were talking about raising children and how rough our childhoods were, and her story simply came out. I think she was relieved to have someone with whom to share it."

Okay. Now I was speechless for a couple of reasons. Number one: Mama had told something to Isabel St. James that had always been such a Secret. Number two: Isabel had also had a rough childhood.

I pulled myself together because now questions started popping into my brain.

"I thought your father was a state senator."

"Yes, that's right."

"But you just now said that you had a hard time growing up."

Isabel blinked about twenty times. "My dear girl, being the daughter of a state senator has nothing whatever to do with having or not having a blissful childhood."

"Oh yeah?" I practically felt my ears grow, waiting for the details of her younger days. Somehow I never pictured Isabel as ever being a girl. For a couple of seconds I wondered what she looked like as a little baby, then kinda steered away from that. I just hoped she was a better-looking baby than she is a grown-up woman. Eesh.

Isabel stared out the windshield at nothing. Her face turned soft and sad, and her eyes seemed to look at sights from long ago. After a little while, it was like someone shook her shoulder and woke her up.

"I don't wish to talk about those days, or even think about them right now. What was it you asked me? Oh, yes! You want me to take that awful person into my home."

"Would you do it for Mama?" I pleaded. "And Mimi is not quite as obnoxious as you might think. And she cooks and cleans."

She looked at me so long without speaking, I thought maybe her brain had gone hard or her lips had frozen together. I put all the hope I could gather into my expression and looked right into her dark brown eyes.

"I'll think about it," she said at last. "I must talk to Ian first, of course. Oh dear! There are so many disturbing possibilities of things that woman might say or do."

I sighed, a little disappointed, but I knew there was a chance she'd agree.

"Okay," I said. "But if you can think fast and talk to him soon, that would be good."

"I thought Grace was acting as a buffer of sorts," she said, "but if Sarah—"

"Her name is Sandra," I said. Ole Isabel has never been any great shakes at remembering names. She called my mama *Lucy* for the longest time.

"Pardon? Oh, yes. Sandra." She waved one hand, like the name business annoyed her. "Well, if she is attempting to bait your grandmother into some sort of fight, it's better that Grace stays away. You mother abhors bickering and quarrels. For now, I shall go inside with you and give Lily a little more support. You mustn't say a word to anyone about your request, though."

I nodded.

"And I can't stay long. I must get Ian's dinner on the table, and I have handouts to put together for Tuesday after the test. Definitions, April, of muscle groups, and names of choreographers from the 1950s. Learn those definitions and names, and be prepared to use them in a sentence."

I stifled a groan that nearly erupted from my mouth anyway. Considering that Isabel was going into the house with me to give Mama a break, I thought it best to smile at her instead. So I did. And I prayed Ian would say, "Sure! Bring Mimi right on over here." My plan would not get Mimi off Rough Creek Road, but it would get her out of the house, and maybe Mama would feel better about the whole thing. I figured it was kinda hard not to think about that old woman if she was right there where you could see her most of the time.

"Those are the last handouts. After next week, we'll start learning steps. I have such plans!"

Sometimes Isabel's plans did not bode well. I heard this announcement with a considerable sinking feeling in my stomach.

"Oh?" I said weakly.

"I am going to incorporate my junior high dance classes with my senior high theater classes," she said with all the enthusiasm you can imagine. "We will be performing a musical at the end of the school year, complete with singing and dancing!"

Just when I thought nothing could get worse, it did. Boy, oh boy, where was an alien abduction when you needed one? Maybe if I went out in the woods tonight, the mother ship would be looking for red-haired people to take to the home planet.

"Wait a minute," Isabel said just as I opened the car door. "I want to ask you something."

I closed the car door to shut out the cold that whooshed in.

"It's about your sister," she said.

"What about her?"

"Is she all right?"

I shrugged. "Ole Myra is always goofy, Isabel."

"I don't want to hear that kind of talk," she said in her teacher voice.

"Sorry," I murmured. "I don't know about Myra. She's been hanging around the mailbox a lot, which I think is goofy."

"Well, darling, she's probably eager for her magazines to arrive. I gave her a subscription at Christmas to *Today's Theatre*, and I know she enjoys those teeny-bopper magazines."

Okay, then. That made a little sense, because Mama would not want her having a bunch of those dumb magazines, so maybe my sister was hoping to get them out of the mailbox before Mama found out. That's probably why she was hiding them under the bed.

"April, I'm concerned that the darling girl has distanced herself from me, and I don't understand why."

"I know. I'm not sure about everything, but I do know she thinks she embarrassed you by the way she botched the Christmas play, and she hasn't gotten over it."

Isabel huffed. "I'm not in the least embarrassed. As I explained to her that very night, her nerves simply got the better of her. If she's going to be on the stage, she must learn to deal with jitters."

"Well, maybe you better tell her where she understands it, Isabel. I think she needs to hear it. And also . . ."

"And also . . . what?"

"Well, she really likes the soaps, and you said they were low class, and I think you hurt her feelings."

"Oh dear! Well, I must rectify this, mustn't I? The darling girl really must understand no serious actor would want to be in a soap opera."

Uh-oh. Myra Sue would not like to hear that.

"Really?"

"*Yes*. A person can have a successful career, of course, but not if she wants the acting community to take her seriously. I really must explain this to Myra."

Well then. There was nothing I could do about it. I doubted Isabel was going to win her "darling girl" over with such information.

When we went into the house, Isabel went to talk to Myra Sue, but whatever was said remained between the two of them, because neither one told me a single, solitary word about it. When I asked Myra, she threw a magazine at me and told me to get out of her room. When I asked Isabel, she just said Myra darling was going through a difficult phase.

Boy, oh boy, did I dread the time when I'd have to go through phases.

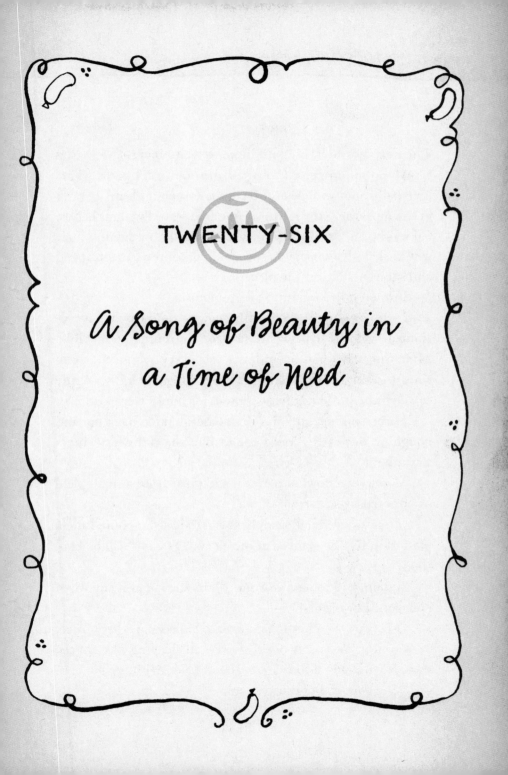

TWENTY-SIX

A Song of Beauty in a Time of Need

☺

The next morning, I did not have to wait ninety-seven years for Myra Sue to get out of the bathroom. And guess what? The bathroom was clean. I have *never* seen it clean at seven in the morning, except when Grandma stayed with us before Eli was born. Usually Myra's wet towels are on the floor, her wet washcloth all soppy in the sink, the toothpaste uncapped and squirted all over the place.

Boy, oh boy. I ought to take a picture.

I gathered my books and homework and carried everything downstairs to place in a stack on the dining-room table. Myra Sue and I had been doing this every school morning since forever, so we could grab everything when it was time to catch the bus, but that morning her books weren't there.

Mimi was sitting at the kitchen table, hacking and coughing her rattly, loose cough like she did every single morning.

Mama set a bowl of oatmeal and raisins and a small plate of buttered toast in front of me.

"Your sister about ready?" she asked as she poured me a glass of milk. She glanced at the clock. "The bus will be here soon."

"I dunno." I looked at Mimi. "Was she about ready when you came downstairs?"

"I haven't seen her this morning." She sipped her coffee. "I got up while you two girls were still sleeping like angels. I'm glad she's back in her own bed. That girl hogs the covers!" She gave us her crusty laugh.

"She didn't sleep with me last night," I said. "She's afraid she'll catch my germs. She and Isabel are just alike."

Mama and Mimi both looked at me like they didn't understand.

"Well, you shoulda seen Isabel yesterday with her mouth and nose covered up with eight hundred Kleenexes while she talked to me. I might sound kinda croaky, but I'm not infectious anymore. Am I?"

I did not *feel* infectious. And I was going to school that day. Then, little by little, as all three of us stared at each other, realization oozed into my brain: if Myra Sue did not sleep with Mimi last night, and she did not sleep in her own bed, then where *did* she sleep?

"Mama," I said, with my voice quivering. "Our bathroom was all clean this morning. Myra Sue *never* cleans the bathroom when she's finished."

I swallowed hard, remembering these last few weeks of her being so secretive and weird and quiet, then yesterday when she was all giggly and giddy. I thought about how she was rummaging around in her dresser drawers. I thought of the neat bathroom, none of her books on the table . . . Something grabbed hold of my guts and my muscles, and I started to shake from the inside out.

"*Mama!*"

I nearly flew up the stairs, taking them two at a time, and burst into Myra's bedroom. Mama and Mimi were right behind me. I yanked open the top drawer where she keeps her undies and socks, and it was empty.

Then Mama opened the closet and we saw, plain as day, a

lot of my sister's clothes were gone. The old, soft-sided flow-ered suitcase that was usually on the top shelf was gone, too.

"Mama, where's her underwear? Where's her shoes and clothes? *Mama, where is Myra Sue?*"

Mama looked at me, her face ghostly white.

"Go get your daddy," she said in a voice so frozen, she did not sound anything like Lily Reilly.

I hardly remember running out of the house and to the barn. I guess it was pretty cold outside, but I didn't feel it even though I wasn't wearing my coat. I do remember seeing the school bus slow down and stop at the end of the driveway, but no one from our family was going to get on that thing that day.

I burst into the barn, and even though I know I'm sup-posed to be quiet and not scare the cows, I hollered as loud as I could, "Daddy! Daddy! Come quick!"

All those stupid cows shifted and stomped and tried to tug their big ole heads free of the stanchions, and when they couldn't do that, they set up to making noise and stomping even more.

Daddy charged out of the feed room, frowning like you wouldn't believe.

"April Grace!" he said. "You know better than—"

"Daddy! Come quick!" I shrieked, all but jumping up and down with anxiety. "Myra Sue is *gone*!"

"Gone? Gone where?"

"We don't know. Oh, Daddy, do you think she was kid-napped?" Which made no sense at all, because a kidnapper would not have taken her clothes, but I was so upset that logic wasn't even considered.

Daddy didn't answer me as he tore out of the barn. I tore out after him, on his heels the whole way to the house.

"What's going on?" he shouted as he opened the back door and we burst inside. "Where's Myra Sue?"

Mama stood in the kitchen, looking more frozen and white than ever. She held a yellow-and-white dish towel and was twisting and twisting it between her fingers. She shook all over.

"I th-think M-Myra has r-run away," she choked out.

"What do you mean, she's run away?"

Mimi came into the room. She held Eli, cuddling him to her, patting his back gently, making whispery, shushing noises near his ear.

"The sheriff's on the way," she said. "Honey, you better sit down before you fall down." She pulled out a kitchen chair with one hand. "Mike, help her to sit. She's been standing there like a statue. She's going pass out if she doesn't move."

Daddy urged Mama into the chair, then he looked around like he didn't know where he was.

"Are you sure she isn't here?"

"We're sure," Mimi told him.

"She's got to be here somewhere," he said. He ran to the back door, opened it, and hollered, "Myra Sue! Myra Sue, get in this house right now!" After a few seconds, he came in and ran upstairs, shouting, "Myra Sue Reilly! Girl, you better answer your daddy!" Then he thundered down the steps, out the front door, and shouted the same kind of words from the front porch.

I went out there, too. I grabbed his arm and dug my fingers in until he looked at me.

"Daddy, her clothes and shoes are gone. That flowered suitcase that Grandma gave her is gone, too."

He looked at me like he didn't know who I was, then scooped me up in his arms and carried me back into the house.

"You shouldn't be outside without your coat," he said. "Go put on a sweater and turn up the furnace till you get warm."

Daisy followed us into the kitchen and stayed near when Daddy set me down.

Mama sat in that kitchen chair, wringing that dish towel in her hands, shaking like the last leaf in a cold winter wind. Daddy poured her a cup of coffee and placed it in her hands. He even wrapped her fingers around it.

"Maybe Myra is at Mom's. Or over at the St. Jameses'," he said. "Or with Forest and Temple."

"I already called everyone," Mama said. "She's not with any of them."

Eli started to fuss, and Mimi gently rocked him back and forth in her arms.

"Lily, honey, this boy's hungry."

Mama turned her head slowly toward Mimi. She stared at her like she didn't hear a word the woman said.

Eli's little arms started waving above his blanket, and he let out a single, loud "Waaa!" About five seconds later, he set up to howling. Mama blinked. I do believe that's the first time she had blinked since she sat down.

"Oh!" she said. "Oh, he's hungry! I'll feed him." She stretched out her arms and Mimi placed the baby in them.

The back door opened and Grandma rushed in. Her hair

hung in little wet curls, and she was wearing sweatpants, her pajama top, her bathrobe, a red slipper on her right foot, and a white sneaker on her left. She smelled of Dial soap and Prell shampoo.

"I got here as soon as I could," she said. "What happened?"

Before you could count to ten, Isabel and Ian charged through the back door, and right behind them came Temple and Forest.

The whole kitchen was full of people and talking and confusion, and poor little Eli was so upset, he cried and cried. He didn't quiet down for a while, even after Mama took him out of the room. Don't anybody tell me that kid isn't smart. He knew something bad was going on in our house, and he didn't like it one little bit. Daisy whimpered because she has never liked it when things get all upset. I led her back out to the service porch, right to her bed, then I kissed her big, fuzzy, white head, hugged her hard, and she gave me a look like she understood how I felt.

"Stay here, Daisy," I told her. "You'll feel better." She settled down, I petted her some more and stroked her head for a little bit longer, and I returned to the kitchen.

I'll tell you something right now: I may have thought my sister was a drip and a dipstick most of the time, and I may have wished she'd move in with Grandma or Ian and Isabel or something like that, but this business of packing her things and running off was nothing I ever wanted to happen. I've seen things on the news about runaways, and it scares the daylights out of me. You know as well as I do that Myra Sue doesn't often have the sense to come in out of the rain, so how was she gonna have sense to take care of herself out there all alone in the world?

I thought about all this, and I saw inside my mind the images of her meeting some awful stranger who would hurt her, or getting lost and freezing to death in a ditch. Or getting run over by a truck, or falling off the side of one of these old, narrow, Ozark mountain roads. Before you know it, all those pictures got into my head and became a thrumming, loud buzz like swarming bees. I could not understand one word of anything anyone said, and I got so dizzy I could hardly see. Before I knew it, I hurled right there on the floor in front of everyone in that kitchen.

"Oh, mercy!" Grandma said, rushing to me.

"Poor little Sunshine!" Mimi gasped, hurrying to my other side.

Clucking like two mother hens, they led me out of the kitchen and down the hall to the bathroom, where they removed my clothes and bathed my face. I'm not sure who did what because right then I felt like I was sitting off in the corner somewhere, watching through dark glasses while everything whirled around me.

"Grace, I think she has a fever," Mimi said with her cool, wrinkled, old hand against my forehead.

Grandma touched my cheek with the back of her hand. She nodded.

"I believe she's had a relapse of whatever has made her sick these last few days. April Grace, you need to go straight back to bed."

"But Grandma, I need to help find Myra Sue . . ." Even as I said it, I felt the room might be slipping away.

"I'll go get your pajamas while your grandma helps you clean up," Mimi said. "Then we're taking you straight to bed. No arguments." I didn't argue.

Once I was in bed, the world around me quieted.

"Grace," Mimi said, all soft and warm, "if you want to go downstairs with the others, I'll stay up here with Sunshine."

Grandma paused, eyed me a moment longer, then nodded. She kissed my forehead.

"You lay still for a while." She glanced at Mimi. "Thank you, Sandra," she said softly, with a small smile. I would have marveled at that, but right then, I hardly noticed it.

Now, to be perfectly honest, I wanted to go right back downstairs, too, because Myra was gone and everybody needed to be helping to find her. But I knew I couldn't. Number one: My whole entire body felt like it was made of foam. And number two: I knew they'd never let me go down there. Number three: If I was sick again, I might be infectious again.

I lay there, weak and jittery at the same time. I kept hearing my own voice saying over and over again, "My sister needs me."

"There, there, honey. Just relax. The sheriff is here now, and he'll get to the bottom of all this. Would you like me to read to you?"

But I didn't want to hear a story. I just wanted to know everything was all right.

"I'll just go sit on the top step and listen," I said, but Mimi pushed me back and covered me up again.

"No, you won't. Your folks have enough to worry about right now."

I had not really thought of that. Me getting sick would just make things worse, and everyone needed to think about that crazy Myra Sue, not dumb ole April Grace.

You know what that Mimi did? I'll tell you. She tucked those covers around me again, she stroked my hair away from my forehead, and then she started singing, just as soft and pretty as anything I've ever heard, as if all those years of smoking had not given her the voice of a bullfrog when she sang. She sang a song I'd never heard in my life, something about how our lives go through seasons like flowers and grass. It was the prettiest song I'd ever heard, and I closed my eyes, listening to the tune and hearing the words.

"That was real pretty," I murmured, about half-asleep.

"Did you like that? I wrote it myself."

My eyes popped wide open, and I looked at that wrinkled face. For the first time, I noticed she had eyes green as the moss growing on the north side of a tree in the woods. When she smiled, I didn't so much notice the brown teeth as I did how that smile made her eyes all soft and shiny like Mama's. Had Mimi always had pretty green eyes like that?

"Would you sing it again?" I asked, closing my eyelids because they weighed a ton. I did not want to go to sleep because I needed to stay awake and think and pray about Myra Sue, but I could not keep my heavy eyelids open a moment longer.

Mimi sang that life's seasons song again, and I couldn't help it. I just drifted away.

TWENTY-SEVEN

Pillaging the Plunder Under Myra Sue's Bed

✷

I'm not sure how long I drifted, but all of a sudden it felt like someone plugged me into an outlet and gave me an electric charge.

I sat straight up in bed, clearheaded, full of energy, and brimming with an idea.

"Mimi!" I nearly shouted. I startled her so bad she practically jumped three feet out of the chair by the window. I reckon she had been sitting there this whole entire time, even though I don't know how long I'd been lying in bed asleep. Quite a while, I reckon, because it was nearly dark outside the window.

"My stars!" she said, putting one hand to her chest as she rushed to me. She turned her head and coughed hard for a few seconds into her elbow, then faced me again and said, "Sunshine, are you all right? I thought you were asleep!"

I threw back the covers and jumped out of bed, realizing a Big Clue or two was probably hiding beneath that landfill of junk under Myra Sue's bed. After all, that mess was so big and so awful, it probably hid life-forms as yet undiscovered by modern man.

"No, no!" she fussed. "Get back into bed. You're sick!"

"No, I'm not!" I hollered. "I've recovered, and I think I know how we can find Myra Sue."

Mimi gawked at me.

"Honey, I . . . What . . . Sunshine, you need to . . . *What are you doing?*"

By then, I was on the floor with the bedskirt yanked up,

revealing that mess Myra Sue had shoved under there on Sunday along with every other thing she'd shoved under there since she was a little kid.

"Help me, Mimi!" I shouted as I started hauling out papers and magazines and trash.

"Honey," she said, catching my arm. "Get up now and crawl back into bed."

I looked at her over my shoulder and saw pure alarm in her face. I bet she thought I was out of my ever-lovin' mind, which I was *not*, I assure you.

"Mimi," I said, grabbing the hand on my shoulder, "I'm not sick. I think that somewhere, in all this junk and trash, there might be a clue about where Myra Sue ran off to." I squeezed her fingers encouragingly. "Help me go through this mess. Please."

"I don't understand . . ."

"Myra spent hours and hours writing notes and stuff, telling Mama it was homework, but it wasn't. She was real sneaky about it, and she even slept with her notebooks."

Mimi sank down on the floor next to me, her face serious. "You think she was writing to someone?"

I nodded and told her about those times I saw Myra at the mailbox. "She was writing to someone, but I don't know who," I declared.

"Maybe she was writing stories and sending them off to get published," Mimi suggested. "I used to do that a long time ago. Stories and poems and songs."

"One thing I know for sure," I said, "is that she was not writing homework assignments like she kept saying she was."

As anxious as I was about Myra, Mimi's statement shocked me a little. For one thing, Myra Sue did not have enough imagination to write stories or poems, and she couldn't carry a tune in a bucket with a lid on it, so I know she hadn't written any songs. And for a second thing, I am the person in the family who'd like to write stories someday.

I wonder if I got that from Mimi, who seems to be a good storyteller.

"Myra Sue would not be writing anything to send off to get published," I declared.

"April Grace, have you told your daddy and mama about this?"

"I guess I should've, but she swore she'd tell J. H. Henry that I loved him—which I do *not*, in the very worst way!— and then she said she'd tell Mama I tore my new coat, and some other stuff. Besides," I sighed, "I didn't want to be a big, fat tattletale."

"I see," Mimi said. "Well, we better see what we can find, Sunshine."

I reached under the bed and pulled out an armful of papers. Then I paused and eyeballed Mimi as she hauled out a pile of dirty socks, some jeans, and underwear.

"What did Myra tell you?" I asked her.

She frowned. "What d'ya mean?"

"When you two went strolling down Rough Creek Road the other day. I saw you, and y'all were talking like two best friends."

Her face cleared. "Oh, that. I saw her outside, and it was clear that she was upset, and when I asked her why she was crying, she told me she felt ugly and dumb. I told her that she was most certainly not ugly or dumb!"

My sister feeling ugly and dumb?

"Are you kiddin'? She has always acted like she thinks she's a cross between Albert Einstein and Vanna White or somebody."

Mimi stared at me with her eyes narrowed slightly, like she was trying to see inside my head, then she lay down flat on her belly and reached way, way under the bed.

"You don't like your sister very much, do you, Sunshine?" she asked. Her voice came out kinda puffy and grunty and muffled.

I had never heard such words spoken, just plain that way, hanging between us like dirty sheets on the clothesline. Just as ugly, too.

I didn't want to think about those words any longer, so I said, "Myra and me don't get along sometimes, but I sure don't want anything bad to happen to her. She's my very own sister." My voice broke and I swallowed hard in case I was fixin' to start bawling like a baby. Then I cleared my throat and asked, "What else did you and Myra talk about? Did she tell you she was gonna run away?"

Mimi scooted back out from where she'd gone halfway into the dusty darkness under the bed and raised herself up on both elbows.

"No, she did not. If she had, I'd have done my best to talk her out of it, and failing that, I'd have told your folks." She had a coughing spell with her head turned to her shoulder, then she said, "She told me she'd wanted to be an actress for a long time, and she told me how she'd messed up the Christmas program."

"I know. That was weeks ago."

"And she feels that she'd let Isabel down."

"Yeah, well, she loves Isabel St. James."

Mimi raised her eyebrows. "Why? That woman is snippy and uppity, and she's not very friendly."

I shrugged. "She's not so bad once you get to know her. And Myra wants to be just like her, and when she flubbed up onstage . . . well . . . that just proved she wasn't like Isabel, I reckon."

"And she's having a hard time understanding that. You know, Sunshine, it's hard when you compare yourself to other folks, because you'll either think you're better than them or worse than them. It's best just to be yourself."

I looked at that purply-red-haired Mimi in astonishment.

"Wow, Mimi. You're smart."

She smiled and ran one hand over my head like I was a sweet little kitten.

"No, Sunshine, I'm not. I've just done a lot of living and I've learned a lot of things. If I was smart, I'd not be in the mess I'm in now."

"What mess is that?"

She looked away.

I knew I should have been scouring through Myra's clutter for clues, but right at that moment, something told me to listen to my mimi.

"Mimi? What mess is that?"

"Oh, Sunshine." She sighed. "I reckon I'm a little bit sick. And it seems I don't have anyplace to go."

"What d'you mean, you're sick? Sick how? What's wrong?"

"Honey, I have lived a hard life, and you can't live a hard life and be a healthy old woman. And now, let's drop it because I should never have said a word. It's just that you're such a smart little girl, it's easy to talk to you, and I guess I sorta forgot there for a minute that you're just a kid."

"You should tell Mama," I said.

She met my eyes and said, "Well, let's not talk about it anymore, you and me. Right now, your sister is the most important thing going on in this family."

She went back to digging stuff out from under the bed, and I could see she had said all she was going to say to me about being old and sick, but you better believe I was going to let Mama know just as soon as all this mess with Myra Sue was over.

"What exactly are we looking for?" Mimi said when we'd pulled out every bit of junk, stuff, and things. She eyeballed that pile around us.

"I don't know, exactly. Like I said, she was scribbling in secret all the time. Just look and see what you find. Of course, I found a list in her coat pocket and it turned out to be nothing, so maybe anything we find here will be nothing, too."

"Let's not give up hope!" she said encouragingly.

So we started sifting through all that mess. We made a trash pile where we put used Kleenexes (eww), two broken hairbrushes, a dried-up apple core, something that looked like a dried-up fur ball that Queenie might have barfed up (but she's never been here, so I didn't know what it was but it went in the trash right quick), plus a broken pencil and two dried-up Bic pens.

I started uncrumpling all the wadded-up papers I found. Some of it was homework. Some papers were tests that sported lots of red checkmarks. Oh boy. If Myra Sue had been doing so much homework, wouldn't she have made better grades than Ds? I bet if Mama and Daddy had seen those papers, they'd have had a fit. Last semester, she brought home all Cs on her report card. Maybe she really had been doing all that scribbling to raise her grades so she wouldn't get in trouble when report cards came out, but I doubted it.

One page I smoothed out was a letter, written to "Dear Sir." It read, "I am a beautiful, twenty-year-old actress, with long, blonde hair and azure-blue eyes. I have a lovely figure. I want to be an actress in the movies, or maybe on television. Being live onstage frightens me, so I need to be on film instead. I am a fan of *Days of Our Lives* and would be perfect on that program, even better than Christie Clark, who plays Carrie Brady." That's where she stopped. It was a purely dumb letter. I found two more almost like it, except "lovely" had been spelled "loverly" and "azure" had been written with two z's. There were some other letters there, too, all to "Dear Sir" and all telling how gorgeous, smart, and talented she was, but none of them were completed. It was like all that writing she had been doing these last few weeks had been practice for concocting big, fat lies.

Wouldn't it be the craziest thing in the whole entire world if my sister decided to run off to New York City and try to get on some crazy soap-opera show? Listen, I've read about New York City and seen pictures and everything. It's a big, scary place. Even ole Myra wouldn't do something so purely dumb as to go there all by herself.

Mimi made a nice stack of the magazines, everything from *Cosmopolitan* (which I'm sure Mama knew nothing about, or it would have been in the burn barrel a long time ago) to *Young Model* to *Tiger Beat*. You know something? Every one of those magazines had mailing labels on them, and the names on those labels were Jennifer and Jessica Cleland. Since Myra, Jessica, and Jennifer were so close and shared everything, it seemed to me my sister might have said something to the other two about this crazy running-away idea.

"Mimi," I said, "take a look at these weird letters I just found."

I handed them over to her, then I got up. I needed to tell somebody to get in touch with those dumb Cleland girls.

"Sunshine!" Mimi said, reaching for me. "Where you goin'?"

"I need to talk to Mama and Daddy." I shook her hand off my arm.

"You shouldn't be up. You're sick."

"I'm fine." I stuck my feet in my fuzzy house slippers and put on my warm, thick robe.

Mama and Grandma were downstairs, both of them pale as skim milk. The expressions in their eyes scared me. Grandma was knitting so fast the needles blurred.

"Mama?" I said. My voice came out weak and frightened.

She turned to me. "Honey," she said, with a version of a smile, "what are you doing out of bed? Are you all right?"

"Mama, Jennifer and Jessica might know something about Myra."

"The sheriff has a list of all of Myra Sue's friends. He and his deputies are talking to everyone."

"How about I fix you a nice ham sandwich?" Grandma asked. She put aside her knitting and got up from her rocker. Grandma has always had the need to cook or stay busy when she's worried.

"I'm not hungry," I said. Any other time, those words coming out of my mouth might have shocked me and everybody else, but right then I knew if I swallowed a bite, it would come back up.

"Maybe you'd feel better if you splashed some water on your face, honey," Mama suggested.

"Where is everybody? I thought our friends would be here."

"They're out lookin', child," Grandma said softly. "Everybody's out lookin' for her, except us. We're stayin' here, looking after you and Eli. Maybe your sister will show up, or call. Now, go splash some water on your face, like your mama said. Maybe a nice bath would make you feel better."

"Maybe," I said, and slogged out of the room. I just passed the telephone when it rang. The sound startled me so bad, I jumped.

"Hello?" I answered. Mama and Grandma rushed into the hall.

"Um, hello? May I please speak to Mia Suzanne?" The voice was very polite but very peculiar sounding, as if the caller spoke from far away.

"You have the wrong number," I said.

"Oh! I'm sorry." And she hung up.

I replaced the receiver and watched while Mama and Grandma went back to the living room, looking defeated.

About twenty seconds later the telephone rang again.

"Boy, oh boy," I thought, reaching for it. "If this is one of those pranksters, I'm gonna give 'er what's coming to 'er!"

"Hello!" I snapped.

"Oh. Um. This is Krista Collier. I'm calling to speak to my friend Mia Suzanne." It was that same voice. She did not sound like a prankster, though.

"There is no Mia Suzanne in this house, and if you—"

Mama yanked the receiver out of my hand.

"Who is this? Where are you calling from?"

I moved over next to Grandma, and she pulled me into the circle of her arms. We hung on to each other as we watched Mama talk on the phone. Mama's eyes got bigger and her mouth opened. She was paler than I'd ever seen her in my life—so pale she was almost blue.

She grabbed a pen from the holder on the telephone table and scribbled something down on the pad there.

"Yes. Yes, thank you. Thank you very much!" she said.

She pushed down the button to end the call, then immediately dialed another number.

"Sheriff's office? This is Lily Reilly. My daughter is Myra Sue Reilly and—yes, that's right, the girl who's missing. I just received a phone call from a girl in Elmwood, Iowa. Her name is Krista Collier. She says that she and my daughter planned to meet at a bus station in St. Louis and were going to travel together to New York City."

Grandma and I gawked at each other. Myra Sue going to New York City? And I'd just told myself my sister would never be that dumb. Good grief. Mama kept talking to that person in the sheriff's office.

"No, I don't know the girl. Apparently she and my daughter struck up a correspondence from a pen pal column in a teen magazine, and it seems they've been making plans on the phone . . ." Her voice broke. "Excuse me," she sobbed, then cleared her throat. "Here's the girl's phone number." She choked out those numbers, then said, "Please. Please, find my daughter. She's traveling alone somewhere, and she's so young. She's . . . She's calling herself M-Mia Suzanne." She stopped and gulped in some air. "She doesn't know anything about the world . . . please . . ."

So that explained all those phone calls Myra Sue nearly broke her neck to answer all the time. Boy, oh boy.

Mama dropped the phone and sank to the floor, crying so hard it was like her body would break. Grandma let go of me, plucked up the receiver, and talked with the person. I squatted on the floor next to Mama and put my arms around her like she was my child. She hung on to me and cried and cried and cried.

I guess the sound of Mama's sobbing reached Mimi. She rushed down the steps, her face full of fear and concern.

"What's happened? Have they found Myra?"

Grandma held up one hand, finished talking with the person on the other end of the phone line, then hung up. She beckoned Mimi, and they went into the kitchen.

I patted Mama's back, smoothed her hair, and gave her kisses until she cried herself out.

"Come on, Mama, let's get up and go to the kitchen. I'll pour you a cup of coffee and bring you a cool cloth for your face."

She nodded, and I helped her to her feet. It was like assisting a little old lady, walking Mama to the kitchen and setting her down at the table.

Mimi put a cup of tea in front of her. "Chamomile," she said softly. "Better for you than the other kind. It's calming."

"Thank you," Mama whispered. She wrapped her fingers around the cup like her hands were cold.

I went to get her a cool, wet cloth for her face, and she smiled sweetly at me when I sponged her skin with it.

"Thank you, sweetheart," she said, pulling me to her and giving me a hug. Then she just held me for the longest time.

From his crib in the bedroom, Eli began to cry.

"I'll fetch him," Mimi said, and was gone before Grandma had a chance to get out of her chair.

Mama took Eli from her when Mimi brought him into the kitchen. He wasn't crying anymore. Mimi seemed to have a knack for calming him down.

"My sweet little guy," Mama murmured, kissing his little face.

"Lily, you feel up to telling us about that call?" Grandma said.

Mama nodded. "Apparently this girl who called a bit ago, this Krista Collier from Iowa, she's a pen pal I never knew Myra Sue had, and apparently they've been corresponding and talking on the phone for a while."

"That's what all that secret writing was about!" I hollered, interrupting Mama.

She looked at me. "All what secret writing?"

"When Myra said she was doing her homework, except I didn't think she was. I think she was writing to that girl."

"And she was writing these," Mimi said, pulling from her pocket those crumpled pages we'd found under the bed.

Mama and Grandma looked at those letters, then Mama looked at me with a frown.

"You knew about this?"

"No, ma'am. I mean, not those letters, specifically. Mimi and I found them under Myra's bed a little while ago. It's just that every time I saw Myra Sue, she was writing. She's never been all excited about homework, but suddenly she was, and it seemed plenty odd to me."

"Why didn't you say something to someone?" Grandma asked. She was frowning at me, too.

"Because . . . because I couldn't *prove* she was doing anything other than homework, and no one else seemed to think the way she was acting was anything to worry about. Everyone just said she was going through a phase and would grow out of it. She wasn't starving herself again. I had no idea she was writing to some girl in Iowa. And besides, she made me promise never, ever to say anything about it to you."

"You should have told me anyway, April," Mama said.

I knew if I had told them earlier, "Ole Myra is doing an awful lot of writing in her room," they would've said, "Good! Your sister needs to study more and bring home better grades." More than likely, they would've been proud that she was working so hard. They probably would've told me not to bother her. But I saw no benefit in being logical at that present moment, so I just kept my mouth shut.

"Well then, I guess maybe I should have spoken up earlier, too," Mimi said, surprising everyone.

"What's that?" Grandma gave her the dirty eyeball. "What do you know about all this, Sandra?"

Mimi sighed. "I really didn't want to say anything." She stopped right there.

"Say it, say it!" Grandma snapped.

"Well, I was hoping to get someone to take me to the store to buy some smokes last night, but when I went to get my purse, I noticed most of my money was missing out of it. Eighty dollars."

Dead silence.

"I hope you're not saying Myra Sue stole money from you," Grandma said.

"Now, Grace, I did not say that." Mimi spoke quietly, kindly.

"It sure sounds to me—"

"Bus tickets cost money," Mama interrupted. "Myra Sue wouldn't have had enough to buy one, even if she'd saved her allowance for a long time."

"That's for sure," I blurted out, thinking about my own allowance.

Again, silence fell over us. Then Mama excused herself and went away from the table with Eli. She came back in a minute without the baby, but with her wallet in her hand.

"I had forty dollars in here," she said. "It's gone."

"Maybe someone broke in," Grandma said.

"And only stole one hundred and twenty dollars?" Mama said. She shook her head. "No. Myra Sue took it to buy a bus ticket." It seemed like something got hold of Mama, and she started to shake again. "Oh my goodness, my little girl, out there somewhere, alone . . ."

Grandma went to her and cradled Mama against her while Mama cried some more. Mimi got up and went outside. She did not wear her coat and she did not take her cigarettes.

"Mama, you want some more of that calming tea?" I asked, wishing I knew what to do. I also wished I had been a big, fat tattletale.

Mama just kept crying and did not reply. I have never felt more lost and guilty and scared in my life.

TWENTY-EIGHT

When You Realize That Soft Voice Speaking in Your Heart Is Probably Jesus

◎

I went upstairs to Myra Sue's room.

I eyeballed all those things we'd pulled out from under the bed. I looked at the empty mercy kit Isabel had given her on the dresser, then stared at the bed where Myra hogged most of the room and nearly all the covers. It seemed to me that her voice echoed in that room, turning into something I could hear way down deep inside of myself.

I remembered when we were little and sat on the floor and played Candy Land, and sometimes jacks. Then I thought about the times when we'd pull a sheet off the bed to make ourselves a tent. Sometimes Mama would let us sleep on the floor in that silly tent. We giggled half the night, pretending we were in the Grand Canyon or Africa, or in a deep, dark forest where strange animals lived. When we'd get to the scary part of our pretending, we'd cuddle up together, watching for bears or dragons. But that was when we were little girls. We weren't little anymore, and it had been a long time since we'd played and laughed together.

What had changed to make my sister do something so dumb, and why hadn't I done something about it?

A huge lump caught in my throat, and I had to breathe hard to get any air around it. That lump had nothing to do with my cold. I wanted Myra Sue back home, all uppity, snippy, messy, and dumb. I didn't care. I just wanted her back here where she belonged, safe and sound.

I crossed the room to look outside. From that window, I could see our side yard, the hayfield, Grandma's little, white house, and the trees and mountains beyond, all bare and cold-looking. The sun hung low in the sky by that time, and the light was turning into a softer, weaker version of itself as it changed to early evening.

A movement snagged my attention. I saw Mimi standing beneath an old oak tree in the side yard. She had her thin arms wrapped around herself, her shoulders hunched and her head down. The wind bumped against her, blowing her shirt-sleeves and strands of that purply-red hair. She didn't move. It was as if she didn't feel it. And then I saw her wipe the heels of her hands across her cheeks as if she were crying.

I wanted to turn away. I wanted to say, "I don't care if she's upset! She's that screamin' Mimi-person who hurt my mama, and who acts like she belongs here when she doesn't. Let her cry her eyes out."

That's what I wanted to say, but somewhere deep inside, in that same place where I missed my sister, I didn't feel that way at all. I felt Mimi's hurt and confusion and loneliness. And knowing she was sick with no place to go, I felt her fear, too. I don't know how I felt it, but I did, and it seemed to tear into my own heart.

It almost seemed to me that Jesus Himself spoke to me in a soft, gentle voice and said, "No matter how ugly and smelly she is, no matter what awful thing she did years ago, I still love her."

I swallowed hard. Part of me wanted to stay right where I was, warm and comfy, and another part said, "She needs you." Maybe that was the Jesus-part speaking.

I put on shoes and socks, took off my robe, and pulled my

coat on over my jammies, then added my gloves and warm hat. I got Mimi's stinky leather jacket out of my own bedroom and went to her out there beneath that old tree.

She looked up as I approached. Her eyes were red-rimmed, and her face looked chapped. She had cried off and wiped away all her makeup. She looked really old and fragile.

"Sunshine," she said softly, "you shouldn't be out here in this wind. Please go back before you have another relapse."

"Here, Mimi, you need your coat."

"Why, thank you, sugar." She fumbled, putting on that coat with shaking hands, then had a coughing fit. She looked so cold, I felt it in my bones.

"Come inside, Mimi." I took one of her icy hands in mine, but she did not move. "Mimi?"

"Wait a minute, Sunshine. I want to tell you something."

"But you're shaking. You're gonna get sick your own personal self."

"I'll be fine, honey." She coughed her crusty cough again. "I just want to tell you I'm sorry."

"Ma'am?"

She started talking, and it was like she could not stop.

"I'm sorry for everything in my life, from the mistakes I made when I was young and gullible to all the foolish choices I made as I got older. My life has been one disaster after another, and look where it has got me: alone, nearly penniless, and without love from anyone." She looked away from me, toward the woods, as if some answer to her problems could be found among the trees. "All I wanted was to be happy. I wanted Lily to be happy, too, but I couldn't provide for her. I had this crazy idea I could be a famous country singer, another Patsy Cline, and I chased after that dream. Little one-room apartments were all I could afford. I waited tables during the day, or went to auditions, then at night I sang in dark, rowdy, sometimes nasty places, just hoping someone would discover me. I couldn't have a child with me in those places, but what was I supposed to do? Leave Lily in a sad, old apartment all by herself while I tried to make a living? Back then it was hard for a woman to make it on her own, especially if she had a child to look after."

"You gave your baby to Aunt Maxie." I heard my accusing tone and didn't soften it, not even a little bit.

She drew her gaze from the woods and looked at me. "Lily's daddy was a handsome, smooth-talking man, but he didn't want us. Aunt Maxie was the only relative me and Lily had. She raised me. I knew she would feed and clothe Lily until I could get decent work. But every job I got paid barely enough for me to live on by myself, and nothing I ever did earned enough to support a child."

"But don't you know Aunt Maxie did not take care of Mama?"

She sorta jerked.

"What?"

I huffed in that cold air.

"Aunt Maxie did not feed Mama right. She did not give her good clothes. She *neglected* her, Mimi. She was *mean*."

Mimi's mouth worked, her lips quivering as if she wanted to speak and couldn't. "Aunt Maxie raised *me*. She wasn't the sweetest woman in the world, but she made sure I had food, clothes, and shelter. She sent me to school, made sure I did my studies. Surely she did the same for your mama."

"You could've called."

"I did! As often as I could." She was silent for a bit, looking sick. "Maxie kept asking when I was coming to get her. I kept telling her 'Soon,' because I thought it would be soon. I was so sure I'd be the next big star on the Grand Ole Opry, and Maxie had agreed to take care of her for me until I could make a name for myself."

She scrubbed her eyes hard, then took in a deep breath.

"I finally got what I thought was my big break, singing with a band in Nashville. It paid good, enough for me to afford a babysitter in the evenings. So I came here and got Lily. But the band broke up not long after that, and I tried to find another band, but there were so many other younger, prettier, better singers than me . . . and I just wasn't good enough."

"Couldn't you have got another job?"

"Sunshine, I was so busy trying to be a country-music star that I didn't bother with much schoolin'. The only kind of work I was fit for was waiting tables or scrubbing floors, and that's what I did. When I couldn't pay the rent, we lost the apartment and had to live in the car. That's no life for anyone, especially a little girl. I brought her back to Maxie, then I traveled all over this country, looking for something that would give us a good life, but I never found it. I didn't want my daughter to grow up seeing nothing but broken dreams and loss. I never came back for her and thought I was doing the right thing."

She gave me a pleading look. "Don't you see? I didn't want to shame her with my failure and poverty." Then she kind of wilted and buried her face in her hands. "I was wrong. I was so wrong and I'm afraid she'll never forgive me."

Boy, oh boy. I heard all this stuff pouring out of Mimi's mouth like she'd bottled it up inside for a hundred years. And I reckon she had. A lot of it made no sense at all to me, but I guess everyone can make lots of mistakes. Something inside reminded me how Isabel and I had misjudged each other last summer. I reckon me and my whole family had done the same with Mimi. Maybe it wasn't just that Mama needed to forgive Mimi; the rest of us needed to ask Mimi to forgive us for misjudging her just because she seemed crude and obnoxious. My heart ached. It was a real, physical pain like someone had grabbed my aorta and ventricles and atriums and all that mess, then twisted it all tight.

"I'm sorry," I said, feeling tears sting my eyelids.

She kinda sniffled a little and tilted her head to one side. "What're you sorry about, Sunshine?"

Boy, oh boy, it's hard to apologize sometimes. I cleared my throat real well and said, "Because I wasn't very nice to you and treated you like you were not family."

"Oh, sweetie," she said, "I come on too strong, so it's perfectly understandable that nobody welcomed me with open arms. I just thought if I came here and tried to be part of the family, act like I was family, then maybe I would be. I tried to be fun and entertaining—"

"You sort of went about that the wrong way," I said.

She nodded. "Yes. I failed again."

"But, Mimi, everyone *needs* to know the truth. We all thought you just didn't want Mama, that you abandoned her to mean Aunt Maxie because you didn't care about anything except yourself and running around. And then you showed up here, and acted like you belonged to us when you were the same thing as a stranger. You even tried to steal Grandma's boyfriends."

Her red-rimmed eyes welled up with huge tears. They ran down her face so fast it was like they raced each other, but she kinda laughed a little.

"Not really. I just wanted to shake her up a little. She and I were girls together. She stole plenty of my boyfriends back in the day."

"Please, Mimi. Let's go inside and tell Mama and Grandma what you told me about everything."

She shook her head.

"I don't think this is the right time, April, not with Myra Sue gone and everyone beside themselves with worry." She broke off and had the worst spell of coughing you ever heard. It was so bad it scared me.

I tugged on her hand, hard.

"Come on, Mimi. I'm gonna get sick all over again if we stay outside in this cold much longer."

That did it. She grasped my cold hand in her even colder one. We walked back to the house, because she knew I needed her to.

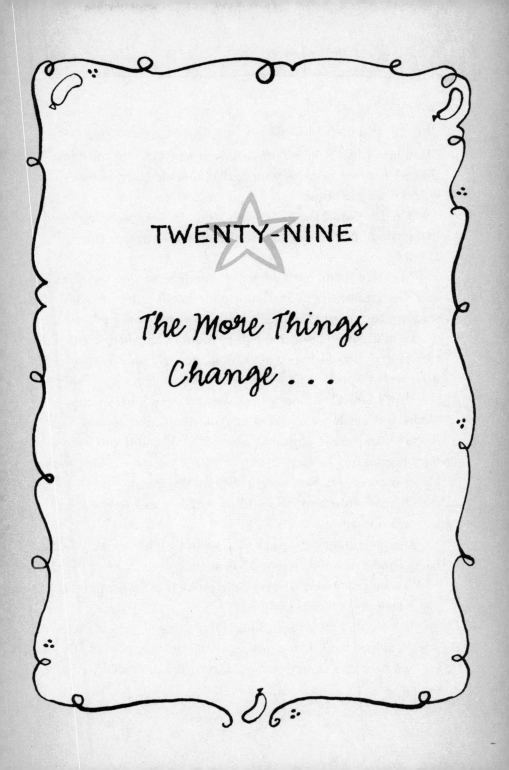

TWENTY-NINE

The More Things Change . . .

☆

Mimi and I had been so intent in our conversation outside that we had not heard anyone arrive, but suddenly, people's voices filled the house.

The Freebirds, the St. Jameses, and Mr. Brett were in the living room with Mama, and it seemed everyone was talking at once.

"They've found her!" Mama shouted the second she saw us. "The authorities in St. Louis found her at one of the bus stations, and they're holding her until we can get there."

Daddy came into the living room with their coats. Grandma followed him with Eli's diaper bag and his baby quilt on her arm.

"April Grace!" Mama said as she shrugged into her coat. "What on earth were you doing outside?" She looked at Mimi. "Sandra, my child has been sick. Why did you have her outside?"

"I'm sorry—" Mimi began, but I interrupted.

"I went out on my own and she tried to make me come in, but I refused."

Mama dragged her eyes from Mimi to look at me. She laid a hand against my forehead, frowning.

"I want you to take a warm bath, put on fresh pajamas, eat a good supper, and pile into bed."

"I'll see that she does," Mimi said, putting an arm around my shoulders, but Grandma edged in there.

"*I'll* take care of her because *I* know how to take care of young 'uns."

Mimi stepped back, nodding, saying nothing. That was mean of Grandma. In fact, the way Mama had talked to Mimi hadn't been very nice, either. Mimi had reacted the same way she always had, a little smile on her face. I'd seen that smile lots of times and had thought it was kinda smart-alecky smile, but now I knew better. It wasn't smart-alecky. It was a hurt smile, a smile that says, "It's okay. I'll hang around and wait." And she'd been waiting for us to love her. *That's* what she'd been waiting for.

Suddenly I didn't care if the world was in chaos around us. Something had to be done, and if the grown-ups weren't gonna do it, I would.

"Isabel and Temple can take care of me," I said, stepping back from the group. "I want Mimi and Grandma to go in the car with you to St. Louis."

Dead silence fell on our house. All those eyes stared at me like I was a three-headed goose, but I did not care.

"That's a long trip for you to make, and you'll not have anything to do but ride along and talk. *And listen.*" I looked at Mimi. "I want *you* to talk, Mimi. I want you to speak up and tell them what you told me." I looked at Mama. "I want *you* to listen, Mama." I turned to Grandma and added, "I think Mimi could be a good grandma if she's given half a chance."

"Oh, now, Sunshine—" said Mimi.

"April Grace!" said Grandma.

"Why . . . ," said Mama.

"I'd like that," Mimi said, very quietly. "If you'd be willing, I'd like to explain, to apologize . . . and to start over."

Daddy and Mama looked at each other, then Mama turned to Mimi.

"We're driving straight up there and back, no stopping for the night."

Mimi nodded. "That's fine."

"There will be no smoking around the baby."

"Of course."

Mama hesitated a moment longer. "All right. You're welcome to come along if you'd like."

Mimi smiled her brown smile. "Thank you, honey. Thank you."

"Mama Grace?" Mama said to Grandma. "All right?"

Grandma did not look too happy, but she nodded.

"Then let's go," Daddy said. "The sooner we can get her, the sooner Myra Sue will be back home where she belongs."

There was a flurry of hugs and kisses, best wishes, and good-byes, then my entire family was gone from the house, out into the cold evening. I watched until the taillights disappeared down Rough Creek Road.

"Well, fellers," said Mr. Brett, looking at Forest and Ian, "we're getting a late start on the milking."

"Yep," Forest said, "we better get on it."

All the men left, and the house felt mighty quiet and lonesome.

"April dear," Isabel said, "go take your bath and put on fresh pajamas, just as your mama said."

"And I'll go brew up some fresh tea for you, and see what I can fix for you to eat," Temple added.

I looked at those two women, more grateful than I can say that they cared enough about me to be there.

"I will. But I need to make a phone call first."

☆

When Melissa answered the phone, I said, "Hey, whatcha doin'?"

There was a silence, then she said, "Nothin'. What're you doin'?"

"Nothin'. Did you know my sister ran away?"

"Yeah. The police were at the school, talking to lots of people."

"She's in St. Louis. Mama and Daddy and Grandma and Mimi have gone to get her."

"All of 'em?"

"Yep."

There was the tiniest silence, then I said, "Melissa, I'm sorry I've been mad at you."

"Me, too."

"I thought you were taking sides, but I realize you were just trying to stand up for Mimi. And you know something? She isn't so bad. In fact, I think she might become a part of the family."

"Really?" I could hear the smile in my friend's voice. "What happened to change your mind?"

I felt kinda odd saying it, but it was the truth: "I finally listened to her."

☆

The sun had been up a couple of hours the next morning when our Taurus pulled into the driveway with everyone crowded into it.

I flung open the front door and went flying down the porch steps. Daddy and Mama pointed through the windshield at me and laughed as I stood there, prancing on the bottom step. The car stopped, and it seemed like forever before all those people piled out of it.

Grandma and Mimi got out of the backseat from opposite sides of the car, and they were talking ninety miles an hour, looking at each other over the roof and smiling at each other like they were friends.

When Mama got out of the car with Eli in her arms, Mimi came up beside her and started baby-talking to him.

"Here, Mom. You want to carry him into the house while I get the diaper bag?" Mama asked, handing him over with a smile. Then Grandma and Daddy came to stand with them. Daddy rested a hand on one shoulder of each grandmother, and they all talked and made goo-goo eyes at Eli and grinned and chuckled and were so friendly and happy that I knew they'd worked things out. Being stuck in a car for a lot of hours has its good points.

Myra Sue had been sitting between the grandmas, and when she finally got out of the car, I threw myself at her.

"Myra!" I hollered.

I hugged that girl so hard I nearly choked us both. She stunk to high heaven, but I guess that with riding on buses, all those smells soaked into her clothes. I've heard bus stations aren't exactly scented with roses and honeysuckle. And by the way, she was wearing a red dress, those high heels, the dangly earrings, and what was left of a whole mess of makeup on her face. It was streaked and smeared. I tell you, that girl was a sight, but I did not care because I was so glad to see her.

"April Grace," she said after a bit, and pulled back. She wasn't mad that I'd hugged her. In fact, she kinda smiled. She had circles under her eyes, her hair was dirty, and she looked almighty tired.

"Are you glad to be home?" I said.

A peculiar expression flickered over her face.

"Yes," she said. "I missed you so much! Oh, it's awful out there away from Mama and Daddy and our home." She looked me in the eye and said, "April Grace, you must promise me you will never run away from home, no matter how bad you think you want something."

"I won't!" I promised. I planned to live right here on Rough Creek Road and nowhere else, if I could ever help it.

"Maybe someday I'll be famous," she said, "but I don't want to go away from here just yet."

Boy, oh boy. That bus trip must have been an eye-opening experience, and I planned to worm every detail out of my sister at some point. Maybe tonight we could pitch a tent in my bedroom and camp out on the floor, and we'd talk about everything. But I had to know one thing right then.

"Did you get in big trouble?" I asked, 'cause I hardly saw how she could get away with running off that way and scaring everybody the way she'd done. But I didn't think she'd get punished when we were all so glad she was home, safe and sound.

"I'm not allowed to talk on the phone or go anywhere with my friends for an entire month, and I can't ever shut my bedroom door again except when I'm changing clothes, and I have to keep my room as clean as you keep yours from now on."

"Good gravy! You gonna be able to do all that?"

She shrugged. "I guess I better. If I don't, I have to move in with you so I can't have any secrets. And I can't wear my *Days of Our Lives* clothes anymore." She looked down at her outfit. "Daddy said I have to dress my age, and I have to give Mama almost all my makeup. She said I can have it back when I'm older."

"Wow. Well, I'll show you how to keep your room clean," I said, although at that moment, I was so glad she was home safe, I reckon I'd have been plenty happy to share my room with her again. For a while, anyway.

Isabel came trotting down the porch steps, her hair sticking up in tufts, and she was still wearing the black slacks and turtleneck shirt she'd worn the day before. When the others went home last night, Isabel stayed with me, God bless her heart. She slept right on the sofa so she'd hear when everybody came home.

"Darling girl!" she said, wrapping her long, skinny arms around Myra and kissing her cheek.

Tired and rumpled as she was, Myra Sue suddenly set up the biggest howl-fest you ever heard, crying her tired eyes out on Isabel's shoulder.

"Isabel!" she hollered, hanging on to that woman while Isabel patted her back and hugged her.

"Don't you ever leave us again!" she said. She looked into Myra's big baby blues. "You hear me?"

"Yes, Isabel dearest," Myra Sue blubbered. "I won't."

We all stood around, grinning and happy, hardly noticing the cold air, when Isabel said, "Come inside where it's warm, everyone. I've got a fresh pot of coffee on."

"That sounds good to me!" Mimi said.

"You and me both," Grandma said, smiling at Mimi. "Just be careful going up the steps, Sandra. You're carrying our grandson."

"I'll be extra careful," Mimi promised. "Come on, girls!"

I was so glad everyone was safely back, and things had worked out, that I stood back for a minute and watched. You know what I saw? I'll tell you. I saw my whole entire family go home, that's what.

THE END

Author's Note

You may be wondering why I chose to set the Confessions of April Grace series in the 1980s—the decade of big hair, shoulder pads, and Bill Cosby. I have a few reasons.

The 1980s is an era that stirs the interest of today's youth. The culture, the fashion, the music—all of these seem somewhat exotic to kids of the twenty-first century. Their parents were young during that time, and the Confessions books are a way to show kids that, no matter what era you grow up in, your problems and issues echo and reflect the problems and issues of days gone by. What you experience is new to *you*, but it's not new.

I wanted to write stories where modern technology does not help my characters solve their problems. April Grace can't Google her concerns and easily resolve her curiosity. She must think and study; she must be innovative; she must turn to others. April and Myra are not in constant contact with their friends via cell phones. Instead, their time at home is spent primarily with their family and neighbors.

I hope the Confessions of April Grace continues rouse the interest of kids while taking their parents on a fun trip back to their own youthful days.